Hide Your Light

by

Penny Arrow

Hide Your Light

Cover Art by *Jennifer Greeff*

The Wild Rose Press, Inc.
PO Box 708
Adams Basin, NY 14410-0708
Visit us at www.thewildrosepress.com

Publishing History
First Edition, 2022
Trade Paperback ISBN 978-1-5092-4574-1
Digital ISBN 978-1-5092-4575-8

Published in the United States of America

Curse or gift, her cryptic visions hold the key to finding a missing child.

Something hard pressed against the side of her face, and her shoulder bent uncomfortably forward, but that didn't seem important. Then the random stream-of-consciousness burbling in her mind was interrupted by a sudden urgent thought:

Why am I on the ground?

She opened her eyes and darkness transmuted into a mass of leafy scrub inches from her face. The damp air reeked of fungal rot and pine sap, her nose an inch from the dirt. Gingerly, she lifted her head, and pine needles fell from her cheek. Dark looming trees and bits of sparkling sky came into view. The left side of her face felt funny and swollen.

She wiggled her jaw to test her range of motion as pieces clicked together in her mind. She was at the Survival Unlimited compound. She'd wanted to see where the girl disappeared.

A tender spot throbbed at the base of her skull. She remembered a shooting pain like a lightning strike, sharp and powerful.

Abruptly, raised voices drove her to her feet in a rush of adrenaline and fear.

Dedication

To my family, with gratitude.

Chapter One

Blue crouched alone in the tunnel's darkness, suppressing her giggles. The grown-ups were right, hide-and-seek was much more fun down here. It was a magical world, all glittery rock and jumping shadows and mysterious shapes when the flashlight was on, and then when she turned it off, the darkness grew as huge as outer space.

Uncle's friend sang out, "Ready or not, here I come!" When she grew up, Blue definitely wanted a pretty silver nose ring like the lady's, as long as it didn't hurt or get boogers on it. The lady's voice echoed like it was coming from all directions. On the way in, Uncle Wes told Blue it was just a little cave and there was no way anyone could get lost, but Blue had found a really good hiding place. It was a deep crack behind a jutting rock, so maybe Uncle Wes didn't know his way around as well as he thought.

The lady's light flashed nearby, and Blue shrank back, but then the light traveled further away. Her voice sounded further, too, when she called out. "Blue-oo! Where are you-oo? I'm coming to eat you-oo!"

A tiny laugh snuck out and Blue clasped her hand over her mouth. It was so much fun in the cave and she wanted to explore after the game. Uncle probably hadn't looked for secret places. He was a grown-up; he might not even fit where she was hiding! If she hunted around, she might find treasure, or skeletons, or blind white fish in a secret river like she saw on TV. Maybe she would discover blind white dragonflies! She collected all kinds of dragonfly stuff at home, and her mom even gave her a dragonfly necklace that Blue wore all the time. But Blue knew dragonflies ate bugs and larvae, and she hadn't seen any bugs down here. Yet. She shifted uncomfortably, feeling suddenly itchy. Maybe she should turn her light on and check.

Footsteps and distant voices interrupted her thoughts, but it was hard to tell where they came from. When the lady had started counting for the game, Uncle Wes said he had to run outside for a second to take a call, so Blue hid, thinking that he would hide too when he returned. But he must have teamed up with his friend to look for Blue instead.

She wiped her glasses on her shirt then snickered. You can't clean the dark off, Blue, she told herself, and set them carefully back on her nose. Then she slid down so her butt rested on the cool stone of the floor. Footsteps passed, and they didn't even pause by the crack. Her hiding place was too good—she might have to give them a clue, like a little fake cough, if they didn't find her soon. Or she could flash her light.

She snuggled into her hoodie, pulling the hem down to cushion herself against the cold, and wrapped her arms around her knees with her hands tucked into the cuffs. Underground, the rocks thought it was still winter, even though tomorrow would be the first day of spring.

When her ankle prickled and made her think of bugs again, she wriggled but kept her light turned off. At first in the woods, the lady had said, "You're probably too scared of the dark to play in a cave," but Blue wasn't afraid of the dark at all. There was nothing in the dark that wasn't there in the light, and she was much more scared of getting in trouble with her parents than of pretend things like monsters. Plus, she was ten, so she was in double digits, which meant teenager, which was practically grown-up.

Sometimes, she felt older than her parents, because they argued about stupid things. Why should Mommy care if Daddy went to Spiritchoolist Church with Uncle Wes or not? The Spiritchoolist people thought spirits were real, and they helped people. It was no crazier than reincarnation, Daddy said, and Mommy dragged them all to Reincarnation Camp last year, so what was the difference? Mommy said it was a bad example to tell Blue that there was no such thing as ghosts, and then start believing in Spiritchoolism just because Uncle Wes did.

Blue shook her head. Grown-ups were crazy, alright. But believing in crazy things was easy in this giant darkness. She usually wasn't afraid of the dark, but what if the Spiritchoolists were right, and there were spirits down here? Hopefully they would be the good helpful kind like Daddy said. But what if they weren't?

She held her breath, trying to hold perfectly still so her clothes wouldn't rustle, but her spine shuddered. What if this tunnel was full of the spooky, angry kind of spirits, like in the movies? Her thumb trembled over the flashlight button, but she yanked it back. No. She was scaring herself with nonsense. She would surprise the lady with the nose ring and Uncle Wes by being the best hider ever, and not give herself away with the flashlight like a baby.

She was practicing her impression of a statue and definitely not thinking of spirits a few minutes later when the voices reached her again, an echoing mixture of soft and loud, which might have been spooky if she hadn't recognized them. It was just Uncle Wes and the nose ring lady again. Were they giving up? She grinned. Finally. She crawled over to the crack in the wall on her knees, prepared to jump out and scare them. Then she made out a string of words in the lady's voice. "Kids are so stupid. I told you it would be easy."

Blue frowned. That was a mean thing to say. Plus, Blue was hiding really well because she was smart, not stupid. Maybe they were talking about someone else. But Blue was the only one invited to play down here, while all the other kids were stuck outside in the woods practicing survival skills.

She sharpened her ears, focusing hard on the blurred words. Uncle Wes's voice sounded annoyed. "Yeah, easy to lure her down here, but now where the hell is she? How can you not find her? This is a cave, not a maze."

Blue was about to jump out, but the anger in his voice stopped her. Would she be in trouble for hiding too well? And what did he mean, lure? She wasn't lured. She leaned against the wall, trying to listen and hide at the same time.

"No worries," the lady said. "She's just playing."

"You better find her in time. Tonight, that's what your grandfather promised. To be safe."

The footsteps paused, and now the lady's low, teasing voice was as clear as if she were standing right next to Blue, speaking in her ear. "Such an impatient man! We've got three days. The equinox would be best, if you ask me. Poppy can be over-cautious."

"Don't play with me!" Uncle said. There was a thump, and then he yelped a very loud, very bad word.

Blue closed her eyes and put her hands over her ears, but when the lady spoke in a grim, serious voice, Blue took them off again so she could hear.

"Keep your hands off me or you'll be sorry."

"Fine, okay. I just—"

"I don't care. There's more, and worse, where that came from." Her tone turned light and teasing again. "Stop worrying, okay? The little shit is not going to hide in a cold, dirty cave for more than an hour. Kids don't do that, especially spoiled-brat rich kids. So chill out. Go up and nail down your alibi. I promise, one hour and she'll be crying for Mommy."

"Great," Uncle said. "Just great. In an hour, there will be security teams all over the woods and the bunker. You won't be able to reach me, I'll be coordinating."

"I got this. Just come down at midnight. That was the plan. Alibi, remember?"

Blue's heart beat so hard her face turned hot. She wasn't sure what an alibi was, but nailing one down sounded pretty bad. According to Blue's dad, Spirit Ridge was the safest place in the world now that Uncle Wes's company had moved in, but Blue had noticed it didn't keep people from sometimes being jerks.

The more she thought about it, the more she didn't like it. Her eyes teared up. Uncle Wes never sounded so mean before. He must be really mad. But was he mad at Blue, or at the nose ring lady? Something was wrong, and Blue's stomach began to ache.

A loud noise like a door slamming echoed around the cave. Uncle had let her unlock the fancy gate in the woods that was hidden by blackberry prickers, to get into the secret tunnel to the cave. But that noise she just heard hadn't been the creaky metal clang of the gate, it had been a regular door-slam. There must be another way in.

Could this be part of the game? Maybe they were tricking her, to see if she could find the door herself. Maybe the door even led home to the bunker. That made sense, because the bunker was on top of Spirit Ridge, and this cave must be underneath it.

Heart pounding, Blue listened again. If the mean lady was gone too, Blue could find the door or the gate. She could find the other kids and the teacher, and tell on Uncle Wes's mean friend for calling her a little shit. She wouldn't say anything bad about Uncle Wes, though, she decided. He was the boss after all, and her godfather, and he probably hadn't meant to scare her.

A shiver went down her back again. Uncle Wes had sounded really mean. Like he did want to scare her, or worse. But she couldn't believe it, and no one else would believe it either. Maybe if she told about the nose ring lady, her parents might agree to move back to their old house in California, and then they would be away from Uncle Wes too. Just in case.

She couldn't hear a single sound, not even the tiniest scrape of a pebble or the echo of a breath. The lady must be gone too. Blue stood up and turned around, listening carefully in every direction. Nothing but silence, and the sound of her own shoes on the gravelly floor. With her heart in her throat, she switched her flashlight on, half certain that the lady's face would be right in front of her, grinning madly, nose ring glittering.

Or maybe there would be a wicked spirit!

The flashlight showed only rock and shadow, but it seemed like now the shadows hid monsters and traps, instead of treasures and cave fish. She breathed the cool musty air, her brows drawing together. There were no wicked spirits. And if the mean lady was here, Blue would hear something, because everything was completely silent, and the lady was never silent, snapping the snaps on her jacket sleeves and fidgeting all the time. She must be gone.

But…which way was the gate? Which way had the slamming door sound come from? Sound wandered so strangely through the twists and turns of the cave.

Hesitantly, her light pooling in a small circle before her, Blue stepped out of her hiding place.

Chapter Two

At one in the morning, Seaview Resort's industrial laundry room was hellish, and it wasn't only because of the heat. The mechanical pounding of twenty oversized washers and dryers and the buzzing fluorescent lights jangled against Robin's nerves, which were not yet attuned to the graveyard shift. Sweat dripped down her forehead as she transferred yet another massive ball of tangled sheets and towels from a cart onto one of the king-sized sorting tables. Green satin crusted with—something—peeped out. She tugged it loose and dropped it into the garbage while keeping her gaze averted.

Despite the disgusting surprises, despite the constant exhaustion which, she had to believe, would pass as she adapted to a nocturnal existence, and despite the heat and noise, there was a kind of contentment in working here alone. There was no one to notice her studying algebra while she sorted, loaded, shook out and folded. No one to notice if she zoned out for a while during one of her thankfully rare cold flashes.

A shriek pierced the din, startling her, and her hands clutched a damp towel as she looked for the source. Washers and dryers thumped as she strained to detect anything over the racket. Nothing, but she couldn't just forget about it. It sounded like a scream. She tossed the towel back on the pile and jogged to the back door. Officially, it was supposed to be left closed for security, but Robin discovered a brick right outside on her very first night, next to a can of cigarette butts. The regular laundry manager who she was temping for must have snuck cigarettes back there, but Robin was just glad to get some air.

She leaned out, stealing a glance at the Pacific Ocean through the beat-up chain-link fence, then scanned the well-lit strip of pavement along the back of the hotel. Her line of sight was interrupted by banks of dumpsters and multiple loading docks. The Seaview was the largest resort in her little Oregon Coast town, and this pot-holed alley behind the scenes was where all of its resources moved in and out.

The shriek sounded again, more clearly now, from an open door near the restaurant. A cloud of smoke rose over a silhouetted figure, and someone's laughter in a lower timbre sounded in return.

Robin's shoulders relaxed. Not a scream, then. Maybe it was the restaurant's closing crew, taking a cigarette break. Robin rarely ran into them. Her carts of laundry were deposited before she arrived by the previous shift, and once Liam dropped her off, she was in her own little world. Her heart calmed, and she sucked in a soothing breath of salt-scented air, resting her eyes on the starry sky. Was tonight the new moon? The stars were brilliant, but then she found the merest sliver of moon near the horizon. Maybe tomorrow.

Math, she reminded herself. And piles and piles of dirty sheets.

After the fresh air, coming in was like walking into a wall of fire. Rebelliously, she left the door wide open. Yanking the elastic band from her ponytail, she knotted her hair up on top of her head. The textbook stared up at her, and she sighed. "Okay, back to it. *X to the M power times X to the N power equals X to the M plus N power,*" she repeated, and turned back to her pile. It had been almost twenty years since she took her GED exam; algebra felt just as useless but twice as foreign this time around. Why, oh why did it have to be a requirement for even an Associate of Arts degree?

She grimly yanked at one corner of a twisted sheet. "X to the M power—"

An icy wave rushed up her spine. She convulsed, releasing the sheet, and caught herself with hands flat against the table. The sweat on her body was a clammy layer of slime and her stomach a hard ball of fear.

Let it be an easy one, please, let it be an easy one.

Just a little cut, one drop of blood, could make the cold flash so much easier. Her uncle dealt with the seizures that way, using the pain and the symbolism of blood and sacrifice as a powerful focus, but cutting herself had become a dangerously comforting habit for her after Daniel, and some of those scars still persisted. Now she endured and ignored. Sometimes it seemed like the flashes were taking the hint. It had been five months since the last one, maybe six.

But this felt like a bad one. She caught herself biting her lip and curling her fingernails into her palms in an unconscious bid for bloody relief, and registered a tiny flame of pride as she forced herself to stop. Then the next wave of nausea rippled through her, and she knew her prayers had been ignored. She wouldn't be able to stay upright.

She collapsed to her knees with what control she could muster, and then to a fetal position on the bare cement floor, cringing away from the sharp corners of the table's lower shelf. Her skull banged against the ground despite her efforts, and pain echoed through her skull; years of kickboxing developed her ability to fall well, but that was on mats, not concrete.

The underside of the table, never cleaned, was a poor distraction from fear and anxiety, but she held onto it as long as she could. Lost socks and bathrobe ties dwelled among dust bunnies the size of tumbleweeds, but it was better than what lay in her own mind. Her stomach wrenched again. Then her vision blurred and the harsh light of the laundry room disappeared.

She'd tried to describe the seizures to Liam before but the chaos was inexpressible. Her mind collapsed under an onslaught of sensation, fighting in vain for a thread of sanity. She told him it was like trying to follow the plot of a TV show playing in the other room while digging for a lost piece of jewelry in the garbage disposal, and then a bulldozer rammed into your house. Or like someone carved an important question for you on a tree, and then felled the tree and fed it through a wood chipper pointed in your general direction, and you had to respond in thirty seconds.

This time, a white spark danced through the chaos, moment by moment, and her mind fixed on it. A dragonfly. A white dragonfly with glowing sapphire eyes flitted along as if above a merry creek. Elsewhere, steel jaws crunched shut with a crack of bone, and something plummeted from a great height. The smell all around was dust and blood. Dust and blood and vomit.

Robin rolled on the floor, hugging herself, as the flash washed her back to the shore of reality. The concrete was chilly against her ribs where her T-shirt pulled away from her jeans. The stench of bile filled her nose; her face was wet and sticky. She forced herself to open her eyes.

A pool of vomit trailed from her face toward the drain set into the laundry room floor. Worse, a pair of shoes were planted right outside the vomit zone. Wedge sandals, pink, with magenta-tipped nails showcased in the open toe.

Robin flinched. She raised her eyes past tanned calves and white capri pants to a pair of small hands on wide hips, and then further to the sneering yet perfectly made-up face of Korina Moralez, Night Manager.

"Get your ass up, and out of here," Korina said. "Jesus, I fricking thought they drug-tested you people."

Robin struggled up on an elbow, head pounding. The echoes of the flash sizzled in her brain, and no words came to her.

"And what's this?" Korina snapped. Her shoes tapped a wide circle around Robin, and she lifted the textbook from the table and dropped it to the floor. "You can't be reading at work!" She sounded scandalized, as if math books were even worse than drugs.

"It's not what you think," Robin said. Her head throbbed, but she climbed to her feet and faced Korina.

"Yeah? You think I haven't seen it all before? Because I have. And I don't turn a blind eye." She huffed and tossed a clean washcloth from the pile on the table at Robin. "Wipe your face. I can't even look at you."

Robin wiped. "It's a medical condition," she said, realizing even as the words came out that it was the wrong strategy. There was no way she could get a doctor's note for her cold flashes. She'd end up institutionalized if she tried. Or medicated.

It didn't matter anyway. Korina just lifted an

eyebrow. "I know. It's called addiction. Get help, get high, I don't care. But get out!"

Humiliation flushed Robin's face, and she opened her mouth, wanting to rage against the unfairness. But what could she say? Nothing that this woman would believe. Robin bent stiffly to retrieve her algebra book and wiped it clean with the washcloth, face burning. As she walked toward the door, grabbing her purse on the way, Korina huffed another sigh and dropped a pile of towels onto the trail of vomit.

****

Robin waited in a pool of light near the lobby, conscious of the desk clerk's curious gaze on her back. She ignored him, clutching her book to her chest and shivering. She was dressed for the laundry's hellish heat, and the ocean breeze was damp and cold. Her head throbbed with every beat of her heart, and she craved home and bed.

Her foster brother's Jeep pulled up and she gratefully climbed in.

"You okay?" Liam asked. He stole a quick glance as he pulled away from the hotel and out into the deserted street. Pillow-creases marred his stubbly cheek and his hair stuck up in all the wrong places. He wore flannel pajama pants and flip-flops with his leather jacket, very stylish. She would make fun if she had any energy left.

Instead she shrugged. "Yeah. No. I don't know. There goes another one, you know?"

"It was a flash?"

"A bad one," she confirmed. "And the manager had to be around to see it."

"Fantastic. Did she call an ambulance?"

"No. She thought I was drunk or high or something.

Just kicked me out."

He winced. "I hope she doesn't tell that to the temp agency."

"Don't worry. She will."

They fell silent. After a while, he said, "Did you get anything interesting? From the flash?"

With her eyes closed, she sighed. "A dragonfly. A trap, like a bear trap, with snapping steel jaws. Somebody falling. And dust. A cold, weirdly mineral smell. Maybe blood too."

"I…have no idea what that means. Watch out for bear traps?"

"I promise, I will. I hear they're everywhere on the coast this time of year."

The tires crunched on their gravel driveway. Motion sensor lights flicked on, illuminating the tiny cottage's dry front lawn. Robin stepped from the Jeep, grabbing at the door for support as her vision turned staticky around the edges.

"Jeez," Liam said, standing at her elbow. "It really did a job on you. I haven't seen you this bad in a long time."

"Must have been saving up. But I'm fine. Just need some sleep. Stupid graveyard shift has been wearing me out."

He fumbled with the front door key. "Might I recommend a shower first? You kind of reek."

She had to brush her teeth and ascertain there were no actual chunks of vomit sticking to her, but the thought of undressing for the shower was too much. Without another thought, she stumbled to her bed and let cool, dark silence overwhelm her consciousness.

Chapter Three

Robin bolted upright, heart pounding. Liam jumped back from where he stood at the side of her bed.

"What?! What's wrong?" she said.

He shook his head with a grin. "I cannot believe your reflexes. One little poke on the shoulder and you're up like a wild boar."

She narrowed her eyes. He wore track pants and a snug black T-shirt, his usual work uniform, that advertised that he practiced what he coached. "What time is it?" she demanded.

"I'm on break." He plopped himself at the end of her bed. "It's nine a.m. I've been at the gym for hours."

She groaned. "And why are you bothering me? You know what time I got to sleep last night."

"Seven hours ago. You're plenty rested." He poked her again, this time on the foot.

She laid back down and closed her eyes, snuggling into her pillow.

"You can't ignore me, little sister. I've seen this before. One little flash and you want to hide under the covers for a week. Well, that's not going to fly this time."

She pulled at the quilt, trying to yank it over her head, but his weight made it impossible. She groaned again. "What's your brilliant plan, then? Are you going to wave a magic wand and make me a fully functioning member of society?"

"Don't you have an algebra test next week? Are you not educating yourself toward a transfer degree that will soon allow you to apply for a bachelor's program? After which, will you not be qualified for many decent-paying jobs in which it will not matter if you have to call in sick or go home sick once in a while, without people getting all judgy and up in your face?"

She squinted at him. "That was the plan."

"Well, it's a good plan. Which you should definitely stick with, because I don't want you moping around the house feeling sorry for yourself. But! I have news."

She waited. Were all personal trainers so dramatic?

He fiddled for a moment with the iPad she hadn't realized he was holding. "I think I know what your flash was about."

He handed it over and she sat up and reluctantly took it from him.

"What am I looking at?" She scanned a screen of internet search results: names she didn't know, photos she didn't recognize, something about a missing child. Nothing, so far as she could tell, about dragonflies.

"You told me once you thought all your cold flashes came to you because they're about things you can change, right? If you can figure them out."

"Yeah," she agreed, not meeting his gaze. She'd told him that after his parents died. When she was apologizing for not saving them.

He squeezed her foot through the covers. "Look at this news story. This little girl, Blue Gracen, disappeared. Yesterday."

She glanced at him quizzically. "Blue? Is that a nickname?"

"Her parents are Hollywood actors, and her middle

name is Eagle." He grinned.

"My vision had a dragonfly, not an eagle. You're making a leap here."

Her eyes fell on the images of the girl displayed amid the search results—a serious-looking child, bespectacled and brown-haired. In one picture, she was stepping down on an oversized shovel, digging in a field. In another, she held a bow and arrow, biting her lip and squinting into the distance. Something about her determination tugged at Robin's heart. But she shook her head. "You're making too big of a leap," she repeated. "What does this have to do with bear traps and rocks?"

Liam scooched closer and grabbed the iPad back. "It's where it happened, and also you might actually be able to help," he said, and tapped out another search.

She peered at the screen and he tilted it toward her. "Eccentric CEO Issues Psychic Invitation," she read aloud, raising her eyebrows.

"That's the one."

She continued, "'Wes Hartwin, owner and CEO of Survival Unlimited Inc., made an unusual appeal in a press release earlier this morning concerning the disappearance of his goddaughter, Blue Eagle Gracen, who has now been missing for over sixteen hours. Unlike most such appeals, this one was directed not at an alleged kidnapper, but at those with extra-sensory perception who may have insight about Blue's whereabouts and situation. No comment was available from Blue's parents, celebrities Marletta Kusak-Gracen and Miller Gracen, long-time friends of Hartwin who have been staying at the site of the new company headquarters, still under construction.'"

Robin stopped reading. "Wow, the cops must love

that. Every nut job in America is going to be calling in."

"It's for real. I looked at the Survival Unlimited website, and there's an open invitation. You have to apply and they screen you. You can give tips over the phone, but they're even going to let a certain number of people visit the site."

"I can't believe the cops are allowing this," she said.

"It's at Spirit Ridge, down near Grants Pass. It's going to be a resort/training camp/showcase for stuff they sell. Out in the middle of the woods, so there's plenty of space."

"Huh." She skimmed further down the article, chewing on her knuckle. Hartwin claimed to believe that "folks with special gifts" could locate Blue faster than the FBI, and he wasn't going to let the investigation be slowed down by "bureaucratic B.S."

An FBI spokeswoman was quoted as saying, "We are following and will continue to follow all worthwhile leads, regardless of the source."

"Huh," Robin repeated.

"See?"

"I don't know." Her eyes fell on a picture of Blue again. Was it possible? Was her blue-eyed dragonfly some kind of dream-icon for the missing little girl? As she'd told Liam, she'd come to believe that her flashes weren't random but connected to her in some way. She couldn't always figure them out, but when she did, they inevitably touched on her life, however obliquely. The flash that had convinced her was the one that predicted her foster parents' fatal car accident, where she'd glimpsed a plastic hula girl dancing underwater. Before she discovered the plastic toy under the seat of the family minivan, hunting for a lost pair of headphones, she'd thought it was about a tsunami in Hawaii. Of course, it still didn't matter, because knowing hadn't helped, and couldn't help, because no one ever listened.

Was the connection here that she could, in theory, join the search for Blue? It was pretty tenuous—if she responded to the invitation, if she was accepted, if being there brought on a cold flash a little more detailed than dust and blood and dragonflies. And it was all circular. Without the dragonfly flash, she wouldn't have considered going, and if she didn't go, she couldn't help.

And hell, if she did go, chances were she wouldn't be able to help. Case in point: her foster parents. Even after figuring out the hula girl would be submerged in their car, all her efforts to warn them had come to nothing.

It was too much. She shook her head. "Hartwin is nuts," she said. "And you are too. After last night, I should try to get flashes on purpose?" She shuddered at the thought. "I'm not that masochistic."

He grimaced but shrugged. "That was way worse than usual, though. The next one won't be that bad. It's an amazing opportunity. Why not help out?"

That was a question with several answers, some of which she could not share. She settled on, "It's a monumentally ridiculous idea. The flashes are not handy tips from a friendly universe. They're a warning that something bad is or was or will happen. And then the warning is shoved into a wood chipper about fifty feet away from me and I get pelted by five random splinters, which my chances of translating are approximately one in a billion. And that helps how?"

As soon as the words burst from her mouth, she winced. Her life might be a wreck, but it was a point of pride that she didn't complain. Liam lost his parents because she hadn't been able to make them believe her. She wouldn't stop talking about her premonition; they'd eventually been so worried about her mental health that they'd committed her to a psychiatric care program. The same people who had rescued her from the downward spiral that began with the onset of her curse had paid the ultimate price for her failure to master it.

Liam shook his head, and they sat for a moment in silence. Then he squeezed her ankle. "Not your fault. You did everything you could."

He had repeated those words so many times over the years that she almost believed that he believed them, and she loved him for it. But he was wrong.

She gently pulled her foot away. "Yeah, well, I might as well get up." She swung her legs off the side of the bed.

He bounced to his feet and gave her his trademark measuring look, gauging her psychological wellness with his eyes. Then he grinned. "Well, I've accomplished something with my day. But damn, girl, I hope you're going straight for the shower because you still smell like puke!"

She peeled off her sock and threw it at him as he ducked and ran from the room.

****

After her shower, Robin wandered into the kitchen and looked at the clock. It was ten already. Damn Liam for getting her up, but there was no way she was getting back to sleep now. Her headache had dissipated, but the emotional residue of the flash haunted her like a bad dream. There had been such a sense of joy in the dance of the dragonfly—and such an aching loss when it was gone.

The other track of her two-track brain held Korina's sneer and the shame that it conjured to know Korina believed her to be an addict.

She made coffee and huddled with her cup at the kitchen table, only to find a note leaning on the fruit bowl: "BTW, Miri for lunch." Which meant Liam's on-again, off-again girlfriend would be coming over. Robin sighed and let her head drop to the table. It wasn't that Miri was so bad—although she kind of was—it was pretending to be normal that Robin couldn't handle.

Her phone buzzed. She lifted her head to look at the screen. It was Greta from the temp agency. Robin hovered her finger over the answer icon, but then she blinked and let it drop. She didn't want to hear it. Even if Korina hadn't described finding her on the floor in a pool of vomit, losing the position was another black mark on her record, and another employer she hadn't been able to keep happy. She'd been on such a great streak too: no flashes on job sites, no problems for months…

Robin slammed the phone down on the table and pushed back her chair. She was tired of hearing herself whine. Liam was right, she could not let herself be brought down by one little flash. There was still time for a run before lunch. Afterwards, she could either go to class—or go back to bed.

****

Relentless drizzle turned the town of Otter Bay dreary and gray. She saw few people as she jogged through the streets. She started slowly, letting her muscles warm up as she made her way past souvenir shops and restaurants, but soon she was pushing herself, her mind emptying of everything but the need to count off another mile. Her route wound past beach overlooks, giving her glimpses of a gray-green ocean, the surf low but tipped with white-caps as a chill breeze blew in.

When she'd washed up here at sixteen, she'd been thin as a stick, malnourished from months begging and stealing on the road. In adolescence, the flashes were frequent and made her nauseous, so even when she had food, she barely ate. Mom and Dad Fox fed her up. After they died, Liam boot-camped her through her guilt-ridden grief by forcing his coping methods on her. Target-shooting, which was Liam's meditation, hadn't taken: she never got good at it, and it was a pain to go to the range. But running filled some need in her, and over time her mood and her health improved, and the flashes decreased.

Still running, she re-tied her ponytail, capturing the annoying wet pieces which whipped her face. She was coming up onto the bridge now, her favorite part of the run where she could watch fishing boats trailing in and out of the bay far below in almost every kind of weather, with seagulls, osprey, even pelicans flying by. Cars and trucks raced by at forty miles per hour. There were no shoulders on the bridge, only the single-file sidewalk shared by cyclists and pedestrians. She braced herself when someone with a baby-stroller appeared ahead in the misty grayness. Robin might have to step off the sidewalk to get around them.

The woman leaned on the balustrade beyond the stroller, which Robin now saw was empty. The child was next to the mother, excited and full of energy as he peered down at the bay. Robin was used to the height, but her gut twisted as the kid balanced on his belly to point at a sailboat far below, his feet in their slip-on sneakers leaving the ground. The mother seemed oblivious, perfectly still in contrast to her son, staring down at the sea as if in a dream despite the drizzle running down her face. Drawing close, Robin could see goose-bumps on her pale and tattooed arm, which was bare to the shoulder. The boy's white-blond hair stuck to his skull and his yellow T-shirt clung to his skin. When he turned to look at Robin, she saw dark shadows under his pale eyes.

The mother showed no sign of moving and cars continued to whiz by without a gap.

Robin slowed to a near stop, jogging in place to show she intended to move quickly around them. "Excuse me!"

The mother jumped and turned. She had the same gray eyes as the boy, the same dark shadows beneath.

"You guys should get out of the rain!" Robin raised her voice to be heard above the noise of the cars.

The boy wriggled on his stomach, pointing down. "Boat!" he said, like a two-year-old instead of the four or five she'd guessed from his size.

The mother grabbed his arm and pulled, and the concrete ratcheted up the boy's T-shirt. Red marks and bruises showed on his ribs, and Robin winced at the way his stomach must be scraping on the rough edge. He didn't react though, even as he was hefted into the stroller. Leaning back he put his thumb in his mouth and stared at Robin with expressionless eyes as his mother wrestled with the kick-brake. She yanked the stroller around and began to walk down the south slope of the bridge. She plodded slowly, like her shivering son and the rain and the wind and Robin jogging behind her were not factors in her world. Robin watched the traffic, finally spotted a gap, and ran a few steps at street level to pass the pair, looking back as she did. The woman's lips were moving, her eyes seemingly fixed on the handle of the stroller, but any words were lost in the rush of wind and cars.

Robin continued off the bridge toward a paved path in the state park, but even picking up the pace couldn't fight the chill that had invaded her. The boy's shadowed glance replayed in her mind, and his breathy, high-pitched "Boat!" The rough way the mother had pulled him off the railing.

The trail was deserted except for a pair of seniors in transparent rain ponchos riding oversized tricycles at a snail's pace, and Robin passed them easily. She tuned into her own breathing, and trying to force the mother and child from her mind. Then she realized—it was Uncle Matt that was trying to surface in memory, Uncle Matt's tattooed arm. The woman on the bridge had Celtic-looking designs similar to his, and when Robin was small, she had been fascinated by them. She could still remember dangling from that muscled arm like a monkey, trying to trace the maze of a Celtic knot with one finger. Uncle Matt's patience had been immense, even when she'd screeched in glee and kicked at his leg for purchase. He had grinned a wide grin that showed off his gold tooth—pirate gold, he always said.

That had been before her mother abandoned Robin and her brother Evan, before Uncle Matt became her adoptive parent instead of just her mother's brother, before she realized that his tattoos and cigarettes and rough talk made her an object of derision among the other kids. It had been long before she understood how much he kept hidden from her, and the reasons for the raised white scars that striped his forearms and the stub where his pinky finger was supposed to be.

But whatever his shortcomings, he had loved her and Evan. She hadn't thought about that part, not for a long time.

When Robin looped around to cross the bridge again a half hour later, she was feeling better, more balanced. The run was doing its work. Her mind wandered randomly without getting stuck on painful parts. She kept her eyes open for the mother and son, thinking they might be staying at one of the little motels or the RV park on the south side of the bridge. But they would be warm and dry by now, the boy in a bubble bath with a rubber ducky, the mother reviving with a hot cup of coffee.

This afternoon Robin would go to class, she vowed. Tomorrow she would call the temp agency and find out where she stood. She would not torture herself by traveling halfway across the state and deliberately trying to cold flash, when she'd been suppressing the curse as much as possible for sixteen years, for good reason.

But that train of thought brought her mind back to Blue Eagle Gracen's bespectacled face, and she wondered what it was like to have famous parents who didn't hesitate to put her in the public eye. The girl had looked a little anxious, nocking a bow twice her size, but who wouldn't? She'd probably been found by now. Just lost in the woods. Maybe Blue had twisted her ankle or fallen asleep. Robin would check the news when she got back home.

It wasn't until she'd traversed to the north side of the bridge that the stroller came into view again, lying on its side far below near the tidal flats, which were accessible only by a steep and rocky path. Heart in her throat, Robin scanned desperately for the mother and child. Her eyes went first to the gray waters of the bay, but then the boy's yellow shirt caught her eye. He sat in the sand, several feet from the wind-driven waves. One bony arm was looped around his bare knees and the other poked at the ground with a stick. The mother was perched on a boulder, still staring out to sea as if mesmerized. Both were soaked. Even from up here, Robin thought she could see the purple of the boy's lips.

Her rising mood was dispelled by grim anxiety. She hurried home. Her phone was on the table where she'd left it, and she, who had minded her own business and lived under the radar for a long, long time, called nine-one-one to report a child in trouble.

And after, without pausing to think, she pulled up the number to call Survival Unlimited's Psychic Screening Hotline.

Chapter Four

Liam walked in as Robin said, "Thank you, goodbye," to the hotline operator. She'd been stretching her hamstring with one foot up on a kitchen stool, and she straightened and pressed end on the phone. She'd paced her way through the house several times over the course of the two phone calls, but her running clothes were still damp, and her hair was lank and stuck to her neck.

"Hey, you went for a run! I'm impressed." He dropped his gym bag by the front door and made his way straight to the fridge for the chilled filtered water.

She set the phone down and lifted the other leg to the stool to stretch. "And you went to work! Good for you."

He made a face at her. "I'm just saying. I wasn't sure you were actually going to get out of the bed. After all, you were up late last night."

"Ha, ha."

He gulped water. "Did you see my note? Miri's coming for lunch."

"Yeah. I didn't know you two were back together." She was carefully noncommittal. Liam and Miri broke up frequently—she thought maybe four times now—because Miri kept falling in love with other people. Liam seemed to think that since she came back to him when each infatuation faded that meant he was special, and eventually Miri would realize that.

"We're getting there," he said. "I know, I know. I'm going to give her ground rules if she wants to be together again."

"Hmm," was all she allowed herself to say.

He piled sandwich makings on the counter. "You going to take a shower? Should I make you a sandwich?"

"Are you telling me I stink again?"

"Yes."

"Oh, well, okay then."

She was in the doorway when he said, "You know, I thought about what you said. You're right. I'm glad you decided not to volunteer for that psychic thing."

Robin's heart sped up. "Oh. Why?"

"Every time you have a flash you beat yourself up. And they never lead to happy endings. So you're right. You should ignore them and move on as well as you can."

Robin turned around and faced him. "I called. I'm going."

He blinked. Opened his mouth. Closed it again.

She laughed a little. "Yeah. I told them about the cold flash I had last night, about the dragonfly. It turns out that it's Blue's favorite animal. I warned them my flashes aren't reliable or clear, but they said come anyway. Mr. Hartwin is sending a travel allowance."

Liam fell into a kitchen chair and blinked. "Holy…Shit. What made you change your mind? Are you sure?"

She thought of the boy under the bridge, and the woman with tattoos like Uncle Matt. "I'm not entirely sure. Of anything. But it feels right." She grimaced to herself. "There's one thing, though."

"What?"

"There's something I never told you. And I'm not sure if it's stupid to bring it up now. But it's a big part of why I didn't want to go." She looked down at her sneakers, avoiding his eyes.

"What is it?"

"It's about how I got here. It's about why I ran away in the first place."

"Miri's going to be here any second. I mean, yeah, I want to hear this. But are you sure this is the time?"

"I want to talk to you before I go. Plus, she's always late. Always."

He glanced at his watch. "True. Go on."

She took the chair across from him and started hesitantly. "You were still a kid back then, so I'm not sure if your parents told you everything I told them. You knew I was messed up, but…"

"Abuse," he said. "Your parents were awful."

Her eyes filled with tears. "It was awful, but it wasn't actually my parents—I didn't have parents. That stuff that I told them about happened on the road, after I ran away. I got picked up by someone who wasn't very nice."

"I'm sorry," he said, eyes dark with pain.

"Just listen, okay? My Uncle Matt, he raised me and my brother after my mom abandoned us. He had the cold flashes too, the family curse. He's the one who told me to flee."

"Why would he do that?"

"Two of his friends disappeared, friends that had their own special abilities. Uncle Matt started having all these gruesome flashes. He was sure there was a killer after people like us. Like me." Robin bit her lip. That was the abridged version. But more information would just confuse things further.

"Your uncle told you, a sixteen-year-old girl, to run away, alone, across the country, based on something in a vision? With a killer after you? There are so many things wrong with that." Liam flushed angrily.

"I was fifteen when I left. And I was supposed to run to one of his friends. Don't say he should have told the police because he did. They thought he was nuts. They sent social workers to the house to assess if it was still a safe environment for me and Evan. Plus, his flashes were way better than mine, clearer. He had a way to focus them that doesn't work for me."

Liam narrowed his eyes. "So, what happened?"

"He was supposed to meet me. I waited for two weeks. He never showed up, but a stranger did. So, I ran."

Liam was silent for a long moment. Then he asked, "Did you ever find out why he didn't come? Your brother lived with him too, right? What happened to him?"

"I did find out. My uncle disappeared, just didn't come home one day. My brother stayed with Uncle Matt's long-term girlfriend, but I lost track of him after he graduated high school. He doesn't seem to be a social media guy."

"That's so sad. Wow. That's so fucking sad. I can't believe you've been carrying this around. And you never told me—why didn't you tell me?"

She watched his face as another layer of realization soaked in. More grimly, he said, "You never told any of us there was a killer after you."

"No," she said. "It wasn't like that. Once the church

people got my Social Security number and stuff, I didn't think there was any way I could be traced. I felt safe. As long as I didn't call attention to myself I could just be Robin Fox, and live a quiet life, and be safe."

"And then you did call attention to yourself and your ability, to try and save my parents."

"Yeah. And that was awful and scary. But even after the news story, nothing happened. No one came to find me. And so I started thinking, I'm on the other side of the country, I have a new name, I'm going to be fine. And I have been. Sort of. I live my little life and stay away from anyone into paranormal stuff. But there's always this little bit of paranoia, that someone, somewhere, is watching for me."

There was a tap on the door. Robin flinched, then laughed.

"Miri," Liam said. He sounded a lot less pleased at the prospect than he had earlier.

Robin laid a hand on his arm. "I'm sorry I hid it from you. I promise, there's no way I would have stayed if I thought that anyone here was in danger because of me."

"You've got to tell me the rest later, okay? I need to hear the rest."

Robin grimaced. "There's not much more. I just wanted you to understand. The guy my uncle thought was after us was part of the psychic community. I can't help worrying. What if he comes to this thing I'm going to?"

"Do you know his name? Have you looked for him online?"

"I know who my uncle thought it was. But he could have been wrong." She shuddered. "I've looked up the guy online once or twice. He's like, a businessman? Old school though, not all social media and publicity."

"Hello?" Miri's voice floated through the door.

"Be right there!" Liam called. He grabbed Robin's hand and squeezed it. "You are so brave," he said. "Are you really sure you want to go? I mean, what if—?"

They both heard a key turn in the lock.

"She still has a key?" Robin asked.

He looked sheepish. "I never asked for it back. I hoped—"

"Yeah." She rolled her eyes and stood up. "Thanks for listening. It made me realize how ludicrous it was, the idea that this random person who may or may not have killed my uncle is going to show up on the opposite side of the country all these years later, just because one little girl got lost in the mountains. I'm going to take a shower. Have a nice reunion."

"Hello?" Miri's heels clicked against the living room floor.

"Robin." Liam rose.

She looked back.

"We're not done talking about this. I still have questions. I thought I knew what your life was like. But now it's different."

Robin shook her head and rolled her eyes. "You just want to talk things to death. Now, go to her!"

****

The bus ticket Robin bought online was for 4:05 p.m., so after her shower, she threw her things into a small rolling suitcase. Miri and Liam were chatting and laughing at the kitchen table when she went in to grab some lunch and snacks for her trip.

"Hi, Robin," Miri said brightly. Robin pasted a smile on her face and pretended she hadn't sworn she would block the threshold with her body before letting Miri get her hands on Liam again.

Miri was oblivious. "See what I found at the Goodwill in Portland? They have the best stuff there." She stood and twirled, displaying a silvery striped skirt that flared out in a retro-fifties way. "Liam's taking me to the swing dance at the Vets' Club tonight."

He raised his eyebrows. "I did not know that. I have client appointments until eight o'clock, you know."

"It doesn't get going until nine. We'll be fashionably late."

"Sounds great," Robin said. "Sorry to miss it. Liam, will you be able to drive me to the bus station around 3:30? Or I could walk," she added dubiously. She'd blow-dried her hair in hopes of making a more professional first impression.

"No problem, I can pick you up between appointments," he said.

"Oh, are you going out of town?" Miri leaned forward, eyes flashing with interest.

Liam and Robin spoke at the same time:

"She's visiting family."

"Business trip," Robin said. "I mean, I will visit family while I'm there, but I'm going for work."

"I thought you were just temping?" Miri said, confused.

"Um, yes. I've got an interview, though. In Grants Pass. A long shot."

"You would move all the way to Grants Pass for a job? And, I thought Liam was your only family," Miri said, wide-eyed.

Robin sighed and looked to Liam for help, but there was none there. "Yeah. This is more of an honorary family member, I guess. It's nothing, I'll only be gone for a couple days. Okay, nice to see you, I should go pack!"

She fled the kitchen but halted in the living room because she'd walked into a cold zone. One step, everything was normal. The next step, her body spasmed, as if her spinal cord was shot through with ice. She thudded to the floor, knees first, and failed to get her hands down. Her chin hit the carpet. Then the carpet was gone; the room was gone.

The inside of the car was soft like Mommy's purse and smelled nice like shoes and boots, but the ice cream was melting already all over her fingers, tipping into her lap, sticky-messy, and the man who gave the ice cream was yelling, and she was crying so loud bigger than a baby because Mommy was getting smaller outside the back window, running after them, and then a big truck banged into her and she was gone—

When Robin came back to herself, she was gagging strands of bile onto Miri's pretty poufy skirt as Miri held Robin's ponytail. Her heart was pounding like she'd run a race and in her mind's eye, the woman was running down the middle of a suburban street, terror on her face, yelling and yelling for the child in the car—and then bang. A truck powered out of a side street, out of nowhere, and she was knocked down and under so fast that—

Robin gagged again.

It had been nothing like a cold flash, except for the very beginning. The rest had been as clear as a dream. Was she really losing it now? Had she finally cracked?

Miri patted her back gingerly, and Robin lifted her head to find Liam's worried face.

"I'm still going," she said.

****

Miri hurried home to change after Liam said, "The flu" and Robin said, "Food poisoning," in an attempt to make her collapse seem less weird. Robin showered for the third time that day, hoping that Liam would be gone when she came out. She had surprised herself with her post-flash declaration, but she'd meant it, and she needed to be alone to think. Plus, she couldn't afford for Liam to keep pushing her about the events of the past.

Nevertheless, he was watching TV with the sound off when she emerged with her hair in a towel and wearing her second-favorite office-casual outfit. A pink patch of rug-rash striped her jawline. Sighing, she plopped next to him on the tatty flowered couch.

"Well," she said.

"I canceled my client," he said, staring at the screen. "He has an irritated hamstring anyway, so I told him to rest."

"Were you thinking of talking me out of going? Because I would understand if you wanted to try. Two really nauseating flashes in a row is not going to make a great impression."

"I wouldn't dream of such a thing." He gestured to the TV. "Look. Blue's been gone for a full twenty-four hours now."

There was a ticker-tape running at the bottom of the screen, reiterating Blue's disappearance and Hartwin's strange invitation.

"This flash wasn't about her. It was different from anything I've ever experienced before. So clear, like I was in her head. A little girl, maybe a toddler or a preschooler? Being taken from her mother."

He looked at her then. "Was it that clear? Do you want to check the news for more kidnappings?"

"There's nothing. I already checked on my phone. And I didn't notice anything useful, like a street sign or a license plate. It was all through the little girl's eyes, and she had eyes only for the mother."

He put a brotherly arm around her shoulders and squeezed. "That sounds terrible. But, if we're going with the theory we talked about before, there must be some way you're connected, right?"

She closed her eyes and rubbed her temples. "I don't know. It was different from a normal flash. The usual rules may not apply. Hell, did I ever say I knew the rules? 'Cause I don't." And that, she'd realized in the shower, was one reason she now wanted to go. It was her first chance to touch base with other talented people who might, like Uncle Matt, know things she didn't about how to manage her curse.

"We'll figure it out," Liam said. "Don't worry. Headache?"

"Not too bad." Aside from the niggling fear that she might be finally going crazy—well, crazier—the worst part was the terrible sense of loss in her chest. Last night's flash, the way her heart broke for the boy on the bridge and his mother, and now this too. "Not too bad," she repeated.

"Robin, listen. Don't let this drag you down. I won't talk you out of going, but I want you to know, I will come and pick you up at any time of the day or night," he said. "I will answer my phone no matter when you call. Don't forget your damn charging cord. And for chrissakes, please stay around people so that if you do flash bad, someone is around to help you."

She managed to smile. "And watch out for a mysterious killer from the past. Got it." She stood. "I should dry my hair. Then we can go."

He looked up at her. "You gotta do what you gotta do. But hey, enough about you. Did I tell you Miri asked me to marry her?"

Chapter Five

The thumb-sucking toddler sprawled across his mother's lap in the seat next to her pushed against Robin's leg with his feet like a cat kneading a blanket. "Sorry," the mother said. "He'll go to sleep soon."

Judging by his alert gaze, Robin suspected that was wishful thinking. "No problem. How old is he?"

"Just turned two," the mother said wearily. She stuck headphones in her ears and closed her eyes.

The boy stared at Robin and wiggled his toes. She turned away, leaning her head against the glass and staring out the window at the green rush of trees and highway. She'd made her choice and here she was. Doubts were trying to worm their way in, but she shut them down; she wasn't going to turn around and go home just because it happened to be a waste of time. Dangerous? No, that was silly. Then why did her heart go double-time whenever she thought about it?

Breathe. Here she was, on the bus. She wasn't turning back now.

On a not much lighter note, she hoped Miri wouldn't drag Liam off to the registrar's office by the time she got home. The woman had nerve; Robin gave her that. It had only been two months since the last devastating breakup. Miri had planned to emigrate to Canada with the new beau—Robin had been rooting for Antarctica. Robin wished she could trust Liam not to fall for Miri's wiles, but her own judgment was suspect too. How much was about Miri—a lot—and how much was Robin not wanting her own life disturbed—some? Sharing a house with the two of them sounded like a terrible idea.

The sky was gray but the road was dry, a good day for travel. This was the first trip she'd taken in a very long time, and she tried to focus on the novelty. Liam forced her out of town once in a while; they'd gone to Mount St. Helens last year, and they went to Portland now and then for a show or a play or a race. She hadn't traveled alone since…well, since the Lost Year. That was her mental shorthand for what happened when she left Connecticut, an easy way of coaxing her brain to skip over it. It was a just-don't-think-about-it blur, right up until she found herself on the Foxes' doorstep. Although she didn't like to think about that much either, that tragically brief return to an almost-normal childhood before the Foxes died and she and Liam suddenly had to grow up.

Towns went past, trees went past, mountains went past, and wherever she went, there she was, in the dark place in her own head. It wasn't a coincidence or random moodiness, she knew. However unlikely it was that some bogeyman from sixteen years ago and three thousand miles away would reappear, some part of her was terrified to be around other people with unusual abilities again.

And another part was longing for it.

As a kid, she hadn't kept track of Uncle Matt's friends, but in the years since, she'd found mention of the two disappearances in old news stories online. One had been a palm reader, an older woman who traveled with Uncle Matt's carnival in the old days before he'd gotten tied down with his sister's kids. The other friend use to come to the house a lot, a geeky twenty-something who hung around with Uncle Matt, drinking beer and talking in the shop, which was the remodeled garage that served as an office/storage area for the landscaping business.

Robin hadn't known at first that they had abilities. Most of Matt's old carny friends were nothing but drunks and liars, his girlfriend Ruthie said, and Robin had no reason to think otherwise. Not until those two disappeared, and Matt realized what was happening to Robin, had he confided anything about his real work, his own abilities, his suspicions.

The seat next to her emptied at some point, and Robin rubbed absently at the chilly place on her thigh, realizing she'd been too caught up untangling her hopes and fears to even notice when the toddler had gone.

She was still sunk in reflection when the bus braked loudly to a stop in front of a shabby pharmacy, but she roused when the driver called out "Grizzly." It was the closest town to Spirit Ridge, the property Survival Unlimited was turning into a headquarters and self-sufficiency themed resort. This was her stop.

She descended the steps, assessing the town. Grizzly's downtown was a few blocks comprised largely of a gas station, a couple of pull-up motels, a bait shop, and a sad-looking grocery store. She knew from Wikipedia that it eked out a living serving campers, hikers, and fishing fanatics. Uber hadn't penetrated yet, but she'd found Mike's Cab Co. listed online, and Mike himself picked her up quickly enough, grumbling cheerfully about missing dinner with his in-laws.

It was dusk when Mike pulled into a pot-holed

gravel drive, marked only by a numbered mailbox.

Robin had expected a corporate sign and a well-paved drive. "Are you sure this is it?"

"No question. I've been up here before with a fare. They just don't like visitors much."

"I thought it was a resort."

"Yeah, well, all the rich people will probably be coming in them four-wheel-drive limo-Hummers what you call 'em. Or helicopters."

"I guess," Robin said.

Glaring electric light came into view after a few switchbacks through dense Ponderosa pines. "Here we are," Mike announced as they pulled into a paved cul-de-sac. A Josephine County Sheriff's Department SUV was parked across from a small guard shack next to a wrought iron gate. Chain-link fence topped with strands of razor wire stretched into the dense gloomy woods on either side. A sign over the gate declared "Survival Unlimited" in silver letters, and the Moebius-inspired logo was repeated on the side of the guard shack.

Mike rolled to a stop, surveying the scene dubiously. "You sure about this? I bet I can get you a room down in Grizzly."

"Completely," she lied.

"You have my number." He shrugged then grabbed her case from the back. When he pulled away, she felt oddly bereft.

The interior light came on in the SUV and the window rolled down, revealing a narrow-shouldered deputy frowning at her with thick eyebrows. Then the window of the guard shack slid open.

"Over here!" a voice called, and Robin saw a freckle-faced redhead beckoning her toward the shack.

"You expected?" the redhead asked briskly. "No press."

"Yeah. I mean, I'm one of the psychics." To her shame, Robin heard her own voice drop on the last word as if trying to keep it a secret.

"What?" The guard pointed to her left ear, blocked by a wireless earbud. "Sorry, crosstalk, could you repeat?"

"I'm Robin Fox. One of the psychics."

The guard scanned her computer screen and nodded, then made a thumbs-up sign to the deputy, who rolled his window back up. "Okay, yeah, I see you. You live in Oregon, we thought you'd be driving in earlier."

"I don't drive; I took the bus," Robin said, hating to admit it. It seemed like the only adults who didn't drive these days were drunks who'd had their licenses pulled.

The guard raised her eyebrows but nodded. "You're late. They were holding off on Orientation for you, but they may have gone ahead."

Robin blushed. "Sorry, I would have explained if I'd known it mattered."

"No worries! I'll get someone to drive you up the hill post-haste. Just a sec."

She pressed a button on her earpiece and spoke. "Robin Fox just rolled up. Can you come get her?" There was a pause. "Oh. Okay, second to last. Still doing the Orientation tonight, then?" Another pause. "I'll tell her."

The guard looked at Robin again. "Yep, Grimley's coming down to get you. Turns out you're not the very last but they're going to run Orientation anyway."

"Thanks. No news about Blue? I had no phone service for a lot of the trip," Robin said.

The redhead's face fell. "No. No news. Otherwise

I'd be sending you up for a party."

Robin kicked herself, realizing suddenly that this woman probably knew Blue personally. "I'm sorry, it must be really nerve-wracking."

"Yeah, you're not kidding. I'm Toofer, by the way. Samantha Toofer, Security."

Robin shook the offered hand, surprised to find a hard ridge of callous. "Do you know, do the cops think Blue was taken out this way?" she asked. "I see you've got a camera." She gestured to the fence post next to the gate.

"You think they tell us? I mean, I've reviewed the footage myself, over and over. It's not like there's a shot of a black panel van driven by a suspicious stranger," Toofer said. "Leads are being followed, blah, blah, blah. Be alert."

That must be disturbing. Robin was paranoid about someone from deep in her past showing up despite the odds, but the folks here had to live with the reality that if Blue hadn't simply gotten lost, one of their own had likely colluded in her disappearance.

Toofer said, "Hey, do you want to sit down while you're waiting? I can let you in the shack."

"No, that's okay. It feels good to stretch my legs after the bus ride."

Toofer shrugged. "Well, if you don't mind then I've got to get some work done."

"Thanks for your help," Robin said. The window slid shut. She peered up the dark drive, a ribbon of black in the thick shadows, and then into the woods which had turned the little cul-de-sac into a bright oasis against the oncoming night. The trees were dense, the streetlight penetrating only a few feet past the fence. It got dark a lot faster out here than it did on the coast. And was so quiet, without wind or waves or traffic sounds. She shivered and wished she'd asked who Grimley was. Why was she so ridiculously nervous? She wanted to text Liam but her pride wouldn't let her. What could he say, anyway? There were probably no killers there, and if there were, they probably wouldn't recognize you, and if they did, they probably wouldn't care about killing you after all this time. Robin already knew all that.

After a long enough wait that she almost pulled out her phone despite her desire to be more self-reliant, headlights appeared above the gate. She'd been expecting something corporate and shiny or prepper-like and Jeepy; instead, the vehicle that paused while the gate rolled slowly out of the way was a cross between an electric golf cart and an ATV, with oversized traction tires, two seats in the front and a mini truck bed in the back.

Robin grabbed her suitcase. The driver pulled up to the guard's hut, and Robin studied him quickly. With thin blond hair like dandelion fluff sticking up in different directions around his weathered face, he looked affably harried. His suit jacket looked high quality to her admittedly undiscerning eye, but it was paired with saggy-kneed jeans instead of slacks. She wondered about the strange marriage of cultures in this place. Could you really be a corporate ladder-climber and an off-the-grid prepper at the same time?

Toofer slid her window back open and smiled. "Hiya, Grim. This is Robin Fox. Robin, this is Peter Grimley, Mr. Hartwin's right-hand man."

Grimley shook Robin's hand. His blue eyes in their nest of crow's feet crinkled with a brief smile, but he drew back to check his watch immediately. "Nice to meet you. Just the one suitcase?"

Without waiting for an answer, he grabbed Robin's case and tossed it into the back. She climbed in, and more quickly than she expected, he powered back through the gate and up the road, maneuvering easily through a series of switchbacks. Because of the vehicle's high tires, her balance felt precarious and she hung onto her seatbelt for comfort.

"I never would have guessed there was a business back here!" she said.

"That's the idea. The lower drive is for camouflage. This part had to be paved, though, or the building crews wouldn't come up."

"I guess your boss really doesn't want visitors. So why invite in a bunch of psychics?"

She mentally kicked herself. So much for the good first impression. But she had no idea what might set off a cold flash—her last decade and a half had been about repressing them as much as possible. Maybe the more she knew, the more likely she might be able to trigger something useful.

Fortunately, Grimley didn't seem offended. He shot her an amused glance. "You read the invitation, right? He's a true believer. And hidden driveway aside, he's not averse to public exposure. There's a TV crew here now. They've been shooting for an episode of *Preppers*, had to stop when Blue disappeared."

"*Preppers*?"

"Don't watch much TV? It's a reality show for the same demographic that buys Survival Unlimited products. Off-gridders, end-of-the-worlders, disaster-preppers."

45

"Fair enough."

They pulled into a large, mostly empty parking lot. It was an island of light amid the black pines silhouetted against the purple sky. To one side of the lot, two large trailers were parked in the grass, and two panel vans with TV station logos pulled up next to them. A plump young woman in a black sweatshirt with the hood pulled up was smoking a cigarette under a streetlight near the vans, and she stared at Robin as the cart rolled past.

The woman's faintly hostile gaze made her uneasy. Robin looked away and realized for the first time what the cart was heading toward.

"Holy crap. It looks like a UFO." She wasn't sure exactly what she had expected, probably a standard headquarters: squat stone or cinder block with lots of windows. But there was no building, just a ring of light around a large uneven dome cresting a tall hedge.

Grimley laughed. "Not in daylight," he said. "Tomorrow you'll be able to see it in more detail. The top of the dome is covered with grasses, but there are vents and skylights and such. It's designed to withstand pretty much everything, so there are heavy duty shutters poised to roll down if the environment becomes inhospitable."

"Are you serious?"

He shrugged, smiling, as he maneuvered around a cluster of SUVs to park at the curb behind an identical cart. He stopped the engine with the push of a button. "Whatever your political beliefs, it's a scary, unpredictable world we live in. At Survival Unlimited, we strive to be ready for anything." He spoke like a tired salesman, gamely delivering the party line at the bar after a long day.

Robin climbed out and looked back across the lot, feeling a chill. The smoking woman was still there, her face in shadow. Robin noticed a huddled group of RVs, VWs, and nondescript junkers set apart from the SUVs, like smokers at a health club. A couple had psychedelic paint jobs, new-age airbrushed logos (Fatima's Fortunes), or both. But it wasn't the paint jobs that drew her eye. One vehicle was plastered with bumper stickers, most printed too small to read. But she saw one she recognized. Uncle Matt had it on his car. A large, stylized L that continued into an angular P at the crossbar.

In the last weeks of her old life, Uncle Matt told her the truth about the church he and Aunt Ruthie belonged to, a spiritualist church that had always been another source of shame for her. The Church of Loomis Powell preached the eternal life of the spirit, which translated into believing in ghosts and reincarnation and mediums. And some of the believers, Matt told her, believed in all that crap because they had special powers themselves. Like he did. Like she did.

She hadn't heard or seen anything about Loomis Powell in so long that she'd almost forgotten its existence. Yet here it was, a relic of her past. Not a good sign.

"Are you alright?" Grimley asked, setting a hand on Robin's forearm. She jerked to attention, realizing that he'd already grabbed her suitcase and come up to stand beside her.

"Yes, sorry. It's been a long day."

"Tell me about it. No one here's gotten more than four hours of sleep since Blue disappeared. Come on, we've got to move. Everyone's gathered for Orientation down on B3."

When they passed through the narrow break in the hedge, the dome's ground level looked slightly more conventional with bare cement walls and deep cut windows. No effort had been put into creating a welcoming appearance, which seemed unfriendly for a corporate headquarters. No signs, no flowers, no welcome desk.

Grimley must have seen her confusion. "Don't worry, it's not all like this, I brought you around the side for the sake of speed. There's a lobby in front; although we don't currently encourage a lot of visitors here, we will when we finish getting the resort village set up. But the search team is based there now. We need to rush, so we're going through the back way and down the staff elevators."

He waved his ID in front of a security panel, and a narrow steel door without an exterior knob clicked open. Robin followed him through, taking nearly two steps for each one of his. She tried to track their path through the building, but despite different carpeting and artwork themes as they turned from hallway to hallway, it felt like a maze.

"What is Orientation?" Robin asked, and he slowed down a bit to answer her.

"Hartwin's way of getting all our 'consultants' on the same page. Blue's disappearance has been devastating. He thinks if he throws enough well-organized resources at the problem, it will be fixed."

"And you?"

"I think trying to marshal a troop of notoriously flaky types, no offense, is going to help him more than it's going to help the investigation. He needs something to focus on, something no one else can do."

She allowed herself an inner smile. She'd been wondering herself if a troop of psychics might hold more than the usual number of eccentrics and prima donnas. "No offense taken."

Chapter Six

They dropped her suitcase off in the small Security Office and Grimley hustled her through another narrow hallway and into a service elevator. B3 was the lowest floor, and Robin's stomach lurched as the elevator dropped and kept dropping.

Grimley noticed her grimace. "There's more mountain under us than there is above," he said. "There are limestone caves in this range, too, but nothing that goes to the center of the earth, I promise."

She smiled weakly. She'd choose heights over depths any day. It wasn't quite fear, but the weight of all the cement and stone above cast a constant shadow in her mind.

When the doors slid open to reveal yet another generic hotel-like corridor, Grimley accompanied her to a set of double doors. "I'm heading backstage," he said. "Go in and find a seat. We'll get started momentarily." He walked further down the hall and disappeared around a corner.

Hesitantly, she pulled open one of the heavy doors.

She found herself at the back of a lecture hall that could probably seat a hundred people in its movie-theater style seating, but currently held about two dozen individuals, clustered toward the stage. Next to Robin, a folding table held a large carafe that enticed her with its rich coffee scent. She filled a mug and made her way toward an open chair, avoiding eye contact and smiling in a neutral way that hopefully masked her anxiety. The curious gazes drawn to her entrance drifted away.

Robin studied the room, as she perched on the edge of the seat and cradled her mug. High above the stage, the bottom of a viewing screen peeped from below a curtain. What did corporate preppers watch for fun, *Mad Max* or *The Office*? PowerPoints about the upcoming apocalypse? She snorted internally at her own lame jokes and wondered if caffeine was a bad idea. Her heart-rate was already elevated, but the hot mug comforted her, and so did having something to do with her hands.

A low hum of conversation buzzed among the people scattered in ones and twos throughout the lower seats. One woman had a sleeping infant in a sling across her chest, and a young man, apparently an assistant, was taking dictation from an elderly man in a three-piece suit. Aside from the infant and the secretary, she couldn't tell who was supposed to have extra-sensory powers and who was along for the ride.

Below, a man in a blue button-down shirt mounted the stage only to pace, head bowed. The room fell silent. The images she'd searched through on the internet hadn't done justice to Hartwin's intensity. He wasn't handsome, but his rangy build and plain raw-boned features exuded power, like the heroically incorruptible sheriff in an old Western.

Grimley slipped through a door she hadn't noticed before, his dandelion hair now slicked down. He joined a second figure standing off to one side of the stage. Hartwin glanced up and appeared to notice the audience for the first time.

"Welcome," he said, his voice more cultured than

Robin had expected. "I thank you all for coming to aid us with your unique gifts. I appreciate, more than I can say, your willingness to help a little girl who is very important to me."

He paused, silence stretching as he swallowed noticeably, then set his shoulders and found their eyes again. "Apologies, I should introduce myself. I'm Wes Hartwin, founder and CEO of Survival Unlimited. Today…today that doesn't seem to matter too much."

The audience murmured warmly in response, but Robin narrowed her eyes. Liam always accused her of reverse snobbery, and she knew her knee-jerk negative reaction to charismatic people was as shallow as an automatically positive response. She tried to force herself to give Hartwin the benefit of the doubt, but the display of distraction and emotional vulnerability felt choreographed to her.

Hartwin spoke again. "As you know, our little village suffered a blow yesterday afternoon, when we realized Blue had disappeared. Blue, or rather, Blue Eagle Gracen, is the eight-year-old daughter of my good friends and business partners, Marletta and Miller Gracen. And she is my goddaughter. She's supposed to be safe here."

Another long pause, looking down, before he continued. "We at first assumed she was lost in the woods. Searches continue throughout this property and in the surrounding wilderness, but…there is a growing concern that something worse may have happened."

The words hung in the room, conjuring unbearable scenarios despite their careful evasion of specifics. Robin shivered.

"Survival Unlimited has a strong online presence

and has been featured in a couple of popular documentary series, so you may know a lot about us already. One of the things you may know is that we have developed a radically open-minded corporate culture. Humans need to adapt when the shit hits the fan, as they say, and adapting, to us, means looking at all the options. That's why you're here.

"Our company sometimes consults with psychics for clues to what the future might bring. Some may deny it, but law enforcement does too, especially in difficult, high stakes cases. We are more than fortunate to be working with an investigator who's not afraid to push the envelope and once used a tarot deck to find a serial killer. I'm pleased to introduce Special Agent Bayley DeBlasi."

DeBlasi was a tall Black woman with dark hair cropped short to show the graceful curves of her skull. Her voice was calm and confident, low-pitched with traces of a Southern accent.

"Thank you, Mr. Hartwin. A note: the tarot deck was a piece of evidence. It was not used in any occult way. With that said, I will gladly accept any legitimate help that is offered. I join Mr. Hartwin in thanking you for your time and efforts.

"But please be warned—I've worked with psychics before. I understand there's no guarantee, that you may have no control over the quality of the information you offer. However, should we determine that for any reason you have fabricated false data, wasting the time of my investigation, then you will be prosecuted."

She aimed a measuring glance around the room, and Robin followed her gaze. The warning elicited a chill of resentment from the audience, and the agent raised her chin and continued. "While you are here, we expect you to relay requests and information through channels. No drama. No wandering the woods, which are still being searched. No press releases! You will, in fact, sign a non-disclosure statement which requires you to remain completely silent about any and all aspects of your experience here until you receive specific, written permission from myself or a representative. I can promise, that will not occur until AFTER the investigation is complete."

An almost palpable sense of disappointment filled the room. Robin imagined abacus beads clacking as the mental recalculations brought potential profits sharply downward. It was hard to capitalize on participation in a well-publicized investigation when you weren't allowed to say a word. She allowed herself a private sigh of relief, though. She might be outing herself, but it would be limited. Her name and picture wouldn't be splashed all over the *National Enquirer* anytime soon.

"Anyone uncomfortable with these rules or unwilling to sign the papers will be escorted from the property. Anyone who needs to consult a lawyer may do so during the time-span of this meeting, after which you will sign or leave."

DeBlasi's gaze picked out each member of her audience again. Robin nodded when it was her turn, appreciating the woman's bullshit-dispelling attitude. Hopefully, any fakers who'd thought to derail the investigation to make a name for themselves now had second thoughts. At the same time, what Robin remembered of her own flashes was often confusing and ambiguous, and might be considered attention-seeking nonsense. After the warning, she would be thinking twice about sharing anything unclear, and others might as well.

DeBlasi continued. "Please take what I've said to heart, and again, my deepest appreciation for your willingness to volunteer your time and effort." One last nod and she exited through a narrow door to the side of the stage area. Hartwin looked torn, as if he wanted to say more, but he followed her out.

Grimley stepped forward and introduced himself. "Myself and my assistant, Fran Rowles, will be your primary contacts," he said. "While we're all hoping for good news and a quick, happy resolution, we're trying to cover all the bases, so please be patient with us."

He gestured to a petite older woman with white hair in an asymmetrical bob, who moved up the aisle, asking names and handing out folders. Robin flipped hers open and found the nondisclosure statement on top. She noticed others snapping photos with their phones, and followed suit, although she wouldn't be sending hers for a legal opinion. It just seemed smart to have a record of what she'd signed.

"First thing to mention; as some of you have discovered, there's no cell service in the building. You'll have to use Wi-Fi, and for that, you'll have to sign in, see your packet for instructions. Alternately, there is a phone available in the office next door, just let Fran know."

He continued, "Fran is a notary public, and she will move through the room witnessing your signatures, so please wait for her. If you're waiting on communication with your lawyer, you can sign at the end of the meeting. And please, smile pretty; she'll be taking a picture for your official ID card, which we'll try to have printed by the time we get out of here. Meanwhile, let's cover some more ground.

"The idea is that you will all pursue your 'unique information sources,' in whatever way you normally do. There's a sheet in your packet where you can outline any special needs that you may have, although we've done our best to anticipate wherever possible. Please hand that in to Fran if it pertains to you."

He pulled a crumpled sheet of paper out of his pocket and ran a finger down it. "Oh right, one last point. While we strive to please, remember we're not a spa or a hotel, this isn't a vacation, and we won't be providing entertainment or room service. Please join the staff in the cafeteria, which is located on the main floor, and open for meals from six to ten a.m., eleven to three p.m., and four to eight p.m.. It provides for a variety of special dietary needs. There's also a small cafe and bar open from noon to eleven p.m.

"As of now, you have a blanket invitation to stay through to the end of the investigation. That may change at any time, depending on the opinions of Mr. Hartwin, Agent DiBlasi, and the ongoing benefit you bring to the situation."

He heaved a theatrical sigh and conjured a wan smile. "Okay, that's my spiel. I hit on everything I intended to, but please do read through the entire contents of your packets when you get a chance. There are more details and more information in there. Any questions?"

When the assistant reached her, Robin pulled out her license and signed and dated her form. Fran stamped and signed as well, then took Robin's picture, which somehow felt more intrusive than signing away her legal rights. She smiled automatically anyway.

A scrawny woman with a Southern accent rose from

her seat up front and asked plaintively, "Will we be given further information about the circumstances of the disappearance, and the poor dear girl? There's been hardly anything on the news!" She turned to face the others, adding apologetically, "I'm Delia Morton, by the way. I have a show about the spirit world on cable in San Francisco?" Morton's orange hair contrasted shockingly with the pink roses on her floral jacket. Robin blinked, wondering how the that played on TV. Maybe the spirits preferred bright colors?

"Thanks for asking, Ms. Morton. I should have said. With the cooperation of the FBI, we've prepared something like a press release, but for your eyes only, which is in your folders. Law enforcement wishes to make very clear, you are not here as 'psychic detectives' but as an information source, therefore the flow of information is *from* you, not *to* you." Grimley smiled and shrugged to soften the blow. "However, as Mr. Hartwin has said, if you have special needs that include the need for specific information, please put it on your request form, and we'll consider it."

"Exact birth dates and times down to the second, that's all I need," a male voice grumbled. Looking around, Robin saw women outnumbered the men by quite a bit, even if she counted a skinny guy with pale hair who was more boy than man. The one who'd spoken looked like a college professor gone to seed, with a poorly shaven neck and bags under his eyes.

"Your name, sir?" Grimley said.

"Rennet. Loren Rennet. Astrologer plus. Plus what? Plus whatever I get from the universe." He sounded like he was warming up for a prepared speech, but Grimley raised a hand.

"Mr. Rennet, thank you. We did anticipate that question. You'll find exact birth dates, times, and places for Blue, her parents, and her grandparents in the packet. Now, if that's all, let's give you some time to return to your rooms and get settled in if you haven't yet. You'll have the run of B2East, which includes your guest suites and a common living area. Your ID cards, which are about to be distributed, will not get you into B2West, where the employees are housed, or back to B3 unless we have another meeting here. However, you are welcome to use the gym on the main floor, and of course the cafeteria. The grounds are still being searched, so the woods are off limits. If you leave the grounds, you'll need to check out and check back in at the gate. Please collect your ID on your way out. Thank you."

Grimley nodded tightly and checked his watch, already poised to walk away. A couple of hands popped up in the audience but Grimley demurred. "I'm sorry, I have to go. For now, please allow Fran to help you."

The older man who had a young male secretary looked incensed by Grimley's refusal and stood abruptly. His neck was adorned by an elaborately arranged silk scarf instead of a necktie, and it niggled something in Robin's memory. Had she seen him on TV, perhaps, when he wasn't so frail? Or might he have visited Uncle Matt?

"Not acceptable!" he called out in a surprisingly powerful voice.

Grimley glanced back. "Excuse me?"

"Don't waste my time! I'm not here to be treated like, like—school children!" He waved his hand vaguely toward the rest of the group. "Do you want my help, or do you not?"

There was a shocked silence, and then someone called out, "Sit down, you old fraud!"

Robin snorted, and she heard at least a couple of other suppressed laughs.

The older man's face reddened, and he turned to face the bulk of the group, sitting behind and above him. "I'm a fraud? I'm a fraud? I see you, CeeCee! I see you, Angel! And you others too. You wouldn't recognize a message from beyond if it hit you on the nose! You have no idea what you're dealing with," he spluttered.

He turned back to Grimley, lowering his voice. "My record speaks for itself, and frankly, I find it insulting that anyone else was invited. But I would not punish a little girl for the mistakes of her elders. Now, get someone back here to take me to where she disappeared!"

His pained assistant was bent over his notebook pretending to write, but he forgot to move the pen. Robin suspected it wasn't the first time his boss had embarrassed him.

Fran whispered something to Grimley, who leaned down to listen closely. When he stood, his face was grimmer than his name. "Ms. Rowles tells me you have not yet signed the non-disclosure form, Mr. Volkov. Moreover, she tells me you were very rude about it."

"I sign nothing without speaking to my lawyer, who is unavailable at the moment."

"I'm sorry, sir. We won't be able to accept your help."

Fran tapped on her cell phone screen faster than a teenager. "Security will be here in a minute," she murmured.

The suited man turned purple. "This is a huge

mistake. There is great evil here, filling the halls of this place, seeping down into the tunnels like water! I can feel it. I can feel it! I'm calling Miller. He invited me personally. Find my little girl, he said." He pulled out his own phone.

Robin felt a chill at the mention of evil. He seemed so certain. If he was legitimate, and they sent him away, it was Blue who would suffer. The other psychics were nearly silent, whispering to each other, watching closely.

Grimley remained unmoved. He turned to the rest of the group. "I'm sorry, I really do have to go. There are matters I need to take care of. Check in with Fran, especially if you have not yet turned in your form. ID cards are up front."

Two guards dressed in black came in through the double doors at the back. Fran gestured to the man with the scarf, who was still trying to call Miller Gracen despite what Grimley had said about the phones. His hands shook as he jabbed at the screen, held it to his ear, and then lowered it and jabbed again. The secretary gathered a briefcase and laptop case and stood waiting to one side. The guards spoke to the older man quietly, and, contrary to Robin's expectations, he smiled coldly and tucked the phone away before following them through the upper door.

Murmurs grew in volume, and Fran Rowles, now at the front of the room, climbed up on a chair and whistled loudly for attention. She spoke in a clear, carrying voice. "As I mentioned to a few of you when we spoke about the non-disclosure agreements—you need your ID number to get on the Wi-Fi. So those folks who still need to contact their lawyers, come up first and get your IDs. You can work on that while we get everyone else squared away.

"By the way, folks, in each of your rooms, you will have a phone. The number is on a sticker on the handset. Thank you." She stepped cautiously down and pulled the cover off the cardboard box that had been left on the table, smiling at the first person in line.

Robin picked up her shoulder bag and joined the queue. She overheard the others talking about the man who'd been escorted out. Apparently he was Alexei Volkov, who had famously consulted for the FBI on multiple serial murder cases, including one that had been turned into a bestselling true crime book.

"Was he serious?" she asked two women who chatted in front of her.

"Oh, honey, who can tell anymore? Ask the FBI!" They cackled uproariously.

She blinked, and one of them patted her shoulder. "He's for real, but he's forever calling everyone else a fraud, so no one likes him. And one of his mistakes got two young girls killed, or at least that's what the tabloids said. Arrogant bastard."

"Don't worry, honey, we don't need him. We've got some heavy hitters here. We'll find that little girl, if she's meant to be found," the other one said.

Robin winced inside. If she's meant to be found? That was the kind of rationalization that made her cringe. If it worked, great, but if it didn't work, it wasn't anyone's fault because there was mystical purpose in the failure. Frustrating.

The line moved slowly. By the time Robin received her ID and directions to install the Spirit Ridge MapApp to find her way around, she was almost reeling. The coffee had given her a shot of energy, but she needed a lot more or a quick nap, stat. She also needed a closer look at the contents of the folder, somewhere without distractions where she could hear herself think.

Out in the hall, she stood in the midst of the crowd, some people trying to get the MapApp working and others still chatting about the Volkov incident. They were of all ages, in poet shirts or gypsy skirts, in business clothes or tweedy suits. Trying to use her curse to find Blue might be impossible, but it was the easier of the tasks she'd set herself. If she wanted to find a genuine psychic who might help her better understand and manage her own powers, and who she could trust, where would she even start?

Volkov had called these people a bunch of frauds. Each member of the group was a cipher to her. The fact that many of them seemed to know one another only made her feel more shut out and unlikely to connect.

According to Uncle Matt, some of the gifted could recognize special abilities in others, or the Church of Loomis Powell could never have formed. Robin certainly didn't have that ability, or she would have run far away from Danny the very first time they'd met.

If she could find out whose car in the parking lot bore the Loomis Powell bumper sticker, she'd have a place to start.

She leaned against the wall and people-watched with one eye on the "loading" bar for the MapApp. It was going to be a strange and lonely few days. She hoped for and dreaded a flash, and she was surprised at the strength of her longing to know at least one of these people was like her. Someone who would understand what it was like to feel cursed, to know things she shouldn't, to struggle to understand messages that seemed like gibberish but must have a purpose, because otherwise they would just be torture.

The little spark that lit up inside her when she realized she might do some good with her ability was faltering. All these people, with successful lives and families and assistants—surely one of them would find Blue. She was putting herself through all this for nothing.

A cluster of people now waited for the elevators and Robin decided to avoid any further interaction for now. The MapApp opened and led her to an emergency stairwell just down the hall.

She pulled open the heavy door.

"Hey! Excuse me!" someone called.

Robin turned to see one of the men from the meeting approaching. He was compact and muscular, with arresting green eyes and collar-length dark hair, and only a couple inches taller than her medium height. Definitely too cute for his own good.

"Yes?" she asked.

"Can I head up the stairs with you? I was on a flight at dawn in Boston. I've just been going from one chair to another ever since."

"Sure." She held the heavy door open as he passed. The stairwell was concrete with metal steps twisting upward. The door clanged and echoed when she let it shut.

Grinning, he stuck out his hand. "Thomas Church, psychic to the stars. Pleased to meet you."

She gave him a perfunctory shake. "Robin Fox," she replied. His squeeze was neither damp nor overly powerful, but she gave him no points, annoyed at his attempt at charm and his intrusion on her solitude.

Her coolness must have been noted, because he

turned down the wattage and allowed space to form between them as they mounted the stairs.

Reminding herself that part of her purpose was to meet psychics, she made an effort, but it came out sarcastic. "So, psychic to the stars. The case will be wrapped up in no time."

"Ha," he said. "Well, between the bunch of us, I'd lay odds we'll find Blue by midnight, despite Volkov getting tossed out on his ear." He paused, maybe expecting a laugh. He didn't get one. After a moment, he asked, "So, what's your schtick?"

Robin had been climbing two stairs at a time, and he'd been easily keeping up, but when he said schtick, she slowed. Had she been insulted by him, or was he just poking fun at the lot of them? Maybe they all joked between themselves that they were con artists, and he was according her the same trust. But did that mean he was for real—or not?

She covered her confusion with the simple truth. "Umm, schtick. Well, visions, I guess. Occasional, ambiguous, and probably not all that helpful, but I felt like I had something to offer. What about you? What does it mean to be a psychic to the stars?"

His face fell. "Oh, you really hadn't heard of me. That's okay! I'm pretty small time, actually. But I was mentioned in the August 14th issue of *People* last year. I did readings at a party that the Gracens attended, that's why I was invited. Scott Fairchild was there. You know, he played the kid in the show about the—never mind."

She appreciated that he'd read the blankness on her face. "Yeah, sorry. I don't read *People*. Or watch much TV. But, you do readings? Like, tarot?" she asked politely.

"It was aura readings, with a Kirlian camera. Normally not my thing, I usually do scrying. But it was a favor for a friend."

"You were invited here, though? And Volkov said he was invited. I wonder how many of us received personal invitations."

He looked at her strangely. "What do you mean?"

"I mean—I don't know anyone here. I just saw Hartwin's announcement online, nothing personal, and called the screening number."

"Oh. I don't know. Probably that's what most people did."

It didn't really matter, aside from making her feel more out of place, if that were possible.

She glanced sideways at Tom and instead of seeing his face, she got immediate brain-freeze, as if iced lightning had come down from the ceiling and hit her on the top of her skull. She was nothing, in nowhere, numb as if encased in a glacier, and then—a glimpse of another face where Tom's should have been, with a different wall beyond. Simultaneously, a deep and awful sound vibrated in her rib cage and made her feel bereft. Her eyes teared with sorrow, and the face was too shadowed and then too bright to make out more than an impression of misshapen-ness. Something was wrong with the eyes, and she tried to focus, but her view jerked in and out with the pulse of a strobe light. The sound continued, one moment soft as a lullaby, the next deeper than a whale song and threatening to shake her rib cage apart with sonic pressure. Behind the figure was a dark wall of stone, which she could taste—rough, dirty, salty.

Everything suddenly stopped, and she was left gasping and blinking in the mundane fluorescent lighting. There was a stair beneath her feet, but she felt wobbly and sank down, guided by Tom's firm grip on her upper arm.

She blinked, still seeing blue flashes in her eyes like floaters that wouldn't go away, and Tom repeated, "Easy, easy. Are you alright? Robin?"

He was so close she would have been offended except she wasn't sure she could remain upright without his help.

She took a shaky breath and steadied herself. "You can let go."

The folder made a convenient writing surface, and she ignored Tom as she tried to record her experience quickly without losing any detail. The salty taste of stone, the sensation of dust upon dust upon dust—it reminded her of the dragonfly flash. She wanted to believe that the blue tracers seen in the corners of her vision meant that it was about Blue, but she wasn't sure. They came right at the end and were barely there.

Tom watched with interest and spoke as her writing slowed to a stop. "You had a vision, didn't you? Did you see her? Can you find her?"

Robin caught the longing in his face. "No, it's not that easy. It didn't even make sense." She set the folder down and rubbed her temples. The silence echoed like a balm, and her heart rate began to slow.

He volunteered, "I only get one or two a year. My spirit guide, Hepzibah, shows up and freaks me out. The visions never make any sense until afterwards, when the pieces start coming together, or sometimes the client understands but I never do."

"Really? You have a real spirit guide?" For a moment, she was floored by his honesty, and also by a weird gratitude. But twice a year didn't sound right. "I mean, you're a professional, right? What do you do the rest of the time?"

He laughed a little. "Well, sure. You tell them what they want to hear, what they need to hear. You mix it up. You got to make a living." He took a deep breath. "But, yeah, my spirit guide is real, or I would never have gotten on this path. I have a connection to water. I met her by accident, in a bathtub. I was about to—" he stopped and blinked into her fascinated gaze. "Gee, anyone ever tell you you're easy to talk to? Let's stop there. TMI, as they say." He offered a wan smile.

Robin nodded slowly and tucked her pen back into the folder. Her purse was still over her shoulder. "Thanks for telling me. That helps." Maybe she would find that most of these people were genuine. That was encouraging, although it sounded like Tom's ability was completely different from hers. She offered a silent thanks to the universe in appreciation for not making her vomit and fall down the stairs, but the other usual symptoms were present: pounding head, dry throat, brain still replaying that disturbing image. All she could do was ride it out.

After a moment, Tom bounced to his feet and reached for her hand. "I'll walk you to your room. You look like you could use a rest."

"Just say it," Robin said. "I look like crap."

"Impossible," he said gallantly.

She rolled her eyes. "Okay, I give up. I guess I do like you."

Chapter Seven

Robin blinked at the unfamiliar wood-paneled ceiling above her, gradually awakening to some uncomfortable facts. Her boots were still on her sweaty feet, her phone was digging into her right hip, and a dark green duvet twisted uncomfortably around her torso like she'd been wrestling with it in her sleep.

She was really here.

She fumbled the phone out to check the time, wondering if the craziness of the day might have led her to sleep through the night, but it was only 9:30 p.m.. A power-nap, apparently, demanded by traveling on an abused brain. She'd had two flashes in one day before, but it had been many years since the last time.

She sat, rubbing at her temples, and looked around. The whole suite was visible from the bed, but it was unlike any hotel she'd ever stayed in, small in size but extravagant in detail—rich colors, soft throw rugs over bamboo flooring, and an attempt to give the impression of sunlight streaming in by using recessed lighting and a plethora of plants. There was a sitting area with a loveseat and easy chair, and a kitchen alcove with a full-sized refrigerator. The theme was Pacific Northwest outdoor, with salmon and bear motifs, and a Pendleton blanket in lime green and black draped over a slatted wooden chair next to the bed. This was definitely the rich man's version of post-apocalyptic comfort.

Her stomach growled. It had been many hours since she'd eaten that protein bar on the bus. She pulled up the MapApp and located The Long-life Café, then gingerly worked her way to the bathroom, discovering her rolling suitcase along the way. In the bathroom—beautifully tiled and with a deep tub that didn't seem to reflect sustainable water-saving practices, but what did she know?—she showered with her head bowed under the hot water, trying to think of nothing. Afterwards, she downed two Tylenol.

Tom Church's face popped into her head as she dressed. He'd said he would check on her later, and she'd been so out of it she had just nodded, but they hadn't exchanged phone numbers and she didn't know which room was his.

For a moment, she paused. Was she considering him a friend already? He'd sounded sincere, but she wasn't sure that spirit guides even existed. Her experience was so limited. Her uncle's church, of course, espoused the reality of ghosts and spirits, but she didn't know what parts of the church were the outer shell of misdirection that camouflaged the genuine power within.

At the same time, even if Tom was for real, he wouldn't understand what it was like to be cursed the way she was. He lived openly with his ability, even exaggerated it, and it didn't cripple him. As a professional psychic who had only one or two real visions per year, he was technically ninety-nine percent fraud.

But she was sure he didn't think of it that way, and perhaps it was unfair. He had years of experience reading people, and entertaining them, and that was perhaps worth something in and of itself. She thought she might allow herself to like him. Not trust him, necessarily, but like him.

In the rush of hot air from the blow-dryer, she remembered something else, or rather, someone else. As she and Tom had navigated the B2 corridor after emerging from the stairwell, with Tom supporting her and trying to find her assigned room as she gamely tried to remain conscious, one of the other psychics bumped into them: a plump blond woman coiffed and heavily made-up but dressed in yellow stretch pants and a sweatshirt.

Tom had let go of Robin's arm to steady the other woman, and then grabbed Robin again as she swayed.

"Oh, excuse me," gasped the big-haired woman. Then she'd looked Robin up and down. "What's wrong, dear? You're white as a sheet!" She had shot Tom a suspicious look.

Robin had reassured her she was fine, just light-headed, and promised to let her know if she needed "anything, anything at all." The woman had handed over a business card.

Robin finished drying her hair and found the crumpled piece of cardstock in her jacket pocket. "Readings. Erin Rainier," followed by contact info. She stuck it in her folder and smiled. Without even trying, she was meeting people and making friends within hours of arrival. Erin's protectiveness had been kind of endearing. Maybe this wouldn't be so bad.

Which was a ridiculous thought, because things were already bad. She pictured Blue's face. Yes, it would be nice to let go of years of paranoia, learn more about her own abilities and become less isolated in her affliction. But she was here to help. It was time to see if she could actually trigger a useful cold flash, something clearer than a person with rocks for eyes.

She paused, still stumped by the meaning of that face. Was Blue kidnapped by a blind man? That sound, that whale song and lullaby sound…It had been haunting. But meaningless to her. Aargh.

Robin patted her cheeks briskly as she stood by the mirror at the door, hoping to add a little color. She still looked pale. Then she froze with her hand on the doorknob as one of her thoughts from a moment ago echoed in her head. The image had finally clicked for her. His strangely distorted face, his darkly shadowed eyes—he had been made of stone. A statue! But his eyes weren't carved smooth like a statue's, they were rough hunks of rock. And he had moved. Whatever he was meant to be, he was alive, at least metaphorically so.

She had no idea how that could be useful, but it was something. She should report it. The idea made her heart beat so fast she could feel her pulse fluttering in her neck like a trapped moth. "I will," she promised herself. She would report it…right after she ate. It was a small step. It didn't have to mean anything. It wouldn't put her in danger.

****

Robin walked through the deserted cafeteria to get to the café, admiring the clusters of plants and trees, and even hydroponic gardens growing things like parsley and cherry tomatoes under hanging banks of grow lights. Where was the power supposed to come from after the apocalypse, she wondered, but they probably had generators somewhere.

The busy social hum in The Long-life Café made her pause in the open door with second thoughts. It was a restaurant and bar with waitstaff moving among the tables, but she'd been hoping for something more casual. A quick scan failed to find anyone familiar except for the woman with the baby, who was chatting animatedly with a dark-haired man and bouncing the bright-eyed babe on her lap.

Robin sat at a tiny round table alone, and despite the busyness, a pot-bellied waiter with a goatee approached within seconds. He had a lanyard around his neck like the one she'd been given, and his ID tag said "ARCHIE." He offered her a menu but she ordered right away. "Can I get a veggie sandwich? Do you have hummus?"

"Sure. You want soup? We have a nice vegetarian tomato basil."

"Okay, sure."

He paused, standing there despite the bustle all around, and said, "You're one of the psychic consultants, aren't you? I don't believe in that stuff, myself."

"That's okay, half the time I don't either," she said lightly.

He glanced around then leaned down to meet her eyes. His were brown and slightly bulging. "I think you're a bunch of liars and cheats."

Her stomach twisted. "I'm sorry you feel that way. Did you have a bad exper—"

He spoke over her as he straightened. "You should leave and let the police get on with things. Tell your friends."

She was speechless. He turned and disappeared into the bustle, and she looked after him. Apparently, the staff weren't all as "radically open-minded" as Hartwin had claimed.

Her stomach growled. Hopefully he would still

bring her food, despite his disapproval.

She was flipping through the Survival Unlimited informational packet when she was flanked by a pair of women in bright fleece jackets.

Robin looked up, offering a tentative smile to the one at her right shoulder. The woman in the fuzzy aqua coat carried a half-empty wine glass and a partly eaten slice of cheesecake, as if she'd been seated elsewhere before losing her table. Her bleach-damaged hair hadn't been re-styled since the eighties and she had deep smoker's lines ringing her mouth. Robin had noticed her at Orientation.

"Mind if we join you?" the woman said, and cautiously lifted herself onto a nearby stool.

"You look a lot better!" someone said from the other side. Robin looked to her left, where she recognized the woman who'd given her the business card, Erin Rainier. Erin climbed onto another stool and edged her own cheesecake onto Robin's tiny table. Her hair was tawnier and she was about twenty pounds slimmer, but she had to be related to the first woman. Her fleece was plum-colored, but they obviously shopped and coiffed at the same places.

Robin said, "Erin, right? I do feel better, thanks. And I'm starving."

"You missed the dinner before Orientation, right? Oh well, you didn't miss much."

Archie the waiter brought Robin's soup and sandwich and squeezed them onto the tabletop without a word or even a glass of water.

"Thanks," Robin said to his back, as he was already walking away.

"This is Madeline," Erin said as if bequeathing a

treat.

"Nice to meet you," the older one said drily. She sounded permanently disenchanted. Her manicure was pastel pink, accessorized by a glitzy wedding ring.

"Nice to meet you too," Robin said.

"I don't think I caught your name," Erin hinted with a flash of white teeth.

"Sorry. I'm Robin. Robin Fox."

"Robin. What a sweet name. Any news yet? Has anyone, you know, found a clue?" Erin asked. "I mean, I'm sure we would have heard if the little girl was found, right?"

Robin shook her head. "I haven't heard anything at all. I was so tired I took a nap. You?"

"Nothing's happened. After the first twenty-four hours—" Madeline shook her head slowly. "Well, it may just be her body we find."

The flat statement lay for a moment between them until Erin broke the silence.

"By the way, what do you do?" She forked cheesecake into her mouth and looked expectantly at Robin.

"Um, I do office work," Robin replied. It was somewhat true. "How about you?"

Madeline leaned across Robin and glared at Erin. "She means, your talent. Are you a palm reader, a mind reader, a...I don't know, a witch?"

For someone who had sworn to herself twelve hours before that she wouldn't be sharing personal information about what could be described as a mental affliction with anybody, Robin seemed to be sharing a lot. She sighed. "I get visions, sometimes. Not very good ones. How about you two? What's your schtick?"

They exchanged glances. Robin was definitely feeling an undercurrent here, but she had no idea what it could be. A strange rivalry between the two. Maybe something to do with their relationship.

"I read tea leaves," Erin said. "I mean, I'm a diviner. I could read all kinds of things, but I just prefer tea leaves. And you know, it's good for ladies' luncheons, they enjoy it. More than reading bones or entrails."

Robin chuckled uncertainly. "Entrails? Who would do that?"

Erin shrugged. "It's a perfectly good method of divination. It's just messy."

Robin smiled, not certain if it was meant to be a joke or not.

"I'm an old-fashioned girl," Madeline said. "Like you, I receive visions from the universe." She gestured broadly to indicate where the universe was. "But mine are distilled into the classic venue of a genuine crystal ball."

"It's the coolest thing," Erin leaned forward to confide. "She got it from her mother, and her mother got it from her mother, and so on."

"Wow, it really runs in your family," Robin said. Little hairs on the back of her neck stood up. She wasn't entirely comfortable with arcane dynasties. "Are you part of the family, too?" she asked Erin.

"Not by blood," Madeline answered for her. "She's my cousin's wife."

"Ex-wife!" Erin said, wiggling her ring-free left hand. "And glad of it!"

"Well," Madeline said. "Sometimes things just aren't meant to be."

They both shook their heads and looked at Robin

expectantly. She was chewing, but had made it far enough through her sandwich that she thought she might claim to be done. Maybe, even with the nap, she wasn't quite ready for socializing. "I've got the beginning of a headache," she apologized. "I think I need a quick walk. Will you two excuse me?"

"Are you going to walk on the treadmill? I'll go to the gym with you. It's late, but I should do something after this cheesecake," Erin offered.

"I need some air; I'll just head outside for a few minutes." Robin stood. "It was really nice to talk to you two. I'm sure I'll run into you later." She grabbed her purse and folder, giving a little wave as she retreated.

As she located a sliding door along the side wall of the cafeteria, she glanced over her shoulder. Madeline was standing at the table Robin had left, digging in an oversized lumpy purse. As Robin watched, she removed a pack of cigarettes and shook them at Robin, motioning for her to wait up. Robin pretended not to notice and slipped out the door.

She found herself on a paved patio dotted with outdoor seating and surrounded by more hedges. The brisk air felt delicious, and she closed her eyes for a moment and just breathed it in. It was not so different from the cool damp air of the coast. Then she picked up an undertone of manure and her eyes popped open. Her online research had mentioned a vegetable garden and chicken coops at the self-sufficiency village. Maybe that smell was from the chickens?

The sky was starry above the tree line, but no moon was visible. From here, she could see a lot of hedge but not much else. Glancing behind, she saw no sign of the fleecy twins, and she wanted to keep it that way. She followed a concrete walkway through the hedge and saw the parking lot, a brightly lit oasis surrounded by dense looming trees.

Her phone buzzed in her pocket. As she reached for it, it buzzed again, and again, notifying her of multiple texts. When she checked the screen, there were nine messages, all from Liam.

"Shit," she murmured. Something must be wrong, or maybe he was having a conniption because she'd forgotten to text when she'd first arrived.

She glanced back again, feeling oddly exposed in the glaring sea of light, and stepped into the shadows of a dirt path to return his text. But voices were approaching. She moved back to the sidewalk with her phone still in hand, keeping one eye out for emerging people and one on the messages.

Liam was worried, nothing more.

She texted:

—It's fine, I'm here. No reception in building, I just now got ur txts, sorry!—

—You strumpy chit-monster! Thought u were dead.—

She grinned and responded:

—Those r not words. I said sorry.—

Three people emerged from the woods, switching off their flashlights as they entered the parking lot and headed toward the bunker. It seemed late for the search party to be coming in, but Robin recognized Blue's parents, Marletta and Miller, from news stories online. Both looked shell-shocked. A man in an FBI jacket herded them from behind, murmuring all the while.

*—Wow, just saw parents, looking pretty low—*she texted to Liam.

—No breakthrus yet?—

—No. One flash. Tell you on phone?—

—At gym, wrking. News 4 later tho. Hartwin history.—

—OK, call l8tr. Have 2 B outside, what time?—

—Make it a.m. Got2 sleep, and u do 2—

"Hey," someone said behind her.

Robin jumped, fumbling and dropping her phone as she turned too quickly. She recognized the woman who'd been smoking in the parking lot when Grimley drove her in. She looked younger up close, and vaguely familiar.

Robin crouched to retrieve her phone, examining the screen quickly for cracks. Saved by her phone case, again. "You startled me!" she said, standing up into a cloud of menthol that nearly made her gag. "Can you put that out?"

"Sorry," the girl said, sounding not sorry at all as she tossed her butt on the sidewalk and ground it out with one black high-heeled boot. She was plump, with piercings in her nose and eyebrow, and her hair dyed a rich purple black. She looked Robin up and down, studying her face carefully as if checking for wrinkles, before shrugging in apparent dismissal. "You with the search party?"

"I was just getting some air when they came out of the woods," Robin told her.

"Huh. Wonder if they found anything." She sounded as if she couldn't care less.

"I'm Robin. Are you with the TV crew? I thought I saw you near the van earlier."

"Kami," the girl said and stuck out her hand.

Robin shook it. It felt small and cold.

"I do lighting," the girl continued. She shrugged, meeting Robin's eyes and offering a half-smile. "It's a job."

"Sounds interesting. So, you guys are waiting around to film when Blue is found?"

Kami shrugged. "If she's found." Apparently done with the conversation, she turned and strolled back toward the RVs. Maybe she needed more nicotine.

Robin watched after her for an instant. An odd duck, with those black-rimmed, assessing eyes. Disconcerting, to say the least.

A glance at her phone showed Liam hadn't added any texts to the conversation. Robin stood alone for a moment. It was late to be taking a walk, the starry sky was beginning to cloud over. But she'd been inside so much today. She should head back to her room for her gym clothes and have a quick workout and a bath before bed, or…she could check out the trail, just take a few minutes to see what the woods were like. See what it might have been like where Blue and the other kids had been playing hide-and-seek. She would go as far as the parking lot lights and the starlight penetrated, and no further.

She ventured onto the wide path, flat and lined with pine needles. From the parking lot, the forest had looked like a single threatening entity, dense with shadow, but among the trees, it felt spacious, with Douglas firs and redwoods and a sparse understory. After her eyes adjusted, the broad smooth path allowed enough light for her to walk safely, at least a little way. It would be a relief to leave buildings and parking lots and people behind and have a few moments of true solitude and clean air.

She did remember that both the FBI agent and

Grimley or Hartwin had said something about not wandering into the woods, but she doubted they were worried about this entry path, where every search party must have trodden the ground a dozen times going in and out. She spotted an energy bar wrapper and put it into her pocket to throw away. Her muscles, stiff from a day of travel, warmed and stretched and she shook off the unease that had dogged her ever since she arrived.

Gradually, though, the darkness grew thicker, the path narrower and impinged by scrub and roots, and reluctantly she turned around. Perhaps tomorrow they'd allow her to join one of the search teams. It wouldn't do her any good to twiddle her thumbs while she was waiting for a flash, after all.

That was when she heard something. She halted, trying to breathe softly, listening. There. Was that a flickering of shadows? Then a sharp pain.

Chapter Eight

Something hard pressed against the side of her face,
and her shoulder was bent uncomfortably forward, but
for a while, that didn't seem important. Then the random
stream-of-consciousness burbling in her mind was
interrupted with a sudden urgent thought:

Why am I on the ground?

She opened her eyes and the featureless darkness
transmuted into a mass of leafy scrub inches from her
face. The air was damp and reeked of dirt and fungal rot
and pine sap, overtly strong with her nose an inch from
the soil. Gingerly, she lifted her head, and pebbles and
pine needles fell away from her cheek. Dark looming
trees and bits of sparkling sky came into view. The left
side of her face felt funny and swollen.

She turned her head gently side to side, wiggling her
jaw to test her range of motion, as pieces clicked together
in her mind. She was at the Survival Unlimited
compound, in the woods. Don't go in the woods, they'd
said, but she'd wanted to go for a walk. Pushing up to
her hands and knees, she felt dizzy, and her side felt sore
where she must have hit the ground, but not viciously so.
She shifted onto her butt and brushed herself off. Her
pants and jacket were damp where they'd been pressed
against the forest floor.

Searching for injury, she found a tender spot at the
base of her skull. She remembered a feeling, like a burn.

No, like a lightning strike, sharp and hot and powerful.

She swallowed, memories clarifying. Marletta and Miller Gracen leaving the woods in a dejected haze. Talking to the girl from the TV station in a cloud of menthol smoke. Walking the trail alone, just stretching her legs, to get a sense of the place where Blue had disappeared. Then, something had alerted her, but…what? She couldn't remember, only the sudden burning pain, her vision gone white as the sun.

Then nothing.

She rubbed at the sore spot. There was no stickiness of blood in her hair, but when she brought her hand around, more detritus fell away and the air stung an open cut on her palm. She brushed off both hands, wincing. She must have tried to break her fall.

In the gloom, she noticed something on her left wrist, at the end of her sleeve. A bumpy, wrinkly shape, like a bundle of moss had wrapped itself around her arm as she fell.

She traced it with a finger, feeling soft velvet—man-made fabric, definitely not moss—and when she pulled it, it stretched. A fabric-covered elastic band. She pulled it off and brought it to her nose. It held a fruity shampoo scent. Robin never used scrunchies because her thick straight hair slipped right out, she needed hair elastics with more friction. Absently she stretched the velvety thing between her finger and thumb and then stopped, her thoughts sharpening to a memory of a pony-tailed Blue in the publicity pics. Robin hadn't noticed what was in the girl's hair. Was there any way, could it be…? But no. So many people had tramped through the woods all day, unable to find a trace of the girl. How could Robin have stumbled onto something of Blue's within yards of the parking lot, within minutes of looking?

Maybe she'd picked it up off the ground before she was attacked and forgot about it. She dug in her pocket and found the energy bar wrapper, which she did remember picking up. Why would she remember that and not the other? But still, that seemed more likely than someone whacking her on the head and then sliding it onto her wrist while she was unconscious. It probably belonged to one of the searchers. She tucked it carefully into her jacket pocket, just in case.

Her thoughts were clearer now, and another question formed, the one she should have considered before anything else. For once, it wasn't a cold flash that had left her non compos mentis. Someone had attacked her. That sore spot on the back of her head was proof. What if they were still here?

Her heart beat faster. Her ears strained, aching with the need to detect any presence.

Small rustles in the underbrush, wind noises. She felt alone. Not safe, precisely, but alone.

Her phone was still in her back pocket, and she pulled it out to see it was after eleven. Unsteadily, she climbed to her feet using a tree trunk for support. There were two new messages from Liam and a missed call. He must have decided to try talking tonight after all. She tapped the screen to compose a reassuring—well, semi-reassuring—text.

—Sorry missed call, had incident but am fine.—

She sent it and tried to decide what else she could say quickly, but she really should get going.*—G2g, more tomorrow. Time 2 call?—*

There a sudden very human sound, and she drew herself up in a rush of fear and adrenaline. Raised voices, not far away. Yelling.

Or, calling her name?

"Robin! Robin Fox! Are you out here? Are you okay?"

She froze, wondering for a moment if it could be a trap, the person who attacked her coming back to finish her off. But there were several voices. It sounded like a search party. She thought she even recognized one of them. Tom Church, Tom the scryer.

"Here!" she called back, her voice rough and small in her own ears. She tried again. "Here! I'm here!" Relief and gratitude warmed her with the knowledge that she wouldn't have to limp back to the bunker in the dark alone. She could have done it, sure, but it would be good not to have to.

Then she felt a chill gathering at the base of her skull, right at the sore spot, and she whispered, "No way. No way!" Her face, flushed hot with emotion and tears, contrasted sharply with the rising explosion of coldness that welled up into her brain. Panic jacked her heart rate up even further, and the mishmash made her light-headed, but she had enough presence of mind to grab the tree trunk again to slow her descent.

There was rough bark, and spongy earth and then abruptly there was the void, the cold nothing with no light, no air, as if she were a fossil in space, her bones a meteorite...until, abruptly, she was elsewhere. It was not chaos. It was perfectly clear.

Eyes closed, near silence, just the sound of her own harsh breathing and her heart pounding too loud in her chest...

"Dog, where are you, Dog?" Poppy's voice barged through the closet door like it wasn't there, and she

hugged her knees tighter, trembling. He sounded angry. She forced herself to open her eyes. Stripy slats of light crossed the doors, looking like ladders in the gloom. Her back burned with insistent raw pain, and she rocked back and forth biting her tongue.

"You've gone too far this time," Sissy said carelessly to him, outside the door. "She's never going to listen to a word you say again. I wouldn't."

Sissy spoke in the same distant tone as always. Three years older than Kami, she was Poppy and Antie's real girl.

"Well, she's not you. And the doctor's on his way," Poppy told Sissy, then, louder, "Come out now, Dog! It will be worse if you make me get you!"

Her shirt was glued to her skin with blood in places, pulling at her wounds with every motion. Her stomach clenched tight with fear, and her face was swollen and hot from crying so much. But her tears had finally run out. Her breath hitched quietly in the silence, like a cooling engine. Poppy was right. She better face him now, because it could be worse. It could always be worse.

"Here! I'm here!" she said, trying to keep her voice steady. "I'm coming, Poppy, I promise."

Carefully, she crawled under the hanging clothes, pant-legs and skirts brushing her head. Her knee came down on something sharp, and she peeped in pain but stifled it quickly. He did not like whining.

She reached up for the knob on the closet door and paused. Out in the room, Sissy was humming tunelessly, probably painting her nails. Poppy was silent. She knew he would be standing there with arms crossed over his chest, staring at the closet door for as long as it took her to come out.

No matter where she hid, he always found her.

Kami's whole body shook, but she turned the knob, and the door fell open. She was weak and collapsed on her stomach at Poppy's feet where his polished brown loafers took up the whole of her vision.

He crouched, and she felt gentle fingers in her hair. "Good Dog," he said. "Good, good Dog."

She relaxed, just as his other hand came down hard with the belt on the already torn flesh of her back.

Robin screamed, loud enough to tear the flesh of her own throat. Her body convulsed, trying to avoid the belt, but then it registered. There was no longer scratchy carpet under bare knees, no more smell of nail polish remover, no warm brightly lit bedroom. She was lying on her side in the dark in the woods, and there were hands on her, people around. She gasped in a deep breath and forced her muscles to relax. It was over. It was only a cold flash. It hadn't been her pain. It wasn't her nightmare.

But—it hadn't really been a cold flash, had it? It was too coherent, too literal. It was more like being in someone else's body, experiencing what they experienced, just like the strange flash at home. Had it only been this morning?! God, what an awful day.

Someone squeezed her hand, and she realized her eyes were shut tight. She opened them, carefully, only to see chaos around her. In the glare of flashlights, several people busied themselves, including someone pacing back and forth mumbling into a staticky radio. A man in jeans and a dark-colored down jacket crouched next to her, checking her pulse, while Tom held her other hand.

She fixed on his worried face. "Not a flash," she

said, needing to explain. Wanting to head off any expectation that she would have easy answers.

"It's okay," he said soothingly. "You don't need to talk." Then he immediately contradicted himself with questions. "What were you doing out here? Did someone attack you?"

Robin opened her mouth, not sure how to explain, or how much to explain. She was grateful when the doctor interrupted her.

"Let's just get her inside. She may have a concussion. Did you fall?" he asked.

She switched her gaze to his. A knit cap obscured his head down to his eyebrows, and the odd angles of light made his face seem sinister. "Someone hit me." She realized she sounded defensive, but she was too tired to explain.

The doctor didn't seem to care. He slipped a brace under her head and motioned to another man. Tom smiled apologetically and released her, backing away. She saw there was a stretcher lined up beside her.

"I'm sure I can walk," she protested, but they were already lifting her. She cried out at as sudden pain sizzled across her back, but quickly stifled it into a groan. What was going on with her? First the vomit-vision, which certainly hadn't been normal, and now this? It felt like she had a belt-stripe welt right across her back, just like the one Kami got from Poppy.

She was being trundled down the path now, her face turned up to the sky. Her internal furor almost drowned out the beauty of millions of stars shining between the trees, but not quite. Then something clicked.

"Kami," she whispered. "The parking lot girl."

Chapter Nine

Her gratitude for being found had been premature. Limping back to her room by herself would have saved her a lot of questions, starting with the medical ones administered by the on-site physician, Dr. Green. Without his knit cap and under normal lighting, he looked much less sinister, with his curly gray hair and a weathered face, but he still poked and prodded more than she would have preferred.

Robin perched on a padded examining table in a curtained alcove that contained a stainless-steel sink and several locked cabinets. The rest of his well-appointed office conveyed part counselor, part physician, and he apparently had multiple PhDs to back it up, according to his wall of qualifications. She endured the barrage of questions with her mind bifurcated: one part secretly freaking out, because she'd reached up the back of her shirt and found actual blood—not just phantom pain, then, from the flash. Unless, somehow when she'd fallen she'd gotten stabbed by a stick and it just happened to be where the pain of the whipping in the vision had occurred? And the other part focused on getting through all the necessary questions as quickly as possible, so she could get back to her room. And freak out.

As he washed and bandaged her scraped hands and examined again the bruise on her jaw and the sore spot on the back of her neck, he asked: "Who is the President of the United States? What day is it? Can you track my finger as it moves across your field of vision? How long did you lose consciousness for? Do you have any ongoing medical issues? What medications are you on? Does anything else hurt?"

She hadn't been able to hide a limp when she was finally allowed to walk, so she had to admit to soreness in her knees and ankles, but she hid or down-played everything else. She fudged the timeline, saying she thought she'd lost consciousness for only a minute, and she hadn't noticed how late it was as she had been walking by starlight. They were so much brighter here than where she lived! It made her sound like an idiot, but she couldn't tell him the truth. If she told him how long she was really unconscious for, which she thought might have been a good half hour, he'd be a lot more concerned. He might insist on a more complete examination and even keep her here overnight. If she allowed him to see her back, he would—what? She couldn't even guess, because she had no idea what was there. But she knew there would be far too many questions, none of which she could answer.

Her mind shied away from thinking about it as if it were a live grenade. Her curse had manifested a cruel new dimension and a new way to destroy her. There was no way she was going to face it or even think about it until she was alone.

When her palms had been cleaned, her jaw iced, and her mental state declared probably free from the negative effects of a concussion, Dr. Green advised her to rest.

"The FBI agent wants to speak with you now," he told her apologetically. "She promised to keep it short."

"I need the restroom first," Robin said.

He pointed to a door in the corner, and she ducked into the little ensuite bathroom and pulled off her jacket. Her button-down shirt was stuck to her lacerated skin from left shoulder-blade to right hip. Gently, she pulled it away and twisted so she could see the wound in the mirror.

It was ugly, especially in a couple of deep spots where the sharp edge of the leather belt must have curved in like a knife. She'd bet, though, that it was only a shadow of the actual wound. Who would do that to a little girl?

Who had done that to Kami?

There was a knock at the door and the doctor's voice followed. "Are you okay?"

"Yes, be right out." She gingerly rearranged her shirt, wondering if there was any way she could filch some bandages from the doctor before she left. Then she hastily flushed the toilet and ran cold water in the sink to splash her face with.

When she came out, standing very upright to keep her shirt from catching on her back, the doctor had left and Special Agent DiBlasi and a uniformed Sheriff's deputy were seated next to the doctor's desk, with a third chair pulled up across from them. Robin limped over and sat down.

"Robin Fox? I'm Special Agent Bayley DiBlasi." She reached to shake Robin's hand, then noticed the gauze wrap and winced, pulling back.

Robin nodded. "I remember you from Orientation." She looked to the deputy, a beefy balding man. He nodded a greeting without offering a name and pulled out a notebook.

DiBlasi leaned forward and spoke intensely. "I'm so

sorry this happened to you," she said. "And I know you must be wanting to rest. We just want to get your account while it's still fresh in your mind."

"She means, what the heck were you doing in the woods," the deputy broke in. "Alone!"

"I don't need a translator, Deputy," DiBlasi said evenly, but she kept her eyes on Robin's face, obviously wanting the answer.

Robin blushed. "Yeah. It seems pretty stupid. I wanted—I'm sure this will sound pretty lame—but I wanted to get a sense of the place where Blue disappeared. I don't really know what happened after that…" Her voice sounded weak to her own ears.

"Well, let's start with dinner. You were seen leaving the café, alone, around ten p.m."

"I don't remember exactly. I walked around for a while and saw the Gracens come out of the woods, and I chatted to someone from the TV station in the parking lot. Then I went down the trail, and I thought it would be too dark, but the stars were really bright. At home there's a lot of light pollution, and it's foggy half the time anyway." Her mind raced even as she tried to sound as vague and harmless as possible. What could she tell them? What should she tell them? She needed time to think about what had happened.

She added, "I still can't believe that anyone would want to attack me. I must have just surprised someone. I mean, there's no reason for me to be targeted by a kidnapper or a—" she was going to say killer, but bit off the word.

"Uh-huh," DiBlasi said. "So no sight, smell, sound of the attacker, just bang, and next thing you know, the search party is calling your name?"

Robin admitted she thought she'd heard a noise. DiBlasi made Robin go over the whole thing again, especially the part where she thought something had caught her attention but she couldn't quite remember what, right before she blacked out.

"And you haven't said anything that would make anyone think you knew where Blue was, or who might be involved with her disappearance? Did you imply to someone, maybe, that you'd had a vision?" DiBlasi demanded.

Tom's face popped into her mind. But he was the one who'd come hunting for her with the search party. He would have had to follow her into the woods, knock her out, give her an elastic band, then leave her there unconscious and start asking people if they'd seen her. She supposed it could have happened like that, but it seemed unlikely.

"If you can't even tell who's sneaking up on you, I'm not sure what good being a psychic is," the deputy muttered.

Robin rubbed at her face. She knew her story sounded idiotic, and didn't blame them for prying for more, but she must have looked convincingly pale and ill, because when the deputy glanced up to frown at her over his notes, he grimaced and turned to DiBlasi.

"Maybe it's time to wrap this up. The doc did ask us to keep it short."

DiBlasi studied her with cool hazel eyes and softened a little. "I might have more questions tomorrow. Can I get your room number? I'll take your cell number too, just in case we need to follow up after you leave."

Robin told her, and asked, "Do you really think this could have something to do with Blue?"

DiBlasi stood and stretched. "Can't rule it out at this point. You're lucky your friend was looking out for you. I don't want to scare you, but if folks hadn't tracked you down...Well. Just, please, no more stargazing. And stay out of the woods."

They left. Dr. Green returned and unfolded a wheelchair. She protested, but he insisted that even though she had no breaks or sprains, she should let herself be wheeled back to her room, climb into bed, and stay there for twelve hours. Groaning, she gave in and tried to brace herself away from the back-rest.

"Relax," the doctor chuckled. "I promise, I'm an excellent driver."

Not good enough, she thought grimly, biting her lip as he wrestled the chair into the elevator. "I thought you weren't supposed to sleep if there was a chance of concussion," she said, aware that she was sounding as crotchety as an invalid.

"You'll be fine, I promise. Plus, I'll make a house-call in the morning."

But I won't be here in the morning, she thought. It surprised her, because she hadn't yet put it into words, but it was true. She was going to leave.

Relief spread through her, lessening some of the pain. Sometimes acknowledging failure was the best you could do. She wasn't proud of it, but she'd come, she'd had two confusing and useless flashes, she'd been scared shitless, and she would run back to Liam with her tail between her legs and a bloody wound across her back. It was for the best.

She rose painfully from the wheelchair when they reached her door and turned to shake his hand. "Thank you for all your help."

****

Robin woke before dawn after an uneasy sleep. Her body had stiffened up overnight, but her back was a little better. It hurt to twist at the waist or lift her arms, and the two deep spots could use some gauze and Neosporin, but she must have stayed on her stomach or her side most of the night because she only had to tug a little to free her pajama shirt from her scabs.

Her mood was terrible but her headache was gone and she had a clarity of thought that had been missing after her crazy, exhausting day yesterday. She didn't belong here. Her flashes were getting worse and weirder, she was of no help to anyone, and she'd wasted law enforcement resources by nearly getting herself killed through sheer stupidity.

As soon as she'd returned her few clothes and toiletries to her suitcase, she slipped out. There were cameras in every hallway, so she didn't feel like she was actually sneaking out, but it would be easier if she didn't have to face anyone. No one would care if she left. She was a victim, not a suspect, and although Agent DiBlasi had intended to speak to Robin again today, she had Robin's cell number if she needed it. Robin didn't have anything to add, anyway.

Her fingers curled around the velvety hair elastic in her pocket. Okay, maybe she had one thing to add. But she wasn't going to, not when it might mean being grilled and not allowed to leave. If the thing really did belong to Blue, they might not let her go.

She passed a few staff people in the hall, some in gym clothes, others dressed for the outdoors. They nodded politely as she made her way to the cafeteria, where breakfast was being set out. Thanking the bleary-eyed staff, she grabbed a coffee and a muffin and left through the same patio door she'd slipped out of last night.

It was not yet fully light, but the air smelled fresh and felt invigorating against her skin. She looked behind her, at the glow of the cafeteria, and the strange world she'd barely begun to get acquainted with. She felt something like nostalgia for a briefly dreamt of future that would not come to pass.

Robin walked through the parking lot while nursing her coffee. She scanned the TV station vehicles, saw no one stirring, and glanced away. She could not think about Kami, about that cold flash that had been strangely clear that was more like a shared memory than a flash. "Here, I'm here," the child's voice had sobbed. No, she would not dwell on it. It must have been long in the past, anyway, even if it was the same girl.

Her aching, stinging back would not let her push it so easily away, as she tried not to allow herself to wonder how scarred Kami's back might be under those black clothes.

Hiking down the driveway to the guard station soothed her black mood. She'd be home by afternoon if she was lucky enough to catch one of the ancient buses. She pulled her case along the pavement, purse slung over her shoulder, the steady sound of the wheels like progress to her ears. Halfway, she realized she should call Liam. In fact, she should have emailed him last night, but she hadn't been considering logistics. Fridays tended to be busy for him, but maybe he could shift some of his appointments and pick her up.

Thinking about what she had to say to him—that she'd been attacked, that she was giving up—made tears come to her eyes, but she couldn't let herself fall apart. When had she become so fragile? This was getting ridiculous.

She stopped, pulled her phone out of her pocket, and texted him to avoid having to say the words. It was barely past dawn, but he would already be at the gym working with his hardcore early morning clients.

—*Pick me up later?*—

Five minutes later, her phone buzzed and she pulled it out again.

—*OK. U done there?*—

She swallowed and texted back:

—*Guess so*—

—*When/where meet?*—

—*Not sure. Will txt when I get to bus, c what will work*—

She put the phone away, feeling both grateful and pathetic.

No deputy was stationed in the turnaround when she reached the gate. A tired-looking bald man drowsed in the security booth. She considered sneaking past, but he was more alert than he looked and waved her over.

"I need to go into town this morning," she said, approaching. "But I don't have a car. I'm going to call for the cab to meet me down at the road."

"Hope you can get a ride this early. You got your ID so I can check you out?" he asked. She pulled off the lanyard, and he ran the card over his sensor.

She tensed, wondering if there would be some message on his system: Crime victim! Do not let her escape!

He handed the ID back with a look of concern. "I might be able to find someone here to drive you to town.

It's early but I bet someone's around here. Might be a little too early—I'm not sure anything will be open over in Grizzly yet."

She smiled, shook her head. "It will be fine. I've got the taxi driver's number in my phone. If it doesn't work out, well, I'm meeting someone," she lied. "I'll just get them to pick me up."

"All righty then, good luck." He shrugged. "Have a good day."

She headed down the steep and gravelly part of the driveway carrying her case by the handle. Her heart lifted a little, so long as she stayed away from thoughts of how she'd allowed herself to hope, and how those hopes had so quickly been crushed.

****

Mike the cabby was happy to pick her up. His little Toyota did a quick U-turn in front of her within fifteen minutes of her call, and she hopped in. The online bus schedule listed the first pick up at 11:05 a.m., and if Liam could cancel a couple of appointments, he'd be nearly to Grizzly by then, so she might as well wait. But there was nothing to do, and she felt anxious, as if someone might come looking for her.

Tom! she thought, and chuckled bitterly at the idea of a search party heading into the woods for her again. Shoot. She still didn't know his room number, and she hadn't thought to leave a note. Well, maybe the doctor would go check on her early, and spread the word that her things were gone. She had Erin's business card, but she had the sense that if she contacted Erin, the whole bunker would be abuzz with speculation about her within minutes.

Maybe the guard would spread the word, and they

would figure out that of course she wouldn't want to stay after being attacked.

According to the cabby, the only thing open this early on a Friday was the diner. He dropped her at a rundown house whose lawn had been converted to a parking lot. The owners probably lived on the top floor, she thought, seeing homey curtains in the windows above. Inside was a counter with half a dozen stools which held a few early morning customers, while the few tables scattered around were still empty. Robin claimed a booth by the front window where she could watch the street, and then ordered coffee, toast, and fruit. She wasn't all that hungry but figured she'd be here for a while.

The waitress, a skinny teenager with titanium braces that matched her titanium nose ring, brought Robin's food. Other customers came and went, filling the diner with a low buzz of sleepy conversation punctuated by the occasional hearty greeting or exclamation. It was soothing white noise to Robin, who flipped through a free newspaper filled with classified ads, horoscopes, and a crossword puzzle.

Her horoscope read: "Thanks to Jupiter's influence, your life is about to kick off a fresh chapter! Hello, reinvention! Channel excess energy constructively. Practical rather than emotional issues tend to capture and engage your attention. Old problems can resurface for further inspection or error-correcting."

She stared at the horoscope for a few minutes. It was right, but also wrong. She supposed it held what everyone wanted to hear: promises of new chances and extra energy. And, everyone had practical issues and old problems that kept recurring. Human nature. It only went to show how easy it was to seem as if you had special insight, when in fact it was a mishmash that would apply to almost anybody, including herself.

She got stuck on the crossword and sighed, staring out the window instead. In the bright morning light, Grizzly was a pretty little town, with narrow streets and old trees pushing up the sidewalks with their gnarly roots. A convenience store and bait shop were right across the street, and she imagined it got pretty busy around here in the summer, with people visiting to camp and fish.

The waitress stopped by to offer a coffee refill, but Robin covered the mug with her hand. "Can I switch to decaf?" she asked.

"Sure, but it'll take a few minutes, we don't usually do decaf this early in the morning! Hey, by the way if you don't mind me asking—are you from that Survival place?"

Robin shook her head. "Not really. Why?"

The girl shrugged. "Just wondering. We've all been waiting for news of that little girl, and I figured you might have the inside scoop. Mike said he picked you up out by there."

"Mike the cabby?"

"Yeah. It's a small town. He stopped by to pick up his breakfast burrito and saw you still sitting here. He waved but I guess you didn't notice."

"Oh." Robin figured there was no presumption of privacy in a town this small. Maybe you had to pay extra if you didn't want everyone to know your business. "I don't know anything, though. I mean, I was only there one day. They didn't tell us much."

The girl lowered her voice. "But they're not letting

anyone in except police and the ESP people, right? Which are you?"

"I'm not police," Robin said. "But I wouldn't call myself ESP people either. Sorry." She looked back down at the paper, hoping the girl would take the hint and go away.

"We get real curious down here about that place," the waitress confided. "Because of Hartwin being from such an old family around here. You know, he didn't hire a single person from Grizzly? He even has cousins here, and he ignored them and brought in all his staff from outside!" She sounded truly outraged.

"Oh yeah? I didn't know that. Did he grow up here?" There hadn't been much information about his early life in the Wikipedia article she'd read.

"He did, he went to school with my boyfriend's dad! I guess he was kind of weird, even back then."

Robin nodded, wondering what the girl meant by weird. "Too bad. I mean, it does seem strange that he would bring his company here and then not hire people he used to know."

The girl shrugged. "What can you do? Rich does not mean nice, that's for sure." That seemed to sum up all her feelings on the matter, and she heaved a sigh then shook it off with a bright smile. "I'll go get your decaf going. You going to order anything else?"

Robin checked her watch. Still over an hour before Liam would get here. "Is there a library in town?"

"Yeah, but it's closed today. It's only open a few days a week. A retired schoolteacher runs it as a volunteer, and she's busy with other stuff. There's a bookstore, though!" She looked pleased to have come up with this.

"I'll see if I can find something to read and come back for my coffee and maybe a pastry or something, okay?"

"Whatever, sure!" The girl smiled. "Here's your check."

Robin paid and strolled to the tiny glass-fronted bookstore, which seemed larger inside than out. The front room was full of multiple copies of bestsellers, kids' coloring and activity books, and travel guides, while the back overflowed with sagging shelves of second-hand paperbacks. Robin quickly selected a copy of *Harry Potter and the Sorcerer's Stone*, wanting an old friend more than anything, but at the cash register, her eye was caught by a small New Age display. On impulse, she bought a deck of tarot cards and a book about how to read them.

"Are you a mind-reader?" the cashier asked breathlessly.

Robin shook her head ruefully. "If I was, I wouldn't need tarot cards, would I?"

On her way back to the diner, she passed a Walgreen's. She could wait until she got home, but she had time now, and if she managed to cover the worst spots on her back with salve and bandages, the car ride would be a lot more comfortable.

She made the purchases then took her bags back to the diner. The waitress had left Robin's table looking inhabited, with the crossword-in-progress and a new mug turned upside down on a saucer. Robin seated herself, and the pig-tailed girl hurried over with the fresh pot of decaf. She recommended lemon pie, and Robin ordered a slice warmed up.

She glanced at the puzzle, then pushed it away,

setting her bags on the table. When she moved the newspaper, the corner of an envelope appeared underneath, and she saw that it had been tucked under her placemat. She tugged it free. It had her name on it. Her real name.

Robin sat back, then forward again when the pain reminded her she was still wounded.

She looked away and then back. "Heather Farrell." She blinked. It was impossible. She looked around quickly to see if anyone was watching but everyone seemed to be minding their own business.

Holding the envelope gingerly, she inserted her finger along the flap as if there might be anthrax inside. Or a snake.

It was a half sheet of lined notebook paper, scrawled upon with big capital letters in black ballpoint pen. YOUR DAUGHTERS HERE AND SHES GOING TO DIE.

It fluttered to the table and she dropped the envelope on top of it, and then her hand on top of that, trapping it. Hiding it.

Her head felt so strange she was sure for a moment that she was getting a cold flash. But nothing came. Her face was numb and the sounds of the diner were far away, as if she'd sunk underwater. The words burrowed through her palm and into her bloodstream toward her heart.

Eventually, her pie arrived.

"Did you—" she cleared her throat. "Did you see who left an envelope for me?"

The girl wrinkled up her forehead. "No one sat at your table," she said definitively. "I knew you were coming back."

"It wasn't you?"

The girl shook her head like she thought she was about to get in trouble.

Robin forced her lips into smile. "It's okay, no big deal. Can I have the check?"

She pulled out her phone and texted Liam, telling him to turn around. She wasn't going home. She couldn't.

Chapter Ten

Blue's heart jumped when she found the double doors at the end of a rough and crooked passageway, impossible to see from within the enormous cavern. With a new energy born of relief, she yanked hard, only to jerk her shoulder painfully in its socket. The doors were locked tight. She sank to the uneven floor and cried for a long time until she grew tired of the sound of her own sobs echoing in the dark. She was too old and too smart for this. And what if a Helpful Spirit heard her and decided she was too babyish to help? She blew her nose on the sleeve of her hoodie and waited in hiding for the mean lady to come back.

Her secret hope was that the mean lady would be in a better mood and not actually be mean anymore, and they could go up to the bunker together and Blue would go home to Mommy and Daddy and it would turn out that Uncle Wes wasn't angry after all. It was silly, she knew, but sometimes grownups were silly. And no one she'd ever met was so mean they'd leave a kid in a cave all day.

When Blue's stomach was rumbling and her mouth had become dry, the lady finally came back, but she was scarier than ever. Blue crouched behind some boulders, close to where they'd started the game of hide-and-seek. The lady paced around and poked her flashlight here and there. She called for Blue, then yelled at her, then talked more quietly in a serious and explaining way, but with mean and scary words. She said she would skin Blue alive, she would electrocute her, she would cut her into little pieces and put the pieces on skewers and toast them over a fire, if Blue didn't come out and come out right now. Blue shrank down in a crevice behind the boulders like a little mouse.

Then the lady's voice changed from serious explaining to pure honey, and that was the worst of all. She apologized for losing her temper and said it was just a game. She said she was sorry to be such a sore loser, and Blue was a very good hider. But now the game was over, and Blue had to come out so the lady could take her back to Mommy and Daddy, who were getting worried.

It should have sounded good. But Blue could hear, in the way that she said it, that the lady hated Blue, and hated Blue's parents, and probably hated all kids and all parents.

Blue was so terrified her pee came out. She pushed herself further into the crack, way back, and kept pushing until she suddenly squeezed out the other side. She crouched there in her itchy, cooling jeans, nearly holding her breath until a long time after the lady stomped out and the doors banged shut again.

When Blue finally turned her light on, she was in a passage that continued both to her right, which might go under the bunker, and her left, which might go under the woods, if she wasn't all turned around in her head. But she couldn't see more than a little way ahead. The walls were uneven and the bumpiness made big black shadows that blocked her view.

She tried to be smart. She remembered the story of the Minotaur in her reading book. Theseus used silk thread to find his way through the labyrinth, but Blue didn't have any thread. She didn't have any bread crumbs, which was okay because that hadn't worked out well for Hansel and Gretel anyway. All she really had was her scrunchy, so she took it out of her hair and set it along the wall near the crack leading back into the main cavern. If no other people or animals—or Bad Spirits— came through here, it should stay put, marking where she'd come from. Meanwhile, she would try something else she'd learned from a story; if you're in a maze, always turn left, and eventually, you'll find your way out.

It couldn't be that far back to the gate in the woods. And maybe there were more ways to get there.

The first time she left the spot with her scrunchy, she ventured only a little way down the passage and then got scared, feeling the weight of the darkness and the stone ceiling and the bunker pressing down on her, and she was so alone and small. Why hadn't she stayed with the other children? She could be home now, in her own dry bed in clean pajamas, having noodle soup and chocolate pudding and Mom and Dad taking care of her. She crawled back to the crack where her scrunchy was, and cried in the dark until her sobs slowed to hiccups. Then, feeling silly to be crying alone where no one could hear her and come help, she took some deep breaths and finally stopped herself, blowing her nose and wiping her face on her sleeve.

When she got her courage up, she ventured a little further the second time, and even further the third. She was proud that she was carefully learning the way, that she was being smart and not getting hurt.

Until she couldn't find her way back, even though

she was sure she'd only turned left and so turning right should have brought her right back to the scrunchy and close to the cavern that would lead to home, if only someone besides the mean lady would unlock the door.

For a while she pretended she wasn't lost, and kept turning right and right and right, sure that the next turn would be the last one. She probably burned through too much of her flashlight power, checking in cracks in case the scrunchy had gotten knocked somewhere by a rat or a bat or some kind of blind lizard. The panic and tears had come and gone again.

Now that she admitted she was lost, and that it might be a long time before she was found (or never, but she tried to ignore the little voice in her brain that added that), she kept moving, trying to cover more ground. She got so tired and hungry she started doubting herself, but she'd made the decision when she was less tired and less hungry so hopefully it was right.

All the while, something was lodged in her chest, a sort of balloon that made her breath come tight and made it even harder to think, so she distracted herself with songs and stories. She liked the sound of her voice echoing softly against the rocks, like someone else was keeping her company. Being silent and alone in all this darkness might be very much like being dead.

She didn't want to be dead. She didn't want the word dead to even be in her head. She didn't want to waste the water that came out of her in tears and snot when she thought of how she didn't want her Mommy and Daddy to be alone without her if she never came back.

So she hummed a very quiet little tune and remembered something from long ago. When she was little, she had an imaginary friend, Georgina, who looked just like Blue but had hair down to her knees because no one made her cut it or even brush it, and her feet were always bare because no one made her wear shoes, and she got to wear princess dresses all the time, even for climbing trees. And she had a princess name, not, as Blue had overheard one of her friends' parents saying, a hound dog name. Georgina would be good company, she decided. Georgina was brave and she wanted to help Blue, but she was also a little afraid of the dark, so Blue talked to her gently and told her not to worry, told her they were being smart, and careful, and would find their way out.

After a while, it stopped feeling like a story she was telling herself, and Blue became certain that if she whirled around next time and she turned the flashlight on, Georgina would be skipping along behind in her bare feet and her princess dress, feeling brave because Blue was so brave, and they would grin at each other, glad they were sharing this adventure.

Then, they found the well.

Blue shined her light about every ten steps, even if she didn't feel anything different on the wall, like a curve or an ending. She was about to turn it on for the thousandth time but realized suddenly that there was gray up ahead. There was light, some kind of light, but so little it was just—gray. Was she imagining it, her eyes making things up in all the boring blackness?

"What do you think, Georgina? Maybe it's finally the way out! We have to check."

When she turned on her flashlight and pointed it toward the gray, she saw an arched ceiling like a church, very high above her. Without realizing it, they'd stepped out of the last narrow passage and into another cavern.

And up up up, there was a narrow crack, and through the crack, she could see stars.

"Oh, Georgina, we found the sky!" she cried softly.

But when she swung the beam downward, her heart wrenched in her chest, because even though she'd been careful to always watch where she was going, knowing these were wild caves not visiting-on-vacation caves— even though she'd been checking her footing in between saving her flashlight—she and Georgina had somehow come to the edge of a pit, which was only a few steps ahead of her.

"Shhh, it's okay," she whispered to Georgina. "No harm done." But she looked longingly up at the stars. If only…well, if only what? If only she had a huge ladder? If only she had a cowboy lasso and knew how to use it? If only she had a trampoline? That slim crack was proof that they were close to the surface world, but it was impossible to reach.

A poem came into her head that she'd learned by heart in second grade. "A flea and a fly in a flue, were imprisoned so what could they do? Said the fly, let us flee; Said the flea, let us fly. So they flew through a flaw in the flue." She would give anything to fly, but maybe at least she could find a flaw.

The pit was deeper than her dad was tall, scattered with large boulders and smaller rocks. She examined it carefully, hoping to find a way to slide down to the bottom and continue on in another passage, because otherwise this was a dead end. How could she turn her back on the sky? They had to move forward.

Her light found a shoe. It was a pretty, sparkly shoe that would match one of Georgina's dresses, if Georgina wore shoes. In fact, it looked like a glass slipper from a fairy tale, but with no high heel. Blue moved the light until she found the other shoe, partly hidden by some rocks a few feet away. It sparkled in the beam of light against a foot made of bones.

Blue screamed and dropped the flashlight, which rolled forward and crashed into the pit. Everything went gray.

Chapter Eleven

"I'm coming," Liam insisted. "You said some of the other psychics have assistants. I'll be your assistant."

Robin paced on the sidewalk in front of the diner clutching her phone to her ear, her frustration rising. The frustration was entirely with herself; of course Liam wanted to come after she told him she'd received a threatening note. And of course he didn't really understand her choice to stay, because she hadn't told him the truth about it. She couldn't, because that would make her years of evading certain facts seem like years of lying. He would hate her. She kind of hated herself.

"What exactly did it say again?" he demanded.

"It said, 'I have the girl. Say nothing to the cops. I'll be in touch.'" Robin bit her lip. She'd worked hard to come up with something that explained why she would change her mind and stay that sounded remotely plausible. "You can't come," she insisted. "Please. I need to do this myself."

How had it come to this? Her carefully edited version of how she'd washed up on his parents' doorstep, homeless and hurting at sixteen, had been hard enough to share. But she'd never told him or his parents anything about the baby. Wasn't it strange, that she could tell Liam about crazy psychic powers and not about something much more common?

At the time, it had simply seemed that a baby who

111

wasn't there was a lot easier to hide than her curse, which was all too visible. But now, she realized she'd wanted the Foxes to see her as a child who needed care and sustenance, and not as a parent herself. Especially not as a parent who'd abandoned her baby, which would make her unworthy of the Foxes' love.

He was still protesting. "I really don't understand. Why are you being singled out? Why wouldn't they go to her parents? Or Hartwin?"

Traffic had increased in Grizzly as the morning waned. A guy pushing a stroller wrangled his way over the bumps and dips in the sidewalk and shot Robin a dirty look. Robin realized she'd been staring and turned to face the diner window.

"It's because I'm not important," she insisted. "I'm separate from everyone, on my own and unprotected. Maybe that's why there's been no ransom demand before. The kidnapper didn't realize how secure the compound is, and had to wait for someone to leave the grounds on their own." Robin was proud of her quick thinking in a twisted, self-hating way. That actually made sense.

"Robin, you've been attacked in the woods, and now you've been contacted by a bad guy. You're not even going to report it, and I'm supposed to just sit back and let whatever happens, happen? I don't think so."

Robin suddenly saw the light. Big brother needed someone to watch over her, but she finally heard the loophole. "Wait a second. I didn't say I wouldn't report it, I just said they didn't want me to report it. You must think I'm an idiot. Or the bad guy must think I'm an idiot. Of course I'm going to the cops. Or rather the FBI. I'll tell Special Agent DiBlasi."

"Gee, I wonder why they think you're an idiot, Miss Wanders-Into-the-Kidnapping-Woods-By-Herself." He sounded somewhat relieved. "I still don't understand why they attacked you. I really don't understand why they gave you her hair thing!"

"It might not be hers, and I might have picked it up myself," she protested weakly, because she wasn't sure she believed that lie herself anymore. The note was making her more paranoid. "But if it is, maybe they gave it to me as proof of life, but they didn't mean to knock me unconscious. I don't know." She hadn't told him the doctor said it looked more like she'd had an electric shock than a knock on the head. That sounded too weird and would raise more questions she didn't have answers for.

Robin saw Mike's cab turn at the corner and waved it down. "Listen, the cab is here. I'll text you later. I promise, I'll talk to the FBI lady."

"No, wait! I never got to tell you. I learned something about Hartwin."

Mike's cab pulled up to the curb. He rolled down the window, smiling goofily. "Ready to head back out there, little lady?"

Robin rolled her eyes. "Just a sec, okay?" She turned her back on Mike, only to see the green-haired waitress watching through the window of the diner. Robin waved. "What is it?" she hissed into the phone.

"When he was a kid, he lived in Grizzly."

"Yeah, I got that," she said. "From his classmate's son's girlfriend, if you can believe it."

"That's not all. Here's the weird thing. There was a disappearance back then, too. I found a one-sentence reference online and had to track the original story down

113

on microfiche at the library. It was when Hartwin was in elementary school. Maybe you can look it up in the local paper, there was just a tiny blurb in the *Oregonian*."

Robin was impressed. Liam wasn't exactly a library and microfiche guy. "Wait a second, you didn't find it. Miri did, right?"

"That's not what's important, genius."

Mike had gotten out of his cab and was leaning against the back hatch waiting for her suitcase. She held up a finger again, making an apologetic grimace. "Who disappeared?"

"It was a little girl in his class. Jennifer Drake."

****

After getting off the phone with Liam, Robin felt guilt settle deep into the pit of her stomach. She had lied outright about what the note said and about planning to tell the FBI. She had lied by omission about the existence of her daughter. And, she hadn't gotten the chance to relate the things she had planned to share. The most recent cold flash. Kami. And the bloody belt mark across her back.

Robin tried to stare out the window of the cab and think about everything, as she had on her previous rides with Mike, but they were spending so much time together, he was beginning to think they were best friends.

"Have your meeting, then?" he asked brightly.

Robin glanced at him. He had a broad, homely face with a friendly grin, and curly ginger hair. He was probably fifty-something and seemed like a nice guy. She should have sat in the back seat, that would have sent a message. But the back seat was half full of junk. Boots, raincoat, paperback books that had seen better days.

Shotgun shell casings.

She knew he'd seen her sitting alone at the diner, and that with the apparent gossip level in this town, he'd learn she'd been sitting alone the whole time she'd been there. She knew how small towns worked and Grizzly was smaller than most.

"Phone meeting," she said. "You know how it is." She made a quick stab at changing the subject. "So, you're a hunter?"

"Sure," he said. "I fill my freezer. Most guys around here do."

"Yeah? You spend a lot of time in the woods?" She wondered briefly if the search teams had consulted locals about what dangers these forests might hold.

"Not me. Maybe compared to some guy who lives in the city, I mean, sure. But not really."

"Oh." Robin looked out the window again.

"You thinking about that girl? Blue?" He flashed her a sympathetic look. "I don't think she's in the woods. If she was lost, they would've found her by now."

"You think so? I've read news stories about adults dying of dehydration ten feet from a well-traveled trail. It must be even worse for a little kid."

He shook his head, snorted. "Not here. Here, there's water all over the place. And the woods aren't that dense, mostly. It's not like there are grizzly bears around here, not for a century! Someone must have took her."

She turned to look at him. "Have you lived here all your life?"

"Mostly, yeah. Why?"

"I heard there was another little girl who disappeared around thirty years back, but I don't know anything about it. I just wondered if people thought she got lost in the woods. Or, like you were saying, if they thought she got taken."

"I was away when it happened," he said, shaking his head. "A young buck myself. But I heard about it. There was all that stuff then about Satanists and such. Some folks were sure she got took. I kind of doubt it though. That one, they'd had a class picnic at the River Park. Said the river was real low that spring, but kids will always find a deep spot. I'm betting she drowned. Sometimes, bodies just don't come up."

Liam had made it sound like something suspicious, but how could it be, if the whole class was there at the river? On the other hand, if it was common knowledge that it was a simple drowning, it wouldn't have been classified as a disappearance.

"Anyone see her go in?" she wondered aloud.

"Nah. That's the mystery of it. She wandered away, I heard. The kids were playing hide-and-seek, and the teachers weren't keeping good enough track of them. It's not easy, you know. My sister was a teacher, up in Portland. Couldn't take the chaos, she quit and joined the Army."

"Wow," Robin said. "That's quite a jump."

"It really is," he said, and allowed the conversation, finally, to subside into silence.

****

It felt like déja vu when red-headed Toofer greeted Robin at the guard shack. There was no deputy on duty, and Toofer called up to the compound to get Robin a ride. "They were looking for you," she commented neutrally. "You must have headed out early. Brought your suitcase and everything."

Robin shrugged. "It's the easiest way to carry my

laptop. I checked with the guard when I left. Is there a problem?"

"No, of course not," Toofer said. "I'm sure they would have tracked you down if they needed you bad enough."

"Right."

It was still cool and clear as Robin paced stiffly back and forth in front of the guard shack. The air felt moist. She could hear the sound of water flowing, and knew that some nearby brook must be feeding into the river below.

It wasn't Grimley but an Asian woman of about thirty who picked her up in the modified golf cart. "I'm Sarah Park, one of the security specialists," she said. "I heard what happened last night," she said. "I'm so sorry. Normally I would have been there to help, but my daughter had a fever."

Robin had to think for a moment to figure out which part of last night she was talking about. "Is your daughter okay?" she asked.

"Yes, she's fine, the fever broke. It's just a bug, but we're all feeling super protective these days."

Robin nodded slowly. "I can imagine." She'd never had the day-to-day experiences of being a parent, and she'd been way too young when she'd given birth. She'd spent only days with the baby, but the connection that had been forged during the months of pregnancy had been real. She'd spent the past sixteen years telling herself, always, that the baby was better off with the normal, stable, well-off parents that Uncle Matt had found for her. Better off without her.

But she'd been wrong. Maybe. Or maybe she was being lied to. Maybe the girl was fine and far away.

The stripe across her back throbbed angrily,

reminding her of one girl who definitely wasn't fine.

Was there a connection between Kami the lighting intern and Robin's daughter? Could she actually be Robin's daughter? But she seemed so old! The baby would only be sixteen now. On the other hand, maybe the blood connection was the reason the flash had been so clear. Uncle Matt and others with the family curse before him had controlled their flashes with blood-letting, but maybe there was more to it. Maybe blood ties counted.

She pushed that away for the moment. The central question had to be, why would Robin's daughter be here, whoever she was? What could she have to do with the missing Blue Gracen?

Robin closed her eyes.

Sarah Park's voice broke into her thoughts. "Are you alright?"

"Sorry. It was a long night. And then I got up so early." Robin yawned.

Sarah looked over at Robin quickly then back to the road. "If you don't mind me asking, why did you get up and leave like that? You caused a bit of a stir."

Robin's mind struggled for a believable lie. "I'm sure it sounds strange to you, living the self-sufficient dream out here, but...I really needed to talk to my brother, after what happened last night. I needed to sit in a normal place, around normal people, and feel—"

"Feel normal?" Sarah nodded. "I get that. I'm sure this place gives off a strange vibe to newbies, even aside from Blue being missing. That's exactly what we're trying to do, make it different. Pull an awareness of the fragility of life front and center in your consciousness, instead of ignoring it. Live closer to the way our ancestors lived, self-sufficient and understanding that life is fleeting and precious. You should see all the drills we normally do: meditation, strength training, survival in all kinds of situations."

"And here I thought you all were in it for the money," Robin joked. But it wasn't really a joke. Despite what she knew about the company, about how the staff had uprooted their lives to make this compound a reality, so far it had been the corporate nature of the environment that kept striking her, rather than any difference in the day-to-day culture of the people who lived here. Maybe that wasn't fair, though. She hadn't seen much, and this was the first non-Blue-related conversation she'd had with a staffer. Unless she counted Alfie, the anti-psychic cafeteria man.

More questions were forming in her mind, but their conversation was interrupted by their arrival at the parking lot.

"Well, that worked out well for me," Sarah announced with a smile as she hopped down from the cart. "It was nice to have a break. And you're not so wacky for a 'psychic consultant.'"

If only you knew, Robin thought as she smiled back. "Same. For a prepper, I mean. Thanks for coming to get me." She grabbed her case and retraced her steps around the hedges toward the cafeteria, while Sarah disappeared through the secured staff entrance near the corner of the hedge. What would Sarah have thought if Robin had a cold flash during their ride? That was always the problem. Robin seemed normal to potential employers and friends, right up to the point where she got weird and scared people away.

****

Her room was in the same mild disarray that she'd left it. She parked her suitcase, freshened up in the bathroom and checked out her back in the mirror over the sink. The lacerations were swollen and pink, but most of the edges had dried together. She dug into the Walgreen's bag and reached awkwardly around to apply the salve and bandages.

First aid accomplished, what should she be doing next? What would Liam do, she asked herself. If he were here, he'd make her check in with the doctor, no doubt. Well, she hadn't fallen into a post-concussion coma, and she'd just put on bandages. Good enough.

Thanks to her promise, Liam was expecting her to come clean about everything. If he had any idea of what she'd neglected to tell him, he'd yell at her until she spilled all the beans. "Sorry, big brother," she whispered.

Guiltily, she sat on the loveseat with her notebook, thinking she should make a list to get all the issues straight in her mind. There were two basic problems, and both were high priority. Blue was definitely in danger if not already dead, and Robin had come here to help Blue and her parents. Her fingers toyed with the scrunchy in her pocket. It was so unlikely that it was Blue's, but what if there had been hair on it, DNA evidence, and her handling had stripped it of useful clues? How could she explain her own cowardice, her own fight-or-flight reflex that had prompted her to pack up and leave before returning with her tail between her legs?

She couldn't explain it. She'd just have to keep playing the idiot. Well, it wasn't such a stretch, was it? She rubbed her temples, feeling tension all through her body, her agitated energy turning her tendons to ropes.

Focus, she told herself. Focus or you're going to end

up sobbing in a corner like an abandoned baby.

For a moment, her brain seized on yesterday morning's flash. She could still feel that awful, yawning sense of loss. It had been like a child wrenched away from a parent. Was it her child, wrenched away from her, so long ago? No, the girl hadn't been an infant. But maybe the child had been kidnapped from the adoptive parents. Robin had never even known their names.

Focus. She ground her teeth, causing her bruised jaw to ache. Lovely.

Okay, the other issue besides Blue was the note. She pulled out the envelope and reread the words, although they were already seared into memory: YOUR DAUGHTERS HERE AND SHES GOING TO DIE. Someone didn't like apostrophes. She studied the handwriting. The capital letters were nondescript block letters. She wasn't a handwriting expert. She couldn't even lean toward male or female. Carefully, she folded the note, put it back in the envelope, and looked at her name. HEATHER FARRELL.

Just like the first time, it hurt her to read it. She lived each day as if she hadn't had a childhood. As if she didn't have a little brother. She blew off questions about those years by lying: My family lives in Canada; We were never close; I'm an only child.

Heather Farrell would have grown up to be someone else. Someone who didn't have to lie.

"Sorry," she whispered to her brother, wherever he might be, whatever life he might be living.

Obviously, someone had wanted to disturb her, shock her, with their knowledge of her real name. But the note—it was so specific. Not just YOUR BABY or YOUR CHILD, but YOUR DAUGHTER. Not many people even knew she'd been pregnant. When she'd gotten big enough that she could no longer hide under baggy sweatshirts, Uncle Matt had sent her to a church friend in Vermont, and the under-the-table adoption had also been arranged through the church. So, it would almost certainly have to be someone he'd confided in. God knew, she hadn't confided in anyone. Daniel had alienated all her friends, and her brother had been caught up his own life.

Unless it was an amazingly accurate guess by someone who'd recognized her from childhood. Knew the LeClairs. Heard some version of the story.

If the note was true, if her daughter really was here—and her mind choked on the possibility to the extent that she forgot to breathe again, just for a moment—that daughter might be Kami, whom she'd had at least one and possibly two unusual flashes about. But Robin hesitated. It just didn't make sense. Robin's daughter would be sixteen, and Kami looked twenty. Eighteen at the youngest. More to the point, Robin's daughter should be living happily with Uncle Matt's old friends in England. She should have a British accent and count her grades in years and call some other woman Mum.

But years of abuse, cigarettes, and too much makeup could have curdled a youthful glow, so she couldn't count Kami out. But Robin hoped and prayed that something else was going on with those flashes. May her real daughter be far, far away, from here, from her, and most of all, from the LeClairs.

"Don't jump to conclusions," she whispered to herself, trying to take strength from the steadiness of her own voice. That, surely, was what Liam would say. Just because someone threatened her didn't mean the threat was the truth. More information was needed. And since she didn't have many routes open to her, she would talk to Kami.

Someone knocked on the door with a jaunty rhythm. "Just a sec," she called, detouring to grab tissues from the bathroom. She blew her nose and splashed cold water on her eyes, hoping her puffy pinkness could be mistaken for exhaustion rather than tears. Well, she was exhausted, deep down in her soul, so there. "Exhausted but determined," she said aloud, testing her voice. Then she went to open the door.

Chapter Twelve

"Thanks for looking out for me last night..." The words died on her lips as she swung the door open.

It wasn't Tom.

Apple-scented hairspray and cloying perfume assaulted her nose and she backed up as Erin moved in for a hug.

"Robin! I'm so glad you're okay!" She squeezed Robin, then grabbed her shoulders and looked intently into her face. "Are you okay? I mean, really okay?"

They were so close Robin could count the crumbs of mascara on Erin's lashes. She pulled back, not wanting Erin to see into her own haunted eyes, and felt the scabs on her back protest.

"I'm fine," Robin said.

Erin pushed past her into the suite and continued talking. "Oh my heavens, you can't even imagine how worried we all were when we heard about the attack. I mean, it could have been any of us!" She flashed a wide-eyed look back to Robin, even as Erin wandered further into the room. The new box of tarot cards sitting on the coffee table drew her attention. "I didn't know you read Tarot!" she cried with obvious pleasure.

"I don't, not really. I bought those yesterday. Just an impulse."

Erin pulled her hand back as if she were about to be burned. "Ooh, maybe you were moved by a message from the Universe. I better not touch them, you have to imprint them with your own spirit if they're going to be your heart deck! Wrap them in silk to protect them, undies or a scarf if you don't have anything else!" She giggled.

"Okay, I'll be sure to do that. Listen—"

"Such a bunch of hooey in here, though," Erin interrupted, picking up and flipping through the Tarot book. "You should ask Madeline for a lesson. The crystal ball is her first love, of course, and where her real talent lies, but she's amazing with tarot as well."

Trying to wrest back some control of the conversation, Robin said, "So, Erin, what's up with you today?"

Erin set the book back down. "Silly me, I didn't say, did I? Mad and I thought you might want to go to lunch before the thing, if you were up to it."

Another voice broke in from the doorway, this one much more welcome. "Look at you, up and around!"

Robin turned, startled to realize she'd left the door open behind her. "Tom! Hi. Yep, still among the living, thanks to you."

He grinned. "I happened to be the first one to notice you were missing, but we would have found you eventually. Someone or other would have gotten a message from their spirit guide, or at least a dream."

Robin laughed and turned to look at Erin. She caught a momentary look of—anger? jealousy?—on Erin's face as she glanced from Robin to Tom, but it was quickly replaced by a smile.

Erin said, "Hi, Tom! I was just inviting Robin to lunch."

"Nice to see you," Tom replied. "Erin and I met

yesterday," he added to Robin. "She and her friend said they saw you leave and we realized that you'd never come back."

"Sorry for all the trouble," Robin said, realizing again what a fuss she'd inadvertently caused.

"No trouble for me, I didn't get bonked in the head," Erin said.

Robin reached up and sheepishly rubbed the back of her head. "It wasn't that bad. I don't think they really wanted to hurt me."

"Let's go up to lunch together," Tom suggested, and then checked his watch. "We should leave about now if we want time to sit and eat."

Robin hesitated, thrown off track. She'd wanted to look for Kami, and had begun summoning her courage to question her. If she allowed herself to be distracted, was it just more running away?

But she had to fit into the group of psychics if she wanted answers. Maybe one of them had written the note. It almost had to be. One of the older ones, who might have known Matthew Farrell or Victor LeClair in the old days. She wanted to talk to Kami again, to look at the shape of her face, the tone of her skin, to see if it was possible that Kami could be her surrendered child. But it could wait for lunch. It would have to.

She pulled on her jacket and slung her purse over her shoulder, making sure the ID lanyard was still around her neck as they headed into the hallway. "What's this 'thing' that's happening after lunch?" Robin asked as she pulled the door shut.

Tom answered. "It's been two days, and so far, there's no new leads on Blue. Nothing shared with us or the public at least. Unless your attack counts as a lead.

We need to muster our resources."

"We're going to be proactive," Erin said brightly. "It was Leelyn's idea, but it's actually really good."

Tom rolled his eyes. "Backhanded compliment, but okay. Leelyn's a medium. The dead speak through her. She says it was their idea, that all of us together can't help but draw the attention of greater powers."

"You mean, a seance?" Robin asked.

Erin said, "No, silly. It's going to be a power circle. We're going to hold hands and focus on Blue. You'll see. It's kind of like, Native American? Or Peruvian. Something."

"Sitting in a circle holding hands? Sounds like a seance to me," Robin said.

"You're really not up on this, are you? A seance is when you're trying to get the attention of one spirit or entity and communicate. This is more like when people all over the world hold hands at the same time and pray for peace," Erin said. "We'll put all of our energy out there with the goal of reaching Blue. The Universe might respond to all of us, to one of us, or maybe Blue will just poof—appear!"

"Huh." Robin was pretty sure that wasn't how the universe worked, but what did she know. "I'll give it a try. So that's right after lunch?"

"Two o'clock is an auspicious time," Tom intoned, and winked at her. "Well, 2:07 anyway. That's what Loren said, and he was promptly contradicted by Natalie, the other astrologer. She's the woman with the prosthetic leg. But she eventually settled on 2:14, and the Circle will still be going, so they're both happy enough."

"Great."

The psychic contingent had pushed together a

flotilla of tables in the center of the cafeteria. Survival Unlimited staff, wearing anything from business casual to coveralls and work boots, eyed the colorfully dressed psychics and gave them a wide berth. The psychics didn't appear to notice, giving off a focused, concentrated vibe, as they prepared for what was coming.

Robin's heart started beating in her stomach. She'd been skeptical and even superior, sneering at the naivete of the plan. But seeing them all together, she suddenly realized she was the ignorant one. She'd rejected her ability and lived in hiding, while all these people had presumably been learning and growing and using their skills.

She was completely out of her depth, and she should have stayed home. Exactly what she'd been thinking this morning, right up until she got the note.

But her conclusion was still the same. If there was a chance that her daughter really was here and in danger, she had to stay. She had to help her.

She stiffened her spine and ignored the pit of dread in her stomach.

As she trailed after Tom and Erin into a long food line, she scanned the room. Very likely, one of these psychics knew who she was. One of them knew her birth family and that she'd fled under a false name. One of them might know what really happened to Uncle Matt. One of them was threatening her daughter's life or lying in order to threaten Robin.

A clean-burning anger was easier to live with than shame and panic, she found, even when it was tinged with fear.

She blindly collected food onto her tray. Tom had

moved ahead and saved a seat for her. Erin and Madeline were nearby, and she saw Erin nudge Madeline, who waved with a flick of her fingers.

Robin sat between Tom and a stork-like man dressed in rough spun robes almost like a medieval monk, his long silver hair pulled back with a silver barrette. She would definitely have noticed him if he'd been at Orientation. He seemed to be concentrating on his food until he turned to her with a reserved smile.

"You are the famous Robin Fox? I'm called Master Leopold by my clients, but you can call me Leo." His voice was mellifluous, his eyes compassionate as he took her hand, changing what she had thought would be a handshake into a firm press between both of his.

She forced herself to stay still for a moment, but when he showed no sign of releasing her, she gently disengaged her hand, pretending she needed to wipe her mouth with her napkin. "Sorry, I'm such a slob. Yes, I'm Robin, good to meet you. Not famous, though, just foolish and unlucky. You weren't at the Orientation, were you?"

"No, I had another urgent situation. I run a small spiritual retreat for the retrieval of past lives, and one of my clients was in crisis. I came as soon as I could. Blue attended one of my workshops, you see, and we formed a powerful spiritual connection."

"I didn't realize that children could—" she trailed off, realizing again how very alien Blue's experience as the child of Hollywood actors had been to her own childhood.

"Of course," he nodded. "One who can access the wisdom of their highest self at a young age has the potential not only to avoid repeating many of the pitfalls of youth, but of transcending mundane existence and becoming a sage and a leader of men."

"Huh. And did this happen for Blue?" She studied his lined face as he considered her question, and detected nothing but sincerity.

"Blue is a very juvenile soul," he said finally. "A beautiful, unique upwelling of energy. Her parents were disappointed that there was no potential for accessing earlier selves, but I made sure they understood what a great honor it was to be entrusted with a new blossom of the Universe. None of us profit by the path of another." He shook his head. "Now I fear for that young soul."

"Yes. Hard not to."

There was something likable about him, which surprised her. Usually she was immune to the kind of charm exuded by men like Hartwin and Leopold. Perhaps the difference lay in the level of sincerity. Leo was undoubtedly a salesman, and a good one; he sold his unusual beliefs to Hollywood actors, after all, and apparently made a living at it. Robin had never before taken the idea of reincarnation seriously, because it seemed obvious to her it was only wish fulfillment, a desire for self-importance. *I may be one of the faceless billions now, but you should have seen me when I was Cleopatra!*

Maybe he was simply among the well-meaning but deluded. Maybe her bullshit detector was on the fritz after wallowing in her own self-doubts for days now. She sighed. It was much harder to judge these people than she had expected. And if she couldn't even tell who was a fake, how could she figure out who was threatening her?

"Excuse me," she said to Leo. She turned to Tom. "I

need to run to the restroom. Where's the circle thing going to be?"

"They've given us an exercise room, like a small gym. It has a padded floor." He shrugged. "I'll wait for you, I don't mind."

Winding her way through the tables, Robin bumped into a woman with a nose like the prow of a ship and cropped, silver-threaded hair. She wore leggings with tall boots and a long scarlet tunic. "Sorry," Robin said.

Instead of pushing past her, the woman paused and looked her over. "You're Robin Fox?" she said in a pleasant, low voice, meeting Robin's eyes with a dark gaze.

"Yes…" She really was infamous now. Word had certainly traveled fast.

"I'm Sidney Doyle. Nice to meet you."

She put out her hand and Robin took it reflexively. Sidney slipped her index finger along Robin's palm in a quick angular motion. Before Robin could react, Sidney smiled and moved past her, back toward the crowd.

Robin knew that handshake. The L, askew and with the tall leg slanted forward to feed into the trunk of the P. The belly of the P was a triangle, so that it echoed the angle of the L. The whole could be traced in six swift stripes. The Church of Loomis Powell.

Robin bit her lip. Was it Sidney's car then that had the church's bumper sticker? Robin had almost forgotten. It was something from the old days, something which might link Sidney Doyle to Uncle Matt, Victor LeClair, and/or the note. She should have asked Tom about the church. Did it even exist these days? It must, or why would Sidney have used the handshake? Unless it was a further intimidation tactic, like the note.

Most of the group around the table had already left when Robin returned, and the few remaining were standing and collecting their trays.

"You look pale. Are you sure you're up for this?" Tom asked, dark eyebrows drawn together.

She picked up her tray, not sure how to respond. She had no reason to trust him, beyond a gut feeling. She took a breath. "Strange question. Have you heard of The Church of Loomis Powell?"

"Sure. The Friends Church. When psychics say it, they don't mean Quakers." He grinned, and then said, "Why, what's bothering you?"

"What else do you know about it? Is it still going?"

"Yeah, I suppose. Younger folks are more likely to use the online PsychicMoot to connect with other psychics, rather than a church group, so maybe the numbers aren't what they used to be, but sure. Let's see, the guy it's named after was historical, hanged as a witch in the end, but during his life he tried to fight ignorance and superstition. Do I get a prize?"

She ignored the question and asked another. "Do you know Sidney Doyle?"

"Well, not know-know. But I've chatted with her. She was sitting, what, three spots away from me. I met her at a conference in Florida. Before she got big. Before we got big," he corrected himself.

"And what does she do?"

"She's really good. She's actually consulted for law enforcement before. She's done talk shows about it, but only a couple. Very tastefully done. She's a classy lady." He glanced around the table. There was no one left. "If you're up for this, we should head in." He started walking toward a doorway near the restrooms. Robin followed.

"Okay, okay. But what does Sidney Doyle do?" She almost shook him.

"Psychometry."

She looked at him blankly.

"The reading of things. Objects. They can absorb emotions, sometimes even specific impressions like bits of memory, if they're handled enough. I guess if there's no CSI stuff, no DNA, they sometimes bring her items to see if she can get anything."

"I'll introduce you, if you like," he offered.

"It's okay. I'm sure I'll meet everyone. We'll probably go around the circle and introduce ourselves, just like in school. Can't wait." Robin couldn't hide the sarcastic edge in her voice, and Tom grinned.

"I can tell, you love that stuff, don't you? 'Hi, my name is Robin, and I'm a psychic. It's been seven hours since my last vision,'" he continued in falsetto.

She was startled into laughter. Grateful for the distraction from her own roiling emotions, she dropped her voice as low as it would go. "Hi, my name is Tom, and I'm psychic to the stars," she said, drawing out the last word.

"Ouch," he said. "Hey, you gotta advertise your talents, no one else will."

They caught up to the rest of group in front of a propped-open door, everyone slowly filing inside. Robin took a deep breath as if she were about to dive underwater, and joined the crowd.

Chapter Thirteen

Someone's too-strong sandalwood scent overlaid the room's natural funk of disinfectant and sweat. Robin sneezed. The space was as big as a school classroom, but it seemed crowded with the mass of bodies, some of them large in girth and/or colorfully dressed. Like most gyms, it was not optimized for sound, and the voices echoed between concrete block walls.

In the midst of chaos, in the center of the room, Robin noticed a seed of peace. One plump woman gracefully and silently folded herself into a sitting position on the mat that stretched across the floor. Those nearest her followed suit, and Robin tapped Tom's arm to pull him out of a conversation and they sat too. Soon, all but a few were quietly waiting for the stragglers to catch on.

"—should really be communing with my crystal right now." Madeline's resentment was clear to the entire room as her voice fell into the sudden quiet. She and Erin looked around. Erin flushed red but Madeline shrugged.

"Sorry," she said with no attempt at sincerity, as they both cautiously lowered themselves to the floor.

The plump woman who'd started the silence folded back to her feet like a yoga master, and Robin recognized her as the woman with an infant at Orientation. She looked to be in her thirties, dressed in layers of scarves and skirts. Her long dark hair was pulled into a messy bun and her olive face was round and shone with concentration.

"Thank you all for joining me," she said. Her voice was very soft, but she spoke carefully and clearly, with a slight accent. She turned in a circle, looking at all the attendees. "I am Leelyn Noguerra, and for those of you who don't know me, I work as a medium. I hope we can accomplish together what we have not yet been able to accomplish alone. We can share some space and silence focusing on Blue, together. A prayer, a meditation, whatever is good for you. We have this room until the 3:30 Zumba class, so…Maybe we can scooch ourselves into a circle? And hold hands, if you want."

There was a rustling, grunting, subdued commotion as everyone attempted to cooperate and follow their own preference at the same time. Robin spotted Sidney Doyle about a third of the circle down from her, comfortably cross-legged, breathing deeply with eyes closed.

Robin watched her for a moment. The church her Uncle and his girlfriend had belonged to had been an embarrassment when she was a kid, and she had learned to keep it secret, part of their background lifestyle that she ignored as much as possible, like motorcycles and weird friends. That had persisted until a few months before everything blew up when Uncle Matt belatedly realized it was Heather, not Evan, who'd inherited the family curse. He told her what the Church of Loomis Powell really was, and that she belonged in their inner circle of people with special abilities as much as he himself did.

Uncle Matt's frightening theory that his friends had disappeared because they were in the inner circle had been far more important to her at the time than the organization itself, and she'd barely thought about it in the years since she ran away. But now the Church was here, or at least one member. She swallowed and tried to clear her mind of emotion.

The quiet continued as a few people who likely hadn't sat on the floor in years groaned their way into semi-bearable postures, and then a brief whispered conversation led to two people darting out of the room and returning with a rolling stack of chairs. Those that found the floor too uncomfortable were helped to set the chairs into the circle. Robin was surprised by the air of cooperation in the room, but even the prima donnas seemed to want to be part of this group effort, plus or minus some grumbling. She fidgeted, feeling the note burning a hole in her purse, which she'd set behind her on the floor. This was going to be a frustrating hour, forcing herself to be still and focus while every train of thought seemed to lead to the need for action.

Just as the room settled down again, a quiet knock sounded on the door and an unfamiliar curly blond head poked in. "Are you guys ready?"

Nods all around. "But Leelyn's already done the introduction," Master Leopold said. "If you want a good opening shot, she should do it again. Would you mind, dear? Or I could do it for you."

The door opened fully, and the blond guy muscled a tripod and camera inside. He was followed by a dark-haired guy carrying a smaller camera, a nylon duffel bag, and a folding stool. Both wore jackets that said Channel 58 in script across the back, with green Survival Unlimited IDs on lanyards around their necks. Robin turned to Tom, her panicky feeling resurging.

"They're filming this?" she asked. "Why?"

"It's just for, you know, posterity." He shrugged. "Don't worry about it. If they decide to use the footage, they need permission from everyone. But just imagine— if we find Blue as a result of this circle, it will be an invaluable piece of video."

"We gave them permission to use any video just by signing our packet," Robin said. "Didn't you read it?" She didn't like the idea that the footage could eventually put her curse—and her face—on national TV, but that wasn't her real issue. What if Kami showed up to do lighting? Robin would have to seize the opportunity to talk to her, even if she had to excuse herself from the Circle to do it. But she hadn't yet figured out what to say or how to address the abuse she'd seen. Her throat tightened.

Kami didn't appear. Robin tried to keep from drumming her fingers on her crossed legs. She chewed her lip as the cameramen set up in two adjacent corners, one on a folding stool and the other upright behind a tripod.

Leelyn acknowledged Master Leopold's offer with a soft, "I'll do it," but hesitated before rising. Her face turned red, and she looked so uncomfortable that Robin wished Leelyn would just tell Leopold and the cameramen to go to hell. Leelyn introduced herself again, self-consciously, then halted and took a deep breath. "I'm so sorry, I hate speaking on camera," she admitted, turning to face the blond guy directly at the end. "Please don't use that. Maybe Master Leopold or someone else can do it, later."

He waved a careless hand. "You're fine. Don't worry."

Leelyn retook her seat and looked around the circle.

"Let's begin," she said, and closed her eyes, making an obvious effort to ignore the cameras and re-center herself.

Robin glanced around for a cue. Most rested their hands palm up on their knees, although a few, like Erin and Madeline and Master Leopold and his neighbors, grasped hands lightly. Tom caught her eye, opening his hand in invitation, but she shook her head. Around the circle, deep breaths were taken. Eyes were closed. Robin followed suit and a thick silence fell on the room, broken by only an occasional muffled cough or cracking knee. After a minute or two she peeked, but nothing was happening, except the blond cameraman was examining his fingernails and the dark-haired one was leaning back against the wall, eyes closed.

She shut her eyes again and breathed deeply like the others, hoping to at least tame her agitation. There was a rhythm in the room as if everyone was breathing in sync, which made her overly aware of her own stilted breaths. Her heartbeat slowed anyway, and she started to feel calmer. Okay, she thought. This is fine. I can handle this. She directed her mind to think about Blue. Poor little girl, with her determined, somehow bruised, expression. She looked like she tried very hard at everything but knew she would forever fall short. Robin wondered if she'd tried to invent amazing memories of a past life at Leopold's clinic, and if her parents had hidden their disappointment when it turned out she was just Blue.

Or maybe Robin was projecting, just as presumptuously as all the others who saw a picture and a few sentences about a celebrity in a magazine or online and thought they understood someone. Just as presumptuously as people who looked at her and saw youth and health and potential instead of the curse that constrained her and the scars of her past. Robin didn't know how Blue felt or what Blue thought, and she shouldn't pretend to.

She sneaked a peek around the circle again. Nothing was going on, but she caught a few other pairs of peeking eyes. Delia Morton, the redhead with the Southern accent, winked at her from across the circle and Robin nodded back. At least she wasn't the only one not lost in communion with the universe.

The painkillers she'd taken earlier had helped dull the soreness of her back, but her cross-legged position stretched her shirt against the bandages and an itching sensation slowly invaded her consciousness. She listened again for the breathing of the group, like a surfer hoping to catch a wave, but the itching intensified. Despite herself, she began to fantasize about rubbing her back against the nearest wall. Or finding a tree, like a bear. The irritation was driving her crazy, and finally she twisted to reach her hand up the back of her jacket.

She scratched gently and with great relief, but one of the scabs chipped off and she felt moisture on her finger. Shoot, another shirt ruined. Hopefully, no one was peeking at her now, because she wiggled like she had a spider in her shirt, trying to move one of the gauze pads to cover the bleeding spot.

The floor rumbled. Her eyes flew open to meet other eyes opening around the circle. Another rumble followed.

"Earthquake!" said the dark-haired camera man, jumping to his feet.

"Stay down," Leopold snapped.

Another rumble followed. Everyone stayed put.

Robin hoped Leopold knew what he was talking about.

"It's not an earthquake!" Leelyn cried. "It's Blue! She's trying to reach us!"

A large woman dressed all in shades of purple flung herself forward off her chair and began to jerk and seize, babbling unintelligibly. Someone cried, "Call an ambulance!" Robin watched in horror, wondering if the woman had a curse similar to Robin's own.

The room rumbled a third time. Leelyn was on her knees with arms flung toward the ceiling as if prepared to catch Blue when she was released from the Heavens. The seizing woman slowed to occasional twitches. Her eyes were wide open and drool on the mat by her mouth.

Nothing happened. Heartbeats passed. All was quiet. Leelyn settled back into a cross-legged position, chest heaving. The purple-swathed woman blinked, wiped her mouth, and sat up with the help of her neighbors.

"Did anyone call for help?" someone asked.

They looked at each other, shaking their heads. The door remained shut. The blond camera man continued filming.

"I'm okay, let's continue," the woman who'd been seizing said huskily. "Really. This is good."

Robin stole a glance at Tom, who was smiling wryly.

Silence resumed. Eyes closed. Breathing slowed. A snowflake landed on her head, then another and another, birthing individual shivers. It couldn't be a flash coming, it was too gentle, too gradual. But it was unmistakable, and she was being pulled in. Her stomach dropped in despair—if there was ever a time when she needed to stay in control, this was it, surrounded by strangers and, possibly, enemies—but at the same time, there was no point fighting it.

And Tom was here, someone she was beginning to consider a friend. She was on a padded floor. A large woman all dressed in purple had just had a violent seizure and gotten back up like nothing happened. Surely, a flash should be a piece of cake, especially one that came on so gently.

Eyes closed, breathing in sandalwood and sweaty mats, feeling the inevitable cold creeping up on her as she tried to hold Blue in her mind. Inhale: Blue. Exhale: Blue. Inhale: Blood. Thick and ripe, curling her tongue, sticking in the back of her throat. A scream, and a dizzying fall, and then it happened again—a scream and a dizzying fall and a scream and a crunch. A jagged black crack among rocks on a sparsely wooded steep slope. Blood, thick and ripe, and gagging.

Then a light pierced where there had been no light, and there was a delicate fairy-tale shoe, almost like a glass slipper.

Inhale: Blood. Exhale. Inhale: Sweat. Rubber mats. Someone's too-strong sandalwood perfume. Exhale.

Robin blinked, seeing the dirt stuck on the edge of her boot from this morning's walk to the guard shack. Seeing the weave of the mat below her. Seeing her hands, hanging onto her legs with white knuckles. She felt fine. The after-image of a shoe was burned onto her retina, but there was no brain-matter-turned-to-hamburger headache. No nausea.

Nevertheless, she would vomit all over the mat in front of her, in the midst of the circle, if that would erase what had just happened.

She had accidentally used blood magic. The way her

uncle had tamed the curse, and her grandfather, and probably generations of Farrells before them. Blood magic light, in this case: a tiny amount of her own blood, spilled by mistake. Not even close to the story told by the scars that had run up and down both of her Uncle's arms like a white spider web through his dark tattoos. He had hinted to her of other ways, but she had refused to listen, right up to the last time she'd seen him, when he had done something awful to save her life. What would he say if he could see what she had done with it?

She'd sworn that she would never use blood to control her curse, and she hadn't until now, so that was something.

The flash had been so painless, so relatively clear. It hadn't had a lot of emotion wrapped up in it, despite the violent overtones. Was it possible that Blue had simply fallen and broken her leg? But there'd been no sign of the dragonfly, and what was the shoe about? Blue had been wearing sneakers when she disappeared, according to the packet, and Robin was pretty sure that shoe in the vision was a type that had been popular when she was little—jelly shoes, they were called, made of sparkle-infused strands of soft plastic that appealed to little girls.

Maybe that would click later. But the clarity and painlessness seemed like an awfully big change for one little accidentally spilled drop of blood. Her uncle, trying desperately to help her deal with the onslaught of flashes, had impatiently told her not to be superstitious, that sacrifice didn't make something evil. But she knew in her bones that it would be a slippery slope, first a little self-cutting, then small animals, and next thing you knew, you were a murderer.

She would not let it happen again. If that was the

cost of taking away the pain of the flashes, she would not pay it.

Around her, all was as silent as before. No one had noticed her flash, and no one had noticed her come out of it.

Then she realized—she'd grabbed Tom's hand, and still held it tight. She glanced at him. His eyes were shut, but he was smiling.

Huh.

She let go, gently, and decided not to think about that right now. Instead, she grabbed her notebook from the purse behind her and scribbled down all the details she could remember, and then sketched the rocks and the jagged crack as well as she could, though it came out looking like a black diamond among gray humps. The shoe was easier. Sparkly, a single slipper like the one in Robin's old Disney picture book of Cinderella, but the lacy effect of the plastic strands made it look even fancier. It sat on a boulder instead of a velvet cushion, and was highlighted by a dusty ray of light in a shadowy place. That, the smell of blood, the shriek…

Blue had definitely been wearing sneakers when she disappeared. Jeans, sneakers, and a white hoodie with a gold number one on the front.

She tucked the notebook back in her bag. The envelope saying HEATHER FARRELL peeked out, and she stuffed it down to the bottom.

****

The circle ended quietly, a torturous length of time later. Leelyn roused herself from stillness, glanced down at her watch, and rose to her feet.

"It's almost Zumba time. Let's take a final deep breath and send all of our hope, all of our strength, to

Blue."

A long moment of silence passed, and Leelyn said, "And now, come back to us. Back to the world. Let's center ourselves in the here and now. Flex your muscles. Feel your bodies. When you're ready, stand up."

The psychics stood, some with a great deal of groaning. There were soft chuckles and soft words, but for the most part, they blinked at each other like kindergarteners roused from a nap.

Robin popped to her feet. She'd been restlessly tapping her fingers against her leg since the flash. Her mind circled around Uncle Matt: his revelation about the family curse, his use of blood sacrifice to control it, his investigation into his friends' disappearances—and then, the baby. When Uncle Matt found out about her pregnancy, and who the father was.

It had been so long ago, and she'd trained herself not to think about those things. But the scabs had begun to rip away before she'd even arrived at Spirit Ridge.

Impatiently she waited as the rest of the group prepared to leave, stacking chairs and gathering purses and jackets. After her flash, she'd watched them all, wondering which one knew of her past life. Now she studied them for evidence of results. Had the circle been effective? Would they tell each other?

"Are you okay?" Tom asked her quietly. "Did you have one of your visions again?"

Robin couldn't deny it after the way she'd grabbed his hand like a date at a horror movie. "Yeah. Not all that helpful, though. Anything for you?"

He shrugged. "It felt very centering. I don't want to lose it. I'm going to go back to my room to gaze into my bowl for a while." He shot her a quick smile and moved past her, leaving her bemused. How many men would admit that?

Others, including Sidney Doyle, seemed to have the same idea. Robin watched her disappear through the doorway, and let her go. Doyle wasn't at the top of her list right now.

Finding Kami was, but as she exited the gym she saw Fran Rowles and a deputy at a folding table in the hallway, apparently making appointments. Some of the group were stopping while others hurried by. Robin bit her lip. She owed it to Blue to report her flashes, and it wouldn't get any more convenient than this.

She joined the huddle near the table. Leelyn was asking about the earthquake. The young deputy with caterpillar eyebrows, who'd been watching the gate when Robin first arrived, grinned.

"You all didn't think you caused the earthquake, right? 'Cause that was just a tremor. We don't get them often, but once in a while. Had one six, seven years ago."

His patronizing tone was irritating, but the fact that he looked barely fourteen made it almost amusing. Leelyn smiled patiently. "An interesting piece of timing, though," she said, aiming her words at Fran. "I suspect that many of us will be contacting you through the course of the day, myself included. It was a powerful experience."

"I'm ready," Rowles indicated her clipboard.

Leelyn turned and noted the others waiting around her. She blushed and gave a little wave as she moved away. She was so self-effacing, but she should be proud of pulling the circle together, Robin thought. Maybe her humbleness worked for her. Directing this group of eccentrics was herding proverbial cats, and a big ego would definitely get in the way.

On the other hand, if someone had keyed into Blue's location and situation during the circle, they would most likely already have broadcast it to the world, not be waiting patiently at the table.

When it was her turn, she said, "I have a couple of umm, visions, to report." Her throat closed up and her foster mother's face flashed in Robin's mind. It had been a long time, but the wounds of trying to warn her foster mother, and of trying to convince disbelieving authority figures of the urgency of her message, were still there. Her inner powerless teenager was still a part of her.

Robin cleared her throat, squeezing the scrunchy in her pocket. She'd finally put it in a plastic baggie that had been crumpled in her toiletry case with one Q-Tip in it. "And something else."

"Urgency?" Rowles asked.

"Urgency?"

"You know, how quickly you think the police need to act on your information."

Robin glanced around her. Others were listening, including the grumpy astrologer Loren Rennet. She flushed. "Not very. I mean, I don't know."

"Name?"

"Robin Fox."

The deputy leaned forward and looked her up and down. "You're the one who got attacked in the woods, aren't you?"

Robin nodded. The hair scrunchy felt like it was glowing through her pocket. Why she felt guilty now, when she was finally planning to come clean, she didn't know. It must have been the deputy's caterpillar eyebrows drawn together in a judgmental frown.

"How about 4:30? We're doing meetings in my office, on B1East." Rowles said. She handed Robin a business card with her office number on it.

"Great." Robin offered the deputy a weak smile and left the table with quickening steps. Now was her chance to get some answers.

Chapter Fourteen

Robin left the bunker through the cafeteria, heart pounding in anticipation and a sympathetic throb pulsing in the whip mark on her back. Finally, she could find Kami. Robin would study Kami's face for family resemblances, look for scars as proof of abuse to confirm it was the same girl as in Robin's flash. She needed to know if there was any way the girl could be her daughter, but at the same time, Robin had no idea what to say. *Are you safe from abuse? Where did you come from, who are your parents? As a very small child, were you removed from someone you loved?*

No one would answer questions like that from a stranger. Robin would have to win Kami's trust.

Robin summoned her courage as she crossed the parking lot. The air was cool and moist, smelling sweetly of pine, the sky a clear cerulean blue above the dense line of evergreen. It lifted her spirits a little, too beautiful to completely ignore. She breathed in deeply, hoping for a hint of menthol cigarettes on the breeze, but detected nothing. The trailers huddled in the unkempt grass on the opposite edge of the parking lot like refugees from a tornado, with a little red hatchback parked askew in front. The two vans with the TV station logo were nowhere in sight.

Robin glanced around the lot. There were fewer cars parked than there had been yesterday. A Friday in the middle of the search for a missing child might be just the start of another weekend to some people. Were the FBI allowing staff to leave? Maybe there was nothing they could do about it—or maybe, they believed Blue was nowhere in the vicinity. The only thing she knew for sure was that she wouldn't be getting the lowdown on the investigation anytime soon, unless she got it in a flash.

A pair of young men with backpacks slung over their shoulders chatted their way to a car without sparing her a glance. She eyed them surreptitiously as they stashed their bags and drove away. The parking lot felt deserted, but since receiving the note in Grizzly, she knew someone must be keeping track of her. Were they watching from one of the cars? Was there an overlooking window in the bunker? There were the security cameras, of course, but the note must have come from one of the psychics, someone who wouldn't have access to those resources.

She froze as another thought occurred to her. Was rushing to speak to a young woman who might be her daughter playing into their hands, whoever "they" were?

It didn't matter, she told herself. She had to do what she had to do.

She continued to the end of the lot. The two trailers had parked haphazardly in the long grass, creating a wide triangle in front where four water-stained canvas camp chairs were arranged in a semi-circle. A coffee can full of soaked cigarette butts and rainwater balanced on the uneven ground between them. Robin studied each trailer, wondering which was Kami's, and wondering if someone inside was studying her in return. She didn't know who or how many people were on the TV crew with Kami, aside from the two men who'd been filming at the psychics' circle.

Nervously, she approached the trailer on the left because the door was slightly closer to the butt can, and the only thing she really knew about Kami was that she smoked. Robin hadn't figured out what to say, but she'd come up with an admittedly lame invitation to get coffee in the cafeteria. If the girl took her up on it, she would keep it light, maybe quiz her a little on what it was like to be part of a TV crew. Curiosity about that was believable. Robin could say she had a friend who wanted to work in television.

She tapped on the flimsy door and waited.

After a moment, she glanced at the other trailer and then the parking lot again, feeling exposed. Still clear. She stepped down, then tried the other trailer with a brisk knock and waited.

Shoot. Still nothing.

What if the little red car belonged to the two camera guys, still safely inside the bunker? What if everyone else was away, taking some weekend time, heading to the big city of Medford for some R&R?

Her heart sped up and she swallowed. She tested the handle. It jiggled only a millimeter back and forth—locked. She peeked into the small sliding window next to the door, and saw a miniature kitchen area where open pop, beer, and food cans crowded the counter space. A giant trash bag lolled half full in the corner with a piece of notebook paper taped to it, which said in bold letters, "RECYCLE, ASSHOLES!" The exclamation point had a skull and crossbones instead of a dot. She couldn't help mentally comparing the notebook paper and handwriting to that of the note, but it was pointless. This handwriting looked more loopy and feminine, but that would probably be easy to disguise, or it might just come out differently if you were in a hurry or angry, or…

Anyway, she couldn't tell if this was Kami's place or not.

Miming the desire to leave a note by digging ostentatiously in her purse for pen and paper, Robin turned and scanned the parking lot again. She shrugged and went back to the first trailer and knocked loudly. Nothing. She waited two seconds then peered into the door-adjacent window. It revealed an identical kitchen furnished with fake wood cabinets, but instead of a proliferation of cans there was an unlit candle in a glass jar, a bag of coffee beans, and a pack of menthol cigarettes on the clean counter.

Aha.

Heart speeding up, she ran a lightning quick cost-benefit analysis. She could leave and return later in the hope that Kami would be around and willing to talk. Or—five minutes inside, and she might have all the answers she wanted. If she didn't get caught.

She'd done B&E before. Sixteen years old, two weeks past giving birth, she'd hitchhiked away from the safe-house in a panic when Uncle Matt failed to pick her up as planned. A sleazy guy old enough to be her grandfather kicked her out of his truck somewhere in the middle of Pennsylvania as payback for rebuffing his come-on. Too afraid to get into another car, in a haze of shock and fear, she'd decided to go off-road and hike the rest of the way to California.

Three days later, starving, shivering, and soaked to the skin from trying to sleep on damp ground in the forest, she'd begun to believe she was going to die. When she had stumbled upon the vacation rentals around the little lake, she was in a feverish daze, startling at every sound. There hadn't been much food on offer—dusty boxes of pasta and cans of soup—but it had kept her alive. She did go back to hitchhiking, of course, because walking was too slow, but whenever she needed to go to ground, she would study maps and look for the low-cost vacation cottages that were unlikely to have security.

Memories of The Lost Year were not shut in a chained-up trunk in her head because it had been a lovely tour of under-used vacation cottages across the country, and she hadn't only stolen dusty old boxes of pasta. It had been hell, and she didn't want to be that person anymore.

But here she was, feeling just as desperate, and nearly as irrational. She glanced over her shoulder with her heart in her throat then turned her attention to the window next to the door. It slid open easily with the friction of her hand against the glass, and the screen followed suit. A fingernail caught and bent back against the metal edge but she ignored it, reaching in hurriedly through an opening barely wide enough for her arm. The lock was a simple push-button knob on the inside of the door, with a sliding bar lock a few inches above it. She released both. Her vertebrae crackled and the scabs on her back pulled painfully as she forced her shoulder to twist and reach as far as possible, but it worked.

With her luck, when she turned back to the parking lot, both vans would be bearing down on her, or the two video guys—but no. The lot was still deserted. She might be on security cameras, but way over here on the far side of the lot? Hopefully not. She swallowed bile and slipped quickly through the door, closing it behind herself and leaning weak-kneed on the other side.

With a start, she glanced around hurriedly. As a teen on the run, she'd learned never to break in without an escape route in mind in case the owners came home. Now, she wasn't sure the trailer even had a back door.

Her ears on high alert for noises from outside, she scanned the interior. The kitchenette led into a dining/TV area with padded bench seating, two scaled-down comfy chairs, a table with a hinged top, and a wall-mounted TV on an adjustable arm. A pocket door was half open, and Robin poked her head into a bedroom with two narrow beds, built in on either side. To her right, another pocket door led to a bathroom, where a candle stood on the bathroom counter amid a mess of cosmetics and a hairdryer. The whole place smelled strongly of pot-pourri. There was no back door. She was trapped.

In a nervous sweat, she entered the bedroom. The built-in bunk to her left was neatly set with a peach comforter and two coordinated throw pillows. The other side had the same comforter, but it was askew with a ratty looking afghan spread over the top. A couple of pictures had been taped to the wall, obviously ripped from magazines: on one, a sweaty bare-chested guy with a guitar and smoldering eyes peering from behind a fringe of ratty hair: on the other, an equally sweaty guy with different-colored ratty hair posed behind a drum set. Someone had a type. She bet it was Kami.

The built-in drawers below had been closed roughly with clothes sticking out. Robin pulled the top drawer open. Black and purple cloth in a wrinkled mess. She disentangled the first thing her hand touched and held up a clingy black t-shirt. Unless there was another female who dressed like Kami and wore about the same size, this had to be her bunk. Under the top layer of shirts, there were a few pairs of wadded up tights, a pair of black chunky-heeled shoes, and multi-colored underwear, but nothing else. No diary, no address book, no convenient pile of notes or letters. She pushed it shut, knowing she should feel slimy for being so intrusive, but unable to feel anything but panic as seconds ticked by.

The drawer below was similar, but with jeans and leggings taking up most of the space. Frustrated, Robin thrust her hands down all the way to the bottom and felt for hidden items. For a moment she was hopeful about a handful of vinyl, but it was a bustier, not a purse.

Next to the drawers, a cupboard door proved to be an access point for plumbing. Above that, an open cubby was crammed with two squished pairs of flats, one burgundy, one black. Behind the shoes were four cartons of menthol cigarettes. That was the clincher, she had no more doubts. Too bad she'd found nothing useful.

Robin stood. She'd been rooting around in a frenzy but the growing ache of disappointment brought her to her senses. There was nothing here, nothing to show Kami's past, nothing to show Kami's connection to her or even, really, what she was like beyond what Robin had already seen. She needed to get out of here and distance herself from the trailer as quickly as possible. Leave no trace.

She strained her ears. There was an electric hum, probably the refrigerator. No sound from the parking lot. Sweeping her eyes around the room one last time, her gaze caught on the hot-eyed musician again. He glared from under the magazine title, GROOVE, printed across his ratted hair.

It was the front cover, she realized suddenly, that still bore a worn address label, half torn away and faded.

She squinted to read it. Pale words swam into her view.

…LeClair.

…shington St.

…ga Springs, NY

LeClair. Impossible. Just—impossible. Here, in Oregon? Here, at the bedside of a girl who might be— no, now had to be—her daughter?

Her heart felt like a hummingbird trapped in her throat, and her skin prickled. For an instant, as dark static invaded the edges of her vision, she was terrified that a cold flash was about to hit. But no, it was just panic. She was going to faint with terror. Was that even possible? She grabbed the edge of the bed, closed her eyes, and forced herself to breathe slowly and evenly.

After a minute, her vision cleared. After another, she opened her eyes and stood up.

Then she swiftly and methodically retraced her steps, leaving everything exactly as she'd found it.

****

At fifteen, Heather Farrell felt like an outsider. She was different from her friends in ways that felt important: like not having regular parents, not living in a nice big house in one of the landscaped subdivisions, not going to Spain in the summer. She and her brother lived with her uncle and his girlfriend in a little ranch house with a pretty front yard. Uncle Matt and his girlfriend Ruthie owned and ran a successful landscaping business, so there was plenty of money, it wasn't that they were poor. But they worked odd hours and smoked cigarettes out back and had tattoos and attended a weird church. Heather's little brother Evan was tall and handsome and athletic, and somehow the things that made her feel different and alone didn't affect him at all.

The friends Heather had, the girls who didn't quite fit into the popular group for their own reasons, talked constantly about sex and clothes and music and movies, and once in a blue moon, the future or the world or what life was about. She tried to join in, but she felt distant and disconnected from everything, and hoped that when she went to college, her life would finally feel meaningful and real.

The first time a flash hit her, a chaos of sensory impressions overwhelmed her in the middle of a history test. A shock of cold, an inability to breathe, and then her mouth filled with the taste of motor oil and her right hand exploded with a shattering pain that made her shriek. And then it was gone as if it had never happened, leaving her white-faced and humiliated, everyone staring until she excused herself. She stumbled to the office with a migraine, and Ruthie, Uncle Matt's girlfriend, brought her home where she slept all the way through to the next morning.

The second time, a week later, she fell down on the sidewalk while she was walking to school. A neighbor walked her back home, scolding her about not eating breakfast, while Heather shook with the residue of despair that clung from a waking dream of knotting a rope. Nothing else stuck in her mind, but she could still see and feel the rough fibers of the rope against a small, smooth hand with perfectly manicured nails, definitely not hers.

That kicked off months of dread and paranoia. She had never grown close to Ruthie, who was a smoking, swearing tattooed fireplug who hadn't finished high school. She'd moved in when Heather was ten, and Heather had never forgiven her for being the opposite of everything she wanted a mother to be. Sometimes she hated Uncle Matt, too, who didn't even try to pretend he was a regular dad. Evan she loved, but he was two years younger and in his own world. And her friends—she might have confideed in them if she was worried about the English midterm or had a crush on a basketball player, but not this.

So she was alone. She scoured the medical dictionary at the public library, the most private option she could think of. Her symptoms sounded like a type of epileptic seizure, which she read could include "altered emotions" and "loss of awareness." She also researched schizophrenia and psychotropic drugs, which seemed more in line with the tiny vivid details that stuck with her after a flash.

Nothing fully explained her condition. The flashes kept coming, each one different but always leaving her whirling with horror and pain. They were so chaotic that she sometimes had no more than a single sensory impression afterwards, a sound or a smell or an image. Her desire to believe that she was the target of someone's campaign to drive her crazy gave way to the knowledge that she was already crazy. Desperately frightened that she'd be institutionalized if anyone found out, Heather put all of her energy into hiding her affliction from those around her. She promised herself that if there was any sign that she might hurt someone in her madness, she would turn herself in. Or kill herself.

Her grades plummeted. She dropped too many pounds and grew hollow-eyed. The school counselor threatened to bring in Heather's 'parents' but she managed, at least temporarily, to convince the counselor she would both try harder and stress out less. At home,

Ruthie kept telling Uncle Matt that Heather was "getting that anorexia" but he was too busy to listen. Heather avoided Ruthie as much as possible by hanging out with her friends, who were also starting to talk to her about anorexia but could be sidetracked by gossip or M&M's.

And then, in the middle of this impossible pretense, when all she wanted to do was curl up and die, there was Daniel.

Daniel LeClair hung out at the SilverFaire Mall where Heather's friends spent at least half their free time. Shaggy-haired, blue-eyed, with shoulders that filled his T-shirts out in a fascinating way, he looked far more sophisticated than the high school boys she was used to. When he chatted her up in the frozen yogurt line in the Food Court, she was tongue-tied as if he were a teen idol.

He was taking a year off before college, he told her. His mother was undergoing chemotherapy and he wanted to be around. Heather considered lying about her age but decided it would be too hard to pull off, especially with her idiot friends making faces in the McDonald's booth ten feet away. Shyly, she told him she was still in high school but instead of shrugging and walking away, he smiled down at her. "You must have an old soul. You've just got this cool vibe, this togetherness, that rolls off you. You're way more mature than most girls your age."

Her torment was invisible to him, she realized. Was it possible that things could get better, that she could have something good left in her life? A faint sense of uneasiness about his motives remained in the back of her mind—why would a hot college guy be interested in a skeletally thin and unpopular high school girl? She squashed it. She deserved something good.

That first day at SilverFaire Mall, Heather left her friends to sit with Daniel. It set the pattern for the next several months; they became more interested in her because of Daniel's interest, but she blew them off whenever he was around, which was nearly all the time. The first time she had a flash when he was around, he was patient and non-judgmental, and Heather stopped dwelling so much on her mental health, concentrating instead on the miracle of finding her soulmate. Being with him, holding his hand, made her stronger. She gained back some of the weight she'd lost, and slept better every night, but she couldn't make herself care about grades, friends, or family. She was past that.

Daniel brought her to the LeClair mansion several times. It was usually deserted except for staff because his father and sister were so often spending time with his mother at the hospital. She never asked why he wasn't with them because she wanted him with her anyway. He took her to exclusive restaurants every week that her uncle wouldn't have dreamed of going to even if he won the lottery. Daniel bought her jewelry with real gemstones, which she started hiding after Ruthie gasped at a five hundred dollar diamond bracelet and said Heather should give it back.

When the pregnancy came, when the flashes increased, when her gradually growing suspicions about Daniel LeClair's motives shimmered into clarity—she and Uncle Matt finally talked. But it was too late for Heather. And too late for Uncle Matt.

****

Robin pulled the trailer door shut firmly, hearing the lock click, and hastened down the flimsy steps. The parking lot was as deserted as before. She put her head down and walked along the curb toward the opening in the hedge that would lead her back inside. Reading the name LeClair on that scrap of paper had felt like the jaws of a trap biting into her. She needed space to move, to think, to run, but she had nowhere to go.

But she couldn't stay still, knowing what she knew. She couldn't stretch her belief in coincidence to cover everything. Two unusual flashes—one of a bereft toddler. One of Kami, physically and psychologically and emotionally abused. One note, with Robin's real name and a reference to her daughter. And now the LeClair connection.

She wanted to vomit. Kami, her daughter, had become a LeClair. After everything she and Uncle Matt had sacrificed to ensure they would never touch her. The words went round and round in her head, almost meaningless in their impossibility. It should not have happened. And yet it had.

Nearly hyperventilating, she checked the time on her phone. Normally, when she felt this agitated, she'd sweat it off on a run or at the gym. Who was she kidding? She hadn't felt this agitated since Liam's parents had died. Since then, she'd been treading the calmest possible waters, ignoring her flashes, not exposing herself to anything except her small circle of safety.

It didn't matter. She couldn't go to the gym. Not only would it be ludicrous under the circumstances, but she also had to collect herself and keep her appointment with Fran Rowles. She just wasn't sure she could handle it.

She texted Liam:
—*Can I call you NOW?*—
Her phone buzzed thirty seconds later.

—Ten minutes, OK?—

—OK—

She paced on the sidewalk, feeling numb.

Backtrack. Was there any other explanation for Kami being linked to the LeClairs besides Kami being Robin's daughter?

Sure. It could all be an enormous coincidence. The anonymous note could be lying. The LeClairs on the magazine address label could be completely different people. The weirdly clear flashes about Kami could have been caused by something Robin ate.

No. That was bullshit. There was no more doubt, not really. Her daughter was here, at Survival Unlimited. Her daughter, who had been living a happy and normal fantasy life in the background of Robin's mind for the past sixteen years, had in reality been absorbed into Daniel's psychotic, dangerous family, and was now, bizarrely, present at the site of another child's disappearance. Present where Robin herself was.

Robin had to focus. This didn't change anything she'd already decided. She had to think about Blue, too—someone else's daughter, undergoing who-knew-what. But she also had to find Kami and confront her. Robin had to learn what Kami was doing here and why the note had threatened her death.

A small part of Robin continued to argue that there must be some mistake. Her flashes were unreliable, the name LeClair wasn't that unusual, plus Kami looked too old, she smoked menthol—and all that makeup?

But most of Robin accepted it, because all along, it was what she'd most dreaded. When Uncle Matt had told her to flee and focus on saving herself if he didn't come, he'd been treating her like a child, and at the time, she'd craved that relinquishment of responsibility. But she should have known better. She should have stayed, should have made certain that her baby was safe, should never have let Uncle Matt shelter Robin from the consequences of her actions and take the risk that lost his life.

A last flame of hope died, one that she had never consciously acknowledged. The hope that Uncle Matt had been in hiding all along, and wasn't dead after all. Uncle Matt would never surprise her by pulling into her driveway unannounced. He would never tell her she was safe and take her home to a happy reunion with Evan. Because the only way Robin's child could have landed in the hands of the LeClairs was over his dead body. She'd known that for him to disappear meant he was most likely dead, but this was incontrovertible proof.

She fiddled with her phone. The sun glared into her eyes as it lowered over the trees. She would only have a few minutes to check in with Liam before rushing to that appointment, and now that the first wave of terror and agitation had passed, she wasn't sure if she could explain quickly enough for the call to be useful. She needed him to help her think this through, she needed to finally tell him the whole truth. But now she was just numb. Dumb and numb.

She gave up on waiting and texted him again:

—*Nevermind. Gtg to appt, but later?*—

She bounced on the balls of her feet, waiting impatiently for Liam to answer, and her phone buzzed just as quick footsteps pounded up from behind her.

Instantly certain that someone was coming to arrest her for breaking into the trailer, she stepped back and threw her hands up in surrender, one still clutching the phone.

A uniformed deputy passed her quickly, jogging to one of the two Sheriff's SUVs in the front of the lot.

Robin lowered her hands. Noises she'd been ignoring clarified into voices, and she turned to see an entourage approaching. Agent DiBlasi and Wes Hartwin were in the lead, her face somber, his relaxed and confident.

Grimley caught up to them at a run and gasped out words. "You're making a huge mistake. I can't believe you're taking this seriously. Wes had nothing to do with it!"

Hartwin paused and faced Grimley. DiBlasi stopped too, staying at Hartwin's elbow, and two deputies closed in from behind.

"Peter," Hartwin said. "Don't worry. They're just doing their job, following every lead, no matter how unlikely. Trust the process."

"But where are they taking you?" Grimley's tone was beseeching, and perhaps in embarrassment, he smoothed his hair with one hand and straightened his spine.

DiBlasi answered impatiently. "He's not under arrest at this time, Mr. Grimley. Your boss has simply agreed to answer some questions. We'll meet his lawyer at the Sheriff's office in Grants Pass."

"But why? This is ridiculous. Wes has an alibi. And he's the last person who would do anything to hurt Blue. How can the FBI give credence to anonymous tips that don't even match the facts?"

Robin dearly wanted to know that too. She wondered if Grimley knew for certain that they were acting on a tip. Were Hartwin's apparent efforts at cooperation and assistance a smokescreen the FBI had finally seen through? Or were they just checking off boxes?

Her mind raced ahead. As selfish as it seemed, if questioning Hartwin led quickly to Blue's location, what would that mean for Robin?

"Trust the process," Hartwin repeated gently. DiBlasi took his elbow and turned him back toward the SUV that had pulled up to the curb. A deputy stood waiting to escort him into the back of the vehicle.

Grimley fell back to stand with other employees who'd followed to watch the spectacle. He met Robin's eyes, and his eyebrows raised to find her there.

Her phone buzzed again, giving her an excuse to look away. Liam suggested five-thirty, after her appointment, and let her know he wasn't too happy having to wait after she got him so worried.

Well, she wasn't very happy either. She followed the group back inside to see if her appointment had been canceled in light of the recent developments.

Chapter Fifteen

Survival Unlimited staff clustered in small groups in the cafeteria, everyone talking about Hartwin's unexpected exit. Voices rose here and there in disbelief or anger, but most faces looked more confused than anything. Robin wondered if the Gracens knew Hartwin had been taken offsite for questioning. It would be devastating to doubt one of your closest friends, but at this point, it would be like finding out you had diabetes when you'd already been shot in the heart.

She passed two of the psychics, Delia and Loren, chatting near the beverage counter. Delia waved, but Robin just nodded and kept going. She'd searched for Rowles' office in the MapApp and was following directions with half her brain, while the other half hopped from Kami's terrifying connection to the LeClairs to the offsite questioning of Hartwin and then back to the LeClairs. She wondered if she might actually have a breakdown here at the compound. What would they do if they found her crying and rocking herself in a random hallway? Maybe the mythical men in white coats would take her away for a nice, peaceful rest.

The MapApp flashed, "You are close!" Robin blinked and looked around. She was in a corridor similar to all the others, perhaps a little more upscale. It felt like the interior of a corporate skyscraper with an eco-friendly theme. Hanging ferns thrived under recessed lighting and various sculptures, blown glass pieces, and fiber art were displayed on occasional tables or built-in cases. Each door she passed had been personalized with handmade tiles bearing employee names. Fran Rowles' tile was hung beside Peter Grimley's, and showed the gracefully etched outline of a running horse on a charcoal background.

Robin hesitated. She'd pushed herself to keep the appointment, all the while suspecting that it would be canceled. Whatever new information had caused Special Agent DiBlasi to take Wes Hartwin away for questioning might make psychic input unnecessary. If the indomitable Fran Rowles wanted to proceed with the interview, was Robin up for it? She might not be in any shape to talk to anyone until she got her head around Kami and the LeClairs and the fact that someone knew who she used to be.

When she held up her hand, it was shaking. She needed to regroup back in her room.

Too late. As she turned to leave, the office door opened and the large woman dressed completely in purple who'd had some kind of seizure during the Circle yelped as they almost collided. "Woops! So sorry, excuse me! You must be next, go ahead." She bustled past Robin, clasping her shoulder as she passed as if they were comrades in arms.

"Come on in," the Sheriff's deputy with the thick eyebrows called out. He was seated at an oval table next to Fran Rowles, who smiled briefly and then looked down at her laptop, typing.

Robin froze in the doorway. Could she simply turn around and walk away? No, she would have to explain, and if she were going to explain, she might as well just—

Deep breath. She filled her lungs with air that still held a trace of the purple woman's lavender perfume, and exhaled slowly. She would not go hide under the bed. In all the shittiness of her life, time had proven her a survivor. And as a survivor, she could help others survive. Like Blue. Maybe even like Kami. Why did she keep having to remind herself of that? She forced a smile, stepped inside, and closed the door behind her.

She glanced around the room as she took a seat across from Rowles and the deputy. A pair of Ficus trees bracketed a large aquarium along the wall to her right. At the far end of the room, an L-shaped desk was against the wall next to two closed doors, with four chairs nearby forming a small waiting area. Several paintings were hung that echoed the wild horse theme from Fran's tile.

The deputy said, "You may recall, I'm Deputy Lincoln and this is Ms. Rowles. You're Robin Fox?" He hovered a pencil over his clipboard.

The white-haired woman shook her head impatiently and leaned forward to offer her small hand to Robin. "Call me Fran. Are you all right, dear? You're white as a ghost."

The simple kindness of Fran's words made Robin's eyes prickle with tears. She squeezed Fran's hand gratefully and took another deep breath. "I'm sorry. I just saw Mr. Hartwin being taken away in the parking lot. It rattled me, I guess. I wasn't sure if I should still come."

Fran shot a surprised glance at the deputy then turned back to Robin. "What do you mean, dear, taken away?"

The deputy busied himself with his clipboard. Robin watched him as she said, "The FBI agent was with him, and some others. They said he was being taken in for questioning. I think to Grants Pass? But not arrested, definitely not arrested," she added quickly, seeing Fran's face collapse in worry.

"That's… shocking," Fran said. "It's just so hard to believe they would even consider…" She laid a hand to her chest. "Oh my."

Deputy Lincoln looked down at the table. "Sorry, ma'am. It was just something that had to be done. No offense."

Fran recovered herself with visible effort. "It's not your fault, I'm sure. All the law enforcement people have been wonderful. It must be a misunderstanding, or something for elimination purposes. A formality of some kind. Although someone should have let me know." She swiped at the screen of her laptop as if looking for a missed notification, but made a face, obviously finding nothing. "I can see how that would have been disturbing," she added to Robin. "I'm so sorry."

Robin shook her head. "It was very civilized. Mr. Hartwin was taking it in stride. It just—threw me for a loop. I've been worrying so much about Blue, and seeing him taken away put things in a different light."

Fran's eyes narrowed, and Robin realized she'd misspoken again. Quickly, she changed the subject. "I'm happy to give you what little information I have, if you're still collecting."

"We are," the deputy said. He sounded less than thrilled, and Robin wondered if he'd drawn the short stick, left behind to transcribe tips from la-la land while others got to interview a far more meaty suspect.

She started tentatively. "Okay, well, I don't know how much help this will be, but I've had a couple of— well, I call them flashes, because they're much more than visual."

Deputy Lincoln opened a notebook, scratched his nose with his pen, then pulled his phone out of his breast pocket and set it on the table between them. "Do you mind if I record?"

"No, that's okay. But I want you to understand, I'm not sure if this will be helpful at all. When most people think of psychics, they think of easy answers. I just get impressions, and I'm never one hundred percent sure what they're about." She was giving too many disclaimers, she knew, probably making herself sound like a liar. Her face warmed in embarrassment.

"Tell us what you've got," Fran encouraged. "Every little bit helps."

Robin related the two flashes she believed were about Blue: first the one from yesterday afternoon, with the horrible rocky eyes. Calmly and distinctly, she relayed every detail, keeping her voice flat and matter-of-fact. She didn't look at them as she spoke, suspecting she would see disbelief hardening in their eyes, but she glanced up when she finished describing the first flash.

The deputy's caterpillar eyebrows were perhaps two millimeters higher than usual, and Fran's face looked as if she'd just seen a deer hit on the highway, but she just said, "Go on."

Robin did, describing the second flash; the shriek, the taste of blood, and the delicate princess shoe.

Then, quickly, before she could lose her courage, she added, "And I need to show you something. I should have told someone sooner; I wasn't thinking straight. I found it last night after I was attacked in the woods."

She grabbed the baggie out of her pocket and slid it toward the middle of the table. They all looked down at it until the deputy slid it closer to himself with a pencil.

"What's this, now?" he said.

"I found it last night," Robin repeated. "It's a hair tie, a scrunchy. It wasn't in a bag when I found it, but I was carrying it and touching it and then I thought, well, what if it has DNA on it—"

She realized she was babbling nervously and stopped. "I'm sorry," she added. "I should have turned it in right away. Most likely it doesn't belong to Blue. There have been so many searchers out there already. Anyway." She stopped herself again.

The deputy nodded slowly. He looked slightly happier with this dubious piece of physical evidence than he had with her description of the flashes. Even better, he didn't look like he was about to arrest her. Yet. "Where exactly was it?" he asked.

"I just, I mean—I found it in my pocket after. After the confusion. After the doctor and the police talked to me." *Which was after I put it in my pocket, after first discovering it on my wrist...*

"You don't remember finding it on the ground?"

"No. But I must have, before I got attacked."

"You're sure it's not yours? An old one you forgot about?"

"I don't use these, ever. They're too loose to hold my hair."

"And no one's ever given you one as a gift? Maybe you said thanks, stuck it in your pocket, and forgotten about it?" Was it her imagination, or was that suspicion growing in his voice?

"No, I would have remembered," she insisted.

"So, it just turned up in your pocket?"

"Yes, I found it when I was back in my room."

Robin could feel her face coloring again. Why wouldn't he just accept it? She hated lying, but there was no way she was going to say that someone had put it on her wrist. It was too personal. It made it seem like a message left specifically for her.

The deputy's radio crackled, and he held up a finger and rose to his feet, pacing to the corner of the room for a pretense of privacy. Robin could only hear spurts of unintelligible voices, and Deputy Lincoln saying, "Copy," and "Copy that," several times before returning to the table.

He glanced briefly at Robin before turning to cut her out of the conversation and addressing Fran. "Sounds like we've both been left out of the loop. Further interviews with the 'consultants' are canceled, and Grimley wants you to call him."

"Is this about Wes— I mean, Mr. Hartwin?" Fran turned pale.

"Call Grimley." The deputy shrugged, then turned to Robin. "All you people are supposed to get dinner and return to your rooms right afterward. It looks like your contracts will probably be terminated." His eyebrows bounced up and down as he grabbed the plastic bag off the table and put it into his own pocket, adding, "Although I suspect we'll be talking to you again, regardless."

He left the room, a spring in his step.

Robin turned to Fran. "I hope everything's okay."

Fran had been biting her lip, but she smiled wearily. "I'm sure it will all work out. Now go on, get yourself some dinner. Thank you again for coming in." She pulled a phone from one of the capacious pockets in the front of her tunic and fiddled with it, obviously waiting for Robin to leave.

Robin shut the door behind her and headed toward the elevator with a mix of relief and dread. Deputy Lincoln hadn't sounded happy, but that didn't mean anything. Maybe the cops had figured out where Blue was. And if she was alive—that would be wonderful. Somehow in her head, Robin had gotten Blue mixed up with the hopeless loss of her own daughter, but in reality, it was a separate thing. Maybe Blue would get a happy ending.

And herself? She paused in front of the elevator door with unseeing eyes. If the psychics were about to be kicked off the premises, she needed to seek out Kami as soon as possible. If she'd been right to think the bulk of the TV crew was off campus for the weekend, she'd just have to leave a message. Now that Robin knew who and where she was, she could not lose her. But at the same time, she had no idea of how deep the connection went with the LeClairs, how long Kami had been under their influence, if indeed she was. If only Robin knew more of the situation, knew how much they'd told her, how much they'd twisted.

Using her ID card, she entered the elevator. The doors slid shut and she paced back and forth in the small space, biting her lip. So many things didn't add up. Had the LeClairs engineered having her and Kami here at the same time? Did Kami know Robin was her mother? Did the Church of Loomis Powell have anything to do with anything? With the prospect of being booted out of Spirit Ridge in the morning looming over her, there was little time to make the connections that needed to be made.

The elevator doors slid open at B2, but Robin stayed inside and hit the button for the main floor. She'd leave a note for Kami. It was either that or break back into the trailer and lie in wait, and once had been scary enough.

The cafeteria was busy. She looked around, half-hoping to see Tom, but no such luck. Sticking close to the wall, she tried to avoid being spotted by the few other psychics she'd met. Her mind raced ahead. What if, contrary to her expectation, Kami was there—what could Robin say?

She pushed outside and sucked in fresh air. Her body was taut as a sail in a storm, and the healing wound from the belt itched between her shoulder blades. Her daughter had been called Dog. Her daughter had been whipped with a belt. That had been her childhood. Robin ground her teeth and tried to breathe deep. The anger wasn't helping, it was making her feel sick.

Someone was smoking on the patio, huddled in aqua fleece and gazing out toward the woods, Robin recognized Madeline, the crystal ball gazer. Robin hurried by, hoping she wouldn't be spotted in the older woman's peripheral vision.

At the parking lot, she paused. One of the TV vans had returned. Her steps slowed and her heart began to pound. Kami might be there. She must be there. Robin and Kami couldn't be this close and not acknowledge each other. What Robin most needed, what she most dreaded, was going to happen. She was going to speak to her daughter, who she had surrendered so long ago.

In a daze, Robin continued to the trailer door and knocked. Her hand shook and her brain buzzed with panic. All she had to say was, "Can I come in, I need to talk to you," but she wasn't sure she could even form words.

No one answered. There was no sound from inside.

She knocked again, then stared at the door, a mix of disappointment and disbelief taking the place of all that anxious hope. So much for her powers of premonition.

Just in case, she knocked on the door of the other trailer. This one was definitely inhabited. Music and voices came from inside. Kami could be in there, spending time with her coworkers.

After a second knock, the camera man with the dark ponytail cracked open the door enough to poke his face out.

"I was looking for Kami," she said, mouth dry.

His eyes traveled up and down her body. The smell of pot leaked through the crack. "They're not here."

"They?" she repeated dumbly.

"Carla and Kami? They're not here." He spoke loudly and overly clearly as if she might be half-deaf.

"Do you know when they'll be back?"

He shrugged and gulped from the can in his hand. "Don't know. Sunday afternoon? Or tonight, maybe tomorrow. Boss doesn't tell us her plans."

"Kami is your—?"

He snorted. "Carla. The producer."

"Oh. I want to leave a note for Kami."

He pulled back, face receding. "Whatever."

"Do you know her?" Robin asked quickly. "Have you worked with her before?"

"Lady, she's just an intern." The door slammed shut. Laughter leaked out underneath.

"Yeah, okay," Robin said to the scarred surface. "I'll leave a note." It was down to a few words on a piece of paper after all. She tore a sheet out of her notebook, folded it and wrote "Kami" on the outside, and then stopped. "I don't know," she said out loud. Finally, she put her name and cell phone number, and scrawled, "Please call me, it's important."

She hesitated, the image of the paper being crumpled and thrown into the trash so clear, it felt like a vision. It was the most likely outcome, if Kami considered the note to be from a random stranger. But there was nothing Robin could think of that would prevent that from happening. Well, maybe the word "mother," but she couldn't leave that lying around where anyone could read it. She sighed, then slipped the folded paper under the door of the women's trailer.

Done.

****

She paused on her way back to the cafeteria, not sure where the boundary of the internal Wi-Fi was, and checked her phone. Liam had tried to call at five-thirty and left her a few unhappy texts when she didn't answer. His last one said:

—*At least text me what's going on!! Nm, don't, I'M COMING 2MORROW!!!!*—

She typed back:

—*Good. Being sent home. All of us.*—

He answered in seconds:

—*Really? Find girl?!*—

—*No. Not sure why.*—

—*Should I come?*—

—*I can take bus. No rush.*—

—*What about craziness?*—

She hesitated. He didn't know the half of it. But now it could all wait for a face to face.

—*Talk tomorrow. Will tell all*—

He subsided. Back in the cafeteria, she gathered food on a tray not out of hunger but because she thought she should eat. She was so numb and empty. Nothing had been solved, she had helped no one, and she'd run into a dead end. Maybe she just needed to rest.

Then, wandering with her tray, she spotted Sidney Doyle sitting at the end of a table across from Master Leopold, their silver heads leaning toward one another. Robin paused and observed. They seemed to be eating peacefully, not conversing much but not ignoring each other either. She hesitated, uncertain whether to approach. She was so damn wrung out. And tired of being frightened. But she would never forgive herself if she let this opportunity slip by.

They looked up curiously as she approached. "Sorry to interrupt. Hello, Leo. Sidney, I was wondering if I could talk to you. Would you have time—?" Robin trailed off, feeling as if she were being judged by both patient faces.

"Come to my room after you eat. Knock when you get there, it's 418." Sidney nodded at her, then turned back to her food.

Master Leopold offered Robin a faint smile. "Perhaps we shall meet again."

****

Half an hour later, Robin knocked on the door of 418 feeling surreptitious. She had stopped back in her own room and sat with her head in her hands, massaging her temples, for several minutes in an attempt to center herself. It hadn't worked, she still felt jittery, uncertain exactly what she was afraid of.

Sidney opened the door immediately and Robin entered a slightly larger version of her own tiny suite: the same color scheme and theme, but a bedroom with a door instead of a one-room studio. A full-sized couch and two armchairs created a cozy sitting area.

"Let me make us some tea," Sidney said. "I'm so glad you were able to come."

Robin perched on a stool at the breakfast bar and watched as Sidney set a pot to boil and gathered mugs and tea. "It's been a long time since I heard anything about the Church of Loomis Powell," Robin said cautiously. "I thought it was just on the East Coast, or maybe disbanded."

"Yes, it was confined to the East Coast at one time. So you had heard of it, I wasn't sure. When?"

Robin stared down at her hands. They'd barely started talking, and already she had given away information. She should have let Sidney lead the conversation. Robin looked up to find the other woman's gray eyes assessing her, and Robin said, "Are you a member?"

Sidney gave a small smile. "I am, although we have all too few, these days. I was hoping to find new recruits, here."

"And you thought I might be a good candidate? Why?" Disbelief colored Robin's tone.

"Well, let's just say I have a talent for sniffing out talent," Sidney said.

Robin narrowed her eyes. Uncle Matt's words about people who were able to sense those with a genuine gift came back to her. "Someone told me you did psychometry. Is that the right word? Object reading."

"That's true, I do. But I'm also sensitive to certain types of power. If I don't sense it, it doesn't necessarily mean they don't have any. But if I do, they definitely do."

Robin nodded, feeling oddly exposed. "So, you

can't say for sure if someone is a fraud?"

"It's hard to prove a negative, and I've known and trusted several people whose special abilities I couldn't sense at all."

Robin wished she could ask how many of the psychic consultants who were present Sidney didn't trust. Instead Robin asked, "How long have you been part of the Friends?"

The water began to boil. Sidney turned her back to pour water from the pot into two heavy mugs. "I only have one kind of tea, so I hope you like it. It's an herbal blend I make myself, from my garden. And there's honey, if you want."

"No thanks, that's fine." Great. Now she could be poisoned by someone's amateur herb gathering.

"Let's go sit down."

They carried the mugs and saucers to the sitting area where Sidney settled on the couch and Robin opposite her on an easy chair. Robin inhaled the gingery steam and set the tea down on the coffee table.

Sidney picked up the conversation. "I've been part of the Church of Loomis Powell for going on thirty years." She shook her head. "Hard to believe it's been that long. And things have changed so much."

Robin bit her tongue, wanting immediately to ask if she'd known Uncle Matt or Victor LeClair. Robin didn't know much about the scope of the Church's activities, but she knew both men had been board members during that period. How could she ask, though, without giving away more than she wanted about her own past?

"The Friends were a lot more powerful when I was younger," Sidney said conversationally, dipping the steeping ball in her tea. "Everyone with any kind of gift wanted to be part of it, mainly because we helped each other. We networked. The group dates from the time of the witch hunts, you know."

"Oh?" Robin was barely paying attention, still struggling with the implications of Sidney knowing Uncle Matt and Victor LeClair. If Sidney was the person who'd left the note in the diner, she already knew who Robin was, so why would Sidney bait Robin? For sadistic pleasure? To disarm her with friendship?

"Fascinating, isn't it? That we have such a long history. Even though the Church is now comparatively tiny, we house a collection of historical documents at the home of one of the Heritage families." Sidney removed the tea ball from her mug, then brought it to her nose. She drew a deep, appreciative breath. "I love the smell. Try it, it should be strong enough."

Robin reached for her mug and pulled the chain, letting the herbs drip before setting the ball on the saucer. If Sidney wasn't the person who left the note, would it be dangerous for her to know who Robin was? Sidney might be a friend of Victor's.

Robin hadn't spoken in too long, and floundered through Sidney's last statement. "I'm afraid I don't know what a Heritage family is."

"No?" Sidney studied her. "I thought you would. It's just what it sounds like. Some gifts come out of nowhere, unpredictable, cause unknown. Others seem genetic, showing up over and over in the same family, down through the generations. Several of those families have been part of The Church of Loomis Powell for hundreds of years." She shrugged. "The Eldridges. The Woodbines. The Farrells. The Kargazis. The LeClairs. A half-dozen others."

Robin stood abruptly. Sidney knew. She must know. "I'm sorry. I have a headache coming on. Do you mind if we do this another time?"

Sidney gazed up at her. She had a kind face, with smile lines far more pronounced than frown lines, and a broad forehead that gave her an open, intelligent look. "You know, if you sit and drink your tea, it might help with the headache. It will relax the blood vessels that constrict around the temples."

Slowly, Robin sat back down. She wasn't sure what game Sidney was playing, or if she was playing a game at all. But there might be no better opportunity to learn what she could from her, and Robin needed information desperately.

What she wanted more than anything was to confide in someone trustworthy and knowledgeable, someone who moved confidently in the world of paranormal abilities and was well-respected. Someone like Sidney seemed to be. But Sidney had said Farrell and LeClair in the same breath. Sidney must have known Uncle Matt and Daniel's father, Victor. That couldn't be coincidence.

Sidney was watching her thoughtfully.

Robin cleared her throat, then sipped the tea. "It's…very good. Thank you. But I'm not sure it would be helpful for me. To join the Church."

"Oh?" Sidney's eyebrows rose.

Robin gathered her thoughts. "I have a history."

Sidney narrowed her eyes, her lips pressing together as she tilted her head.

A loud banging from the door interrupted. Someone called through in apparent panic: "Sidney?! You there? Sidney, it's me, it's Jim! Angel's gone!"

Chapter Sixteen

A large man with an exuberant gray beard and thin gray ponytail pushed past Sidney into the suite. The T-shirt restraining his pot-belly was pink with a rainbow on it. His eyes dismissed Robin and flicked around the entire space as if Angel might be hiding behind a piece of furniture.

Sidney closed the door and watched him for a moment with arms crossed and eyebrows drawn together. Then she moved to lay a hand on his arm. "For gods' sakes, Jim. This isn't helping. Sit down and tell us what's going on." She gestured to Robin. "This is Robin, one of the psychics. Robin, this is Jim, Angel's dad. Angel's one of the consultants, too," she explained. "He's the youngest one here, just a kid, but he's been on the circuit for ages. Not that there are many events these days, but we see each other now and then, don't we, Jim?"

Jim came back to himself, at least a little. His gray eyes, creased with anxiety, focused on Robin, and he enveloped her hand with a calloused two-handed shake that shook the fringes on his black leather vest. "Sorry for the drama," he said. He lowered himself to the couch and pulled a giant pink bandana out of one hip pocket to wipe his face. "I didn't mean to come off all crazy. I'm worried as all hell. That's why I came to see Sidney. It's good to meet you, though, Robin."

"You too," she said. "I don't want to intrude. Hope you figure things out. Sidney, thank you, I'll talk to you later."

Sidney frowned. "Oh no, you don't. We're not quite done, I think." She gestured so authoritatively that Robin found herself sitting back down. Sidney turned to Jim. "You don't mind if Robin stays, do you?"

"Not at all, maybe she can help. Angel's gone, been gone for hours. This isn't like him. He always lets me know what he's up to. Maybe not right away, but not like this. He's thoughtful, a good kid, and we were planning to play chess after the Circle."

Sidney perched next to Jim, and patted his knee. "That does sound worrying, but it's probably nothing. It usually is, with teenagers. Did you bring me something?"

It seemed like a non-sequitur to Robin, but Jim nodded.

"It's just a little thing I found in his room that I don't recognize. It might not have anything to do with him going off..." His voice trailed off as he dug in his pockets again. "Aha." He pulled out the crumpled pink bandana, shook his head, tucked it back in and pulled a red roll of cloth out of the same spot like a magician's scarf trick.

Jim deftly spread it out on the coffee table. The ring on his left forefinger caught Robin's attention as he moved: a chunky silver skull with sparkling diamond eyes. She frowned, reminded of the rock-face man in her flash.

The object that appeared in the center of the red bandana was less interesting. A set of earbuds curled in a nest, the wires black with purple earpieces. Robin leaned close to see that the earbuds, too, had little skulls on them. She had a pair just like them, only in blue—Skullcandy brand.

"These aren't Angel's," Jim said. "He packed his favorite pair of over-the-ear headphones, and they're on the nightstand next to his bed. These were on the dresser. He hates putting things inside his ear, never buys this kind. Plus, I've never seen them before."

Robin held her tongue, still not sure what was going on. But even normal teenagers wandered off sometimes, it was part of being a teenager. And surely it was hard to keep track of their things.

Sidney appeared to have no such reservations. She rubbed her hands together briskly, then picked up the earbuds and cradled them in both hands, her eyes closing. Robin glanced at Jim's face. He was spellbound, holding his breath. She looked back to Sidney, whose face was serene.

Sidney laughed a little and said, "Music, of course. Okay, the music is pretty loud." She bopped her head as if hearing the beat. "She's sharing it with Angel. She's really cute, Jim, kind of plump, black hair, I think."

Her eyes popped open, and she carefully set the earbuds back on the coffee table. "That's about it. They didn't absorb much of an impression."

Jim wrinkled his nose. "I haven't seen any girls around here. No one under twenty-five, anyway."

Robin cleared her throat to interrupt. "So, you hold the thing and you can tell what last happened to it. Or something?"

Sidney chuckled. "Yes, sort of. It's usually only the most vivid of impressions. I'm reading an invisible human residue left on the object rather than the object itself, and some things aren't very absorbent."

"So Angel was holding these, or listening to these, thinking about a girl?"

"I think they both held these. Angel feels things intensely, he leaves a lot of residue, so I can sense him even though he only had these for a short time. But I can feel the girl too, just a ghost of an impression." She closed her eyes again. "I can sense her state of mind when she listens to music, and she listens to a lot of music. She's restless, almost angry."

Jim whooshed in relief. "A girl. Okay. I guess I should have guessed, I just didn't think there was anyone young enough here. But okay, he found someone. Good for him."

"You can actually tell what she looks like?" Robin persisted.

"Not always. But I got an image through Angel's eyes. She made quite an impression."

Robin was feeling a little sick. She turned to Jim. "How long has Angel been missing?"

"Well, it's been hours, like I said. I walked him down to the cafeteria and ate lunch with him, then he went to the Circle, and I haven't seen him since. He's been kind of antsy, hasn't had a chance to do his psychic thing yet, so we were going to play chess. I told him if he won we could maybe go out to dinner, find some music tonight downtown, drive back tomorrow. He was like, 'I'm going to kick your ass, old man.'"

"I didn't see him at the Circle," Sidney said slowly. "Did you, Robin?"

"No. I'm still not a hundred percent sure who we're talking about. But I didn't notice anyone who looked like a teenager. There have been so many new faces here, though, I might not have noticed."

184

"Angel? You'd recognize him for sure," Jim said. "He's famous. And he's vain. Boy's got more product in his hair than a beauty salon. And blue eyes that practically glow."

"Famous for what?" she asked.

"His parents had him on the evangelical circuit for years. Four years old, five years old—all the way until he was seven. People would pay a mint for him to lay his hands on them. This little boy, hair and skin so pale he practically looked like an albino, but with these light blue eyes…He looked like an angel. And fragile, skinny as hell." Jim's voice turned sad and ruminative.

"Jim was one of the roadies," Sidney said. "When the marriage broke up and Angel's parents started slinging accusations at each other, Jim got called to testify in court."

"Both of them tried to bribe me to implicate the other one with terrible things, like child abuse. But the worst thing is, it wouldn't really have been lying either way. Without laying a finger on him, they'd totally fucked him up. My crew shielded him as much as we could as it got worse and worse, but everything from them was poison. I kick myself to this day that I didn't just take him away when I first realized how bad they were."

Vague memories of tabloid pictures stirred in Robin's mind. The conservatively dressed holier-than-thou parents, once-beloved TV show hosts with their perfect marriage and angelic child, glaring daggers across a courtroom. "Oh, yeah. I think I remember that. You sued for custody, right?"

"Didn't get it. Had to change my 'lifestyle,' apparently roadies don't make great parents. But two years later, I finally got approved as foster dad and then was able to adopt him. So it's all good."

Robin wondered if it was actually good for Angel, to be living the life of a working psychic as a teenager. It was hard not to like Jim, though.

"What are his abilities?" she asked. The remark about him laying hands on them on the revival circuit had twinged her skepticism bone. She'd always assumed that the blind suddenly able to see and the crippled rising from their wheelchairs at those shows were just that—a show.

"He's a psychic healer. But not the way you're thinking. Not the way his folks wanted people to believe," Sidney said.

Jim explained. "The kid can read auras. Your intentions, your mood, all the good and bad deeds you've done—it all feeds into this energy field that hovers around you. It helps if he touches you, but some people's auras are so strong, he says they glow from across a football field. And he can't exactly 'fix' things. But sometimes, sometimes—he can help a lot. Balancing your aura can change how you feel, physically, and that can change how well you are." Jim ran out of words and stopped talking with his head hanging.

Sidney caught Robin's expression and laughed. "It's not nonsense, really! Angel's very gifted."

Jim said, "When I met the kid, I thought his parents had brainwashed him into thinking he was magic. Or he was trying to please them and pretending. But no. He can do this crazy thing, and he's done more good in his short life than most folks do in a lifetime."

Robin's eyebrows went up, but she nodded. With an ability like that, what had it been like for him to live with toxic parents? Never mind what they said or did, he would have known exactly how they felt, how twisted they were. It hit too close to home. She shuddered.

Sidney broke in. "Hang on. So you walked him to the door of the small gym, but he didn't attend, and you haven't seen him since? That means he's been missing since about two o'clock."

"I walked him to the hallway," Jim said. "We were still chatting. He was six feet from the door when I left him." A thread of fear had returned to his voice.

"Maybe that's when he ran into the headphone girl again," Sidney said. "And he decided to hang out with her instead of with all the old folks. Understandable. He might have been dubious about how his aura-reading would be helpful in the Circle."

"And then maybe the two of them heard we were all getting kicked out tomorrow, and decided to live it up," Jim said. "It's not like him, but if he really liked her, and this was his only chance to spend time with her..." He sounded like he was trying to convince himself, but Robin's uneasy feeling was hardening into a pit in her stomach.

"I think you better tell Security," she said.

They both looked at her blankly.

"I mean it. Maybe he is just with some girl," like Robin's mysterious, abused, psycho-raised daughter, "but remember yesterday? I went into the woods for a little stroll and ended up unconscious. And Wednesday? When Blue disappeared off the face of the earth? This isn't a good time to just hope for the best."

Jim's beard bristled as he clenched the muscles in his jaw. "You're right. Of course, you're right. I should have gone straight there. It's tough being a dad; you don't want to step on their independence. But it's not safe here. How could I have forgotten that?" He stood, and Sidney stood too.

"Thank you, Robin. I knew we needed you here," she said. "I hope to talk to you again, soon. Jim, I'll go with you to Security. Maybe they'll take two concerned voices more seriously than one."

Robin followed them to the door, hoping her half-formed fears were simple paranoia. If the girl who'd shared music with Angel was Kami, so what? Just because she'd been raised by the LeClairs didn't mean she'd been tainted by them. Two oblivious teenagers making out while the world collapsed around them was kind of a sweet story. But then she remembered just how desperately she'd wanted to believe in that brand of normal when she was a teenager, and what the ultimate price had been for the illusion. Daniel LeClair had turned her innocence against her.

Robin's stomach twisted with sudden fear, but she stopped herself before opening her mouth. She must not project her own experience into everyone else's problems. Angel was probably fine.

"Good luck. I'm sure he'll turn up soon," she said. "Let me know if I can do anything to help."

"Thanks," Jim said.

Sidney and Jim moved off quickly toward the elevators, and Robin turned toward her room. She let herself in, gratefully closing the door behind her. For a moment she stood in the silence, relishing the solitude which instantly turned down some of the static in her anxious mind.

The lights were dim and she didn't bother to brighten them as she slumped on the bed. She should send an email to Liam, make arrangements for tomorrow. She should think through what Sidney had said about Loomis Powell, and figure out how much Robin could trust Sidney. Robin should come up with another way to contact Kami or figure out if Robin could afford to hire a private detective, to investigate Kami's history and relationship with the LeClairs.

Robin's mind was as bruised as if she'd been hit with a series of cold flashes, and the mattress beneath her seemed imbued with extra gravity. There was nothing she could do right now, nothing useful. Nothing that was time sensitive.

She fell back on the bed and, tugging the quilt over herself, allowed sleep to pull her down.

****

BEEP. BEEP. BEEP.

An alarm was going off, ear-splitting and insistent as a fire alarm. Blindly, she reached for the clock, but there was no clock. She fumbled for her phone, heart pounding in time with the klaxon. The alarm was unbearable. Her phone wasn't there. Her phone couldn't make that deafening awful noise anyway. Tangled in the quilt, she fought to a sitting position and tried to find the source of the racket. It was everywhere, thunderous enough to vibrate her skull and scatter her thoughts. She put her hands over her ears and stumbled to the light switch.

As the lights came on, the alarm abruptly ceased. Her relief was intense but short-lived. The screen across from the loveseat flickered on and a bell-like tone emanated from the speakers. She turned to look. A haggard Wes Hartwin appeared on-screen as the sound faded.

"Attention, everyone. Apologies for disturbing you," he said gruffly. Robin stared, feeling as if she must still be in a dream. Had Hartwin rigged all the TVs with some kind of central override switch? A loudspeaker system wasn't good enough for him? That probably wasn't the biggest issue here, but it seemed strange and intrusive for his face to suddenly be in her space.

She shook her head and tried to focus, her mind fuzzy from the abrupt and awful wake-up call.

Hartwin's larger-than-life bloodshot eyes stared from the screen. "Please remain calm. Lockdown has been triggered but will be resolved as soon as possible. Team G, Drill scenario 6. Team P, Drill 4. Subject R.F."

Lockdown. What the bloody fuck did he mean by lockdown? He couldn't seriously mean they were going to close down the bunker and shut out the world. Right? Because that would not end well. This was a corporation, not a religious cult.

Hartwin ran his hands through his hair, reminding her briefly of Angel's worried dad with his telltale gesture of desperation. Silence stretched painfully as he seemed to be gathering his thoughts. She waited, holding her breath, for clarification or for him to chuckle suddenly and say it was all just a test of their emergency broadcast system, everybody go back to sleep. Then the microphone picked up a crash off-camera. He turned his head, eyes widening in startlement, and stuttered, "Who—What the hell are you doing up here?"

The screen flickered and went off, as did the lights. Darkness thickened around her, unrelieved by any tiny gleam of light. Robin stood alone, as cut off from the world as in a sensory deprivation tank, with no company but the sound of her own breath. The bunker closed around her with all the weight of its cement and steel.

She shuddered. But it wasn't just from the sudden onset of claustrophobia, or fear of lockdown, or dread of what this might mean. This was a chill that started at the base of her spine and shot powerfully upward like a lance of ice. Horrified recognition coursed through her, and she jerked herself away from the potentially lethal corners of the coffee table, twisting as she fell.

Chaos. Pain. Her mind jittered for sensation, any clear sensation, amid colors and shapes and textures and odors that competed for attention in an unbearable cacophony.

It went on for hours, or days, or years, bombardment without surcease.

Then, hush, came a wind. Hush, hush, came a soothing wind.

Branches rustled. Insects scurried. Deep inside, silence. The slow drip of water carving stone.

Panic. Strangeness. Chaos threatening to return.

Then, hush, came a wind.

Hush, hush.

A face with unblinking crystalline eyes, and the rough rub of stone.

Her consciousness recoiled again, but despite herself, she started to calm. Peace sank into her like the chill of the earth. A slow, easy peace.

Hush.

She stopped struggling. Darkness filled her. Rain fell and seeped into the ground and was drawn into the trees and was dripped into the spaces of her mind. Stone endured and water carved and the currents of air ceaselessly flowed in unseen tides. Tiny bright lives flowered and ended: scurrying, nestling, building, passing.

Hush, came a wind, carrying with it news of the world, molecules of pine, of diesel, of steel, to mix with dust, and loam, and damp fungi.

Her breath matched the rhythm. It was a different kind of consciousness, but it was real. If she panicked, if she clung to it, it would slip away. She relaxed, let it wash over her. She was as slow, as solid, as centered as a mountain.

And into the rhythm of sun and rain and wind and growth and death, a small, warm, human hand crept trustingly into hers. She gasped, then shouted. Blue!

It echoed around her—Blue! Blue! Blue! Blue! Everything shattered as her voice broke the vision. No more hush of the wind. No more rustle of branches. No more depth of the caverns beneath. All gone. Her hand was emptier and colder than it had ever been, and her heart was so hollow, nothing but a husk.

Chapter Seventeen

Ba-bump. Ba-bump.

Her heartbeat, slowing to normal, led her back to awareness.

Her eyes flew open to find herself engulfed in gloom, the only light coming from an emergency strip glowing halfway up the wall all the way around the room, creating a sickly yellow-gray light. She blinked in confusion, not sure at first where she was. Spirit Ridge. Her suite. There was the coffee table with her purse on it. There was her unopened box of Tarot cards. Rolling over, she spotted her suitcase next to the rumpled bed.

She blinked. The last thing she remembered was calling Blue's name.

She had felt Blue. Robin knew where she was, she was certain of it. But—Wes Hartwin. Before she flashed. He'd been talking gibberish on TV. Lockdown. He wanted to lockdown the bunker. Right before her flash, his face had changed. Something had happened, and the power had gone out.

She shook her head and rolled up to a sitting position. Out of habit, she rubbed at her temples, then realized something.

Aside from her confusion about what had happened before the flash, she felt fine. No brain-tissue-turned-to-hamburger headache. Was it—had she tapped into blood magic again?

No. It had been different. She had been offered a way to tame the chaos.

Sitting on the carpet next to the coffee table, she reconstructed the flash in her mind, then dug in her purse for her notebook. She flipped it open and scribbled, then stared at the few words she'd written, barely visible in the gloomy yellowish light.

Spirit Ridge—spirit!?

Wind=blood?

The page was barely legible in the gloom, but the words tattooed themselves across her mind in glowing letters. Uncle Matt's lifetime of scars, his sacrificed fingers. Was there an alternative? Her stomach twisted. She had hated what he did. But he had sacrificed for her. If it hadn't been necessary—had anything been necessary? Her years of trying to suppress what she was? Yes, she'd been hiding from a killer, but she'd also been trying to free herself from the dark shadow of what she thought her curse entailed.

Slowly, she pressed the notebook shut, as if trying to keep something in. Not repressing her flashes meant trying to record everything, but she couldn't wrap her head around it right now. It was too much. She had turned away from Uncle Matt when she'd seen him use blood to focus his power. Had been as disgusted as if he'd admitted to necrophilia. Her flashes had always been barely intelligible and chaotically painful without blood, and she'd believed that her suffering was her own form of sacrifice, an unwilling payment for knowledge that she didn't even want, punishment for being so irrevocably broken.

What if her guilt and self-hatred hadn't ever been necessary? What if her ability only demanded a kind of focus?

Hush, came the wind.

No. It couldn't be true. It might not even work away from here. She had felt another being. Another consciousness, sharing the rhythm of the mountain. Rock-faced man.

Tears came to her eyes and she blinked them away. Right now, it didn't matter. All that really mattered was finding Blue. That was why she had come here. And if she had also found her long-lost daughter, if she had also reminded a killer that she existed—those issues would have to wait.

She rose and brushed herself off, breathing deeply in an effort to stay in the moment, undistracted by the past or by emotion. The room felt so surreal with the lights like this. She tried the light switches and opened the refrigerator to no avail. Why hadn't the backup generators kicked in? Wasn't the bunker supposed to continue running smoothly in the face of anything, up to and including nuclear disaster? Could this be intentional?

She slung her bag over her shoulder, laced up her boots, and zipped her jacket, wondering where to start. Without power, the bunker's server wouldn't be supporting the MapApp, and she had no idea how to access the caves under the building that she'd sensed during her flash.

She peered out into the hallway through her door's peephole. The emergency lighting cast yellow-gray light at waist level, and everything looked deserted. Down the hall, the emergency stairwell door was outlined with fluorescent paint that glowed in the strange light. The gloom and the silence made it feel very late at night. How long had she been out? Before the lockdown alarm, she'd been napping, and then unconscious during and after the cold flash. It could have been hours.

When she dug her phone out of her bag to check the time, the screen was blank, the power drained. She hadn't plugged it in before her nap, and now there was no power. Useless. She crammed it back into the bag.

She hesitated, then walked down the hall to Tom's door and knocked lightly. The sound echoed in the deserted hallway, and she looked around uneasily. The door swung open. A slice of warm dancing light appeared, and Robin stepped closer. An unintelligible sound came from inside, a muffled screech, and the crack yawned open to reveal not Tom but Erin and Madeline. Before Robin could wonder if she'd knocked on the wrong door, Erin grabbed her arm with a harsh grip, yanking her in, as Madeline reached to push the door shut behind her.

"What the hell?" Robin reflexively jerked her arm, breaking Erin's grip. She backed against the door, facing both women. Their faces were grim and leaping shadows cast by candlelight added years to them both. The room beyond was similar to hers, but lit by nearly a dozen white pillar candles.

Tom was tied to a chair at the round kitchen table, with pantyhose around his arms and torso and his wrists pulled behind him. It looked ridiculous, like whoever had tied him up had learned from watching Scooby-Doo reruns. When she met Tom's eyes, he made another muffled grunt through the bandana knotted around his mouth. A trickle of dried blood flaked at his temple, and she guessed he'd been there for a while.

Madeline and Erin weren't her idea of scary, at least

without weapons, but it was two against one as long as Tom was out of the picture, and based on his head wound, they weren't afraid of doing damage. If he used some of the muscle in that wiry body, he might be able to work loose of the pantyhose which were probably too stretchy to make effective bonds. She and Tom together could take out the Big Hair Gang in less than a minute.

It would be a different story altogether if they did have a weapon, and she reminded herself not to underestimate them. They must have taken Tom by surprise and clocked him a good one with something.

She shifted her eyes back to the women, who were crowding her but apparently hesitant to lay hands on her.

"Am I interrupting something? What the hell is going on here?" Robin demanded. She reached behind herself for the doorknob. If she could get into the hall, she could yell for help. But there was no room to open the door without putting herself in reach of the two women.

Erin flashed an insincere smile. "We were waiting for you. I figured you'd show up here. Girls like you always fall back on the nearest attractive man when the going gets tough."

Robin snorted despite the humorless situation. "You know, I was mostly coming over to see what time it was. My phone is dead. But I can ask someone else. I'll just be going now."

"No. You're staying. We need to keep you safe," Madeline said. Shoulder to shoulder, they crowded closer. There was still no sign of a weapon, not even whatever they'd used to bash Tom.

Robin looked past them and raised her eyebrows at him to indicate that he should stand. He frowned, which accentuated the dark shadows under his eyes. From the knot on his temple to the leprechauns on the pajama pants he wore with a plain gray T-shirt, he didn't look capable of an escape attempt. He was just going to have to pull it together.

Robin squared off and glared at the cautiously advancing women. "I thought we were in lockdown. No one's going very far, right? What the hell do you mean, safe?"

Erin and Madeline took half a step closer. She was shorter than both of them, but younger and more muscular, and they'd obviously noticed.

Robin flicked her eyes to Tom again and saw he'd gathered himself to act. As he stood, the chair stayed attached to him at first, tilting against his back, and then the pantyhose stretched and slid grudgingly along the varnished wood. The chair fell away and tipped sideways to hit the tiled floor with a bang. Erin and Madeline whirled to see their prisoner standing with loosened hose drooping around his hips and his pajama pants dangerously low.

Tom looked as startled as they did and hurried to yank up his waistband from the back.

"Free your hands!" Robin called and hurtled toward Erin but Robin didn't have space to work up much momentum. Erin grabbed Robin, swearing, and managed at first to keep her feet. Robin jerked at the back of Erin's knee with her own calf and brought both of them down, Robin landing heavily on top. Erin swiped at Robin's eye, bucking beneath her as hard as a mechanical bull in a cowboy bar. Robin rolled to one side and lost her grip, wincing as her back banged the tile floor. Erin landed an elbow in her stomach, and Robin gasped in pain.

"Help me, goddammit!" Erin yelled. Madeline had backed away, cringing, her eyes going from Erin to Tom and back.

Robin pushed the pain away and grappled back on top. She struggled to grip both of Erin's arms. Erin lashed upward and snapped at Robin's chin with her teeth, and Robin recoiled but held fast.

There was a loud thump, and Robin tore her gaze from Erin for a moment. Tom, freed from the chair, still was wrapped in pantyhose with his hands and feet tied together. He'd fallen to the floor, and was lifting his butt over his wrists to bring his hands to the front.

Belatedly, Robin saw Madeline had collected her courage and was winding up to swing her purse at Robin's head. Robin ducked, and most of the force of the blow was lost, but the part that landed didn't feel good. Madeline pounded her back and shoulders with the oversized bag, and Robin hunched and hung on to the still-struggling Erin as tightly as she could, hoping Tom would jump in soon.

"Get a knife!" Erin screamed. Her movements had become weaker, and there was an edge of panic in her voice.

"A knife?!" Madeline sounded horrified but when Robin glanced up, she had dropped her purse and was wrenching open a drawer.

But Tom was there, finally free and on his feet. He yelled, "Hold it!" and closed the space between them with one long step.

Madeline whirled around and flung her hands up in surrender. A paring knife clattered across the counter. "Don't hurt me! I had to! I'll be good, I swear!" She sank to the floor.

Tom, who hadn't touched her, looked nonplussed.

"Jeez, Madeline, have some backbone!" Erin burst out in frustration.

Tom loomed over Madeline for a moment, but she only scooted against the cabinet, covering her head with her arms. "Stay there!" he ordered, and moved to help Robin, who edged herself off of Erin so that Tom could hold her arms on the floor above her head.

Robin sat up and shook her own aching arms. She took a deep breath and stared down at Erin, wondering what to do with the two crazy women.

"What the hell is going on?" Tom said, and when Robin glanced up, she realized he was asking her, not Erin or Madeline. He sounded angry, but he looked less threatening than weary as he met Robin's eyes. "Just who are you?"

"What do you mean?"

"These 'ladies' clobbered me in the head because they wanted you, Robin! Why would they do that?"

"I have no idea!" Even as she said it, she wondered if that were true. She knew a little about two things that were going on—the disappearance of Blue, and the reappearance of Kami. She just couldn't see how that would lead to this fracas.

Erin said, "Oh, don't pretend you don't know. This is all about you! You and your stupid power."

"What's all about me? What do you know about my power?"

"Don't say another word," Madeline told Erin. She looked scared and resentful, hunched against the cabinets like an animal afraid to leave its den. "Let 'Robin' play all the games she wants. It won't matter in the end."

"What games?" Tom asked, looking at Robin.

"Yeah, what games?" Robin said, looking at Madeline with narrowed eyes. "You wrote that note, didn't you? Do you work for the LeClairs? Is that it?"

"Clare who?" Erin said. "Don't know her."

"Victor LeClair? Daniel LeClair? Ring a bell?"

"Well, I know that name. Victor LeClair is a philanthropist," Tom said slowly. "He's super rich. He's usually a sponsor at the New Age conferences where a lot of the psychics network. And he's the guy behind PsychicMoot.com. What does he have to do with anything?"

Madeline extended one shaking arm toward her purse, and Tom released one of Erin's wrists long enough to knock it away and set the purse next to himself.

"Can we tie them up or something before we continue this conversation?" Robin said. "I'd really like to get up."

"You're not tying me up," Erin growled.

Tom said, "Oh, you'd rather stay down here? Because hey, if that's your preference, we can just hog-tie you to the base of the table. That's the fun one where your hands are tied to your feet behind you. Don't think I won't do it. As a matter of fact, that sounds a lot easier than letting you get up." He grabbed some of panty hose that had fallen to the floor.

"No!" Erin said. "Whatever. Yes, I'll get up."

Robin climbed off of Erin's legs, Tom released her arms, and they both helped her off the floor. She tensed as if she was about to make a run for it, but they held her arms tightly and she grudgingly sat down. Robin snugged the panty hose around her, making sure they were a good deal tighter and more strategically placed than they had been for Tom, and then they pulled Madeline to her feet and tied her likewise.

"This is not something I thought I'd ever be doing," Robin remarked finally, as she pulled the last knot tight around Madeline's ankle. Robin rose to her feet. Her shoulders relaxed, just a little, now that the two women were restrained.

"You have no idea what you're in for," Erin said, voice acidic. Her hairdo was awry from their scuffle on the floor, and smeared mascara made her look as if she had two black eyes. She should look ridiculous, tied up with pantyhose, but ill will rolled from her in waves.

"Shut up, Erin," Madeline hissed.

Robin's tension ratcheted up. "Oh yeah? Tell me, then."

Erin pressed her lips together and raised her eyebrows.

"Is it something to do with Victor LeClair?"

Erin studied the ceiling.

Robin clenched her fists. "Did he pay you to attack me? Was it you who hit me in the woods?"

Tom stepped closer and laid a hand on her shoulder. Robin stiffened and he removed it. "I don't think she's going to talk to you," he said quietly.

Robin ignored him and bent so that she was inches from Erin's face. "What the hell is going on? What do you know about my daughter!"

"You're losing it," Madeline observed. "Trust me. You'll find out everything you need to, in time."

Erin sputtered with laughter. "Yeah, why don't you just sit down and relax? All will become clear, in time," she intoned.

Robin straightened and forced herself to breathe

deeply. What had the women said, earlier? They needed to keep her safe? Clearly, they knew something, but by wasting her time interrogating them, she might be playing into someone's plan to keep her out of the way— of what, she had no idea. But she wasn't going to stoop to torture to find out.

Deliberately, she turned her back on them and met Tom's concerned face.

"How about you and me talk away from little pitchers," she suggested, gesturing toward the tiny sitting area.

He looked relieved. "Sure. Let me grab some ice, my head is pounding like a drum."

Robin plopped down on the loveseat, trying to let go of the anger that had flooded her. She was still smarting from the fight, especially where Erin had elbowed her, but that was nothing compared to her mental agitation. She rubbed her temples.

Tom reached into the freezer of the unlit fridge and pulled out an ice cube tray. "Shoot, they're half-melted already." He dumped them into a dishtowel anyway and put the dripping bundle in a bowl before coming to sit with her.

"What did they hit you with, anyway?" she asked.

He pointed at a brass knick-knack about six inches tall on the kitchen counter. "It must be from their room. About an hour after the power went out and the lockdown started, I came back here and took a shower before all the water cooled down. I lit some candles to brighten the place up. When they knocked, Erin was bracing up Madeline and said she'd twisted her ankle and asked if I could help. I invited them in, Madeline sat down and I knelt down to look at her ankle. Erin beaned

203

me. I'm lucky I don't have a skull fracture."

Robin glanced at Erin and shook her head. "Yeah. She's stronger than she looks. It could have been a lot worse. Is your vision blurry? Let me see your pupils." He leaned close and she peered into his blue eyes. His pupils seemed the same size.

"No. Aside from a throbbing headache, I think I'm okay." He leaned back and put the ice pack on his head with his eyes closed. The towel dripped on the upholstery. After a few moments, he sighed and set the ice pack on the floor. "So."

"I'm so sorry," she said. "They attacked you because of me."

"It's not your fault," he said. Then he looked at her, eyes holding no trace of their usual humor. "At least I don't think it is. Do you want to tell me what's going on?"

She lowered her voice. "I honestly don't know. Not entirely. But I have a guess. And I think I know where Blue Gracen is."

He opened his eyes wide. "Really? Did you have another flash?"

"I did. She's under the bunker. Did Hartwin or anybody mention caves? Tunnels?"

He shook his head. "There was nothing like that on the maps they gave us. Are you sure?"

"I'm positive. And she's not alone. Something or someone is with her, but I think she's okay. At least she was okay. But we need to find her, or let the cops know where she is."

He was shaking his head. "You know we're trapped, right?"

"The lockdown? Yeah. I heard that announcement

Hartwin made. But that just means we're locked in the bunker, right? We can still go talk to Security. Or the deputies."

"No, we're locked in this hallway. When it first happened, everyone panicked. We wanted to get upstairs, talk sense into Hartwin, remind him that the FBI doesn't like to be shut out. It became clear pretty quickly that our ID cards no longer worked to open doors or access the elevator. Even the emergency stairwell is locked tight."

"That's crazy," Robin breathed. She remembered again the glimpse of Hartwin's panicked face she'd seen on the television screen. "I heard a loud crash right at the end of his little announcement. I thought he might be under attack. And then the generators didn't switch on. Maybe it's not Hartwin doing this."

He shrugged. "You could be right. But does it matter? We only know there's no more Wi-Fi, no cell phone service, and no way out of this hallway, at least not until the cops get things under control."

Robin took a moment to let that sink in. The thick concrete walls around her, the gloom, the horrible green strip of emergency lighting—it didn't just feel like a prison, it was a prison. "Good thing I'm not claustrophobic," she tried to joke, but her voice cracked.

He frowned, studying her face. "You're not. Are you? Listen. Don't worry about it. Whatever's happening up there, it's out of our hands right now, but it won't last long. I'm betting the FBI is dealing with whatever defenses Hartwin thinks he's got. We've got water, air, shelter, and all the food people had stashed in their suitcases, so we're perfectly safe. And you said Blue was safe, too. We'll just hang in there for a few more hours, and it will be fine. In the meantime, you can tell me your theory about these two and whatever the hell they have to do with Victor LeClair."

Robin glanced over at Madeline and Erin, who seemed to be concentrating on their own hushed conversation. It was reassuring that she couldn't make out more than an occasional word. When they noticed Robin looking, Madeline said, "Can you please, please, get me one of my nicotine patches? I'll give you a clue if you do."

"Madeline!" Erin cried.

"I wasn't going to tell her anything good," Madeline said defensively. "Duh."

Robin rolled her eyes and turned back to Tom. "Maybe if we separated them we could get Madeline to talk. Do you think it counts as torture to deny her nicotine?"

"Come on, stop procrastinating. What's going on?"

She sat back, stung by the half-humorous accusation. She wasn't procrastinating. But he was right in one way—she hadn't decided to completely trust him, either. She'd come here on a whim, but she hadn't necessarily been looking for an ally, had she? She'd wanted to find out about the lockdown, the power outage, and maybe, just maybe, to share her flash about Blue.

He'd earned at least a little of her trust, though. It was pure paranoia to imagine him in cahoots with Madeline and Erin, getting hit on the head and tied up on the off chance she would confide in him.

"Okay," she said finally. "I'll tell you." And because she didn't know any other way to tell it, she started back in the summer of the year two psychics disappeared from her uncle's group of friends, when Heather Marie Farrell thought she was going crazy, and Matthew Farrell started tracking a killer and lost track of the niece he should have been watching for signs of the family curse.

Tom was startled by the name Daniel LeClair, she could tell, but she stopped watching his face as she related the story of how badly her teenage self had fallen for him, and how betrayed she'd felt when Uncle Matthew had warned her against Daniel. How even more betrayed she'd felt when she'd realized he'd been right. Then, the adoption that was arranged to keep her daughter out of the hands of the LeClairs, Uncle Matt's disappearance, and Heather Farrell's desperate flight across the country and transformation into Robin Fox.

"My daughter is here," she told him finally. "It's Kami. She's an intern with the TV crew. And somehow, someone knows about the relationship. I was about to leave after the attack in the woods but someone followed me to Grizzly and left a note telling me she was here and threatening her life, so I had to come back. I didn't know who she was then, only that she was here. And I haven't been able to warn her since I figured it out."

Tom was silent for a long moment. Finally he said, "So now you think it was Madeline who left the note? Which would mean she knows your real name. Which you think means that the LeClairs have found you, and found your daughter, and traced you both here. It's a lot to assume, isn't it? Except, Madeline and Erin did want to attack you…"

Robin told him some of the pieces she'd left out: the flash of Kami's childhood, and the magazine cover on Kami's wall.

"Okay. So they found Kami a long time ago, you're

thinking? And abused her, the poor kid. But still, I don't understand why they would threaten her life. As if they wanted you to stay and protect her. Why would they want that?"

She shook her head. "I don't know. But I'm probably the only one left in the world who knows Uncle Matt thought Victor LeClair was a killer. Maybe they hadn't been able to find me until I poked my head out of the woodwork, and now that they have, they won't take the chance of losing me again."

Tom shook his head. "Victor LeClair. That's mind-blowing. He's just a boring old rich guy. A nice one, at that, a soft touch for charities. He gives away tons of money, hosts fundraisers. If Victor's a bad guy, it's not showing in his actions, at least publicly."

"How does he make his money?"

He shrugged. "We'd have to look it up, but I have no idea. PsychicMoot.com is relatively big, but it's no Facebook. I always assumed it was old family money, but I don't know."

Over the years, along with fantasies of her daughter growing up happy and healthy in some kind of idyllic English country manor, she'd imagined lives for her enemies too. In her head, the wicked LeClairs had been amassing power underground like supervillains, not making friends and pretending to be philanthropists. But she knew what she'd seen in her flash, and she'd stake her life on it being true.

In the face of her silence, Tom asked, "Is there any way it could have been someone else?"

"Not unless he has an evil twin," she said wryly. "I don't know what to tell you. I think he's just good at masking himself. And way back when, Daniel admitted that making me pregnant was part of his father's plans."

She saw that Tom still had his doubts, but she refused to share the other piece of evidence that was on her mind, both because it was too painful, and because it wouldn't seem like proof to anyone who didn't know Uncle Matt's word was as good as law. The last time she'd seen her uncle, he'd told her his suspicions had hardened into certainties. And he shared more information about the family curse; if the sacrifice was big enough, you could not only see what was hidden, but influence the probabilities. He cut off his own finger with rose-clippers to influence the future and try to ensure her safety. She'd been so horrified, so angry, and would feel forever guilty that she hadn't accepted his last act of love with more grace.

Instead of explaining that to Tom, she repeated, "I saw Victor's true self in that flash, even though I failed to recognize him. He called my daughter a dog. He hurt her and messed with her head. She was just a child!" Her voice had risen, and tears sprang to her eyes. She rubbed at them, angry at herself for looking weak, and turned to glare at Erin and Madeline until they looked away.

"Okay," Tom said. "It's hard to get my head around, but I believe you. And I have to tell you something, too. It's going to sound weird, because I told you before how rare it is for me to hear from my spirit guide Hepzibah. But after the Circle today, I felt like there were thunderclouds right above my head, like power was amassing around me. I came back to my room and tried scrying. Nothing at first. But I felt so strange, kind of itchy all over. Like she was right there on the other side, willing me to reach out to her."

He grinned wryly. "I'm not trying to make this

sound dramatic, I swear. I guess I'm the one procrastinating now. I need to tell you this, but I don't want to tell you this, plus I'm afraid you won't believe me. Guess you know how that feels."

Not trying to make this sound dramatic, her foot, she thought wryly.

"The water shimmered, and then Hepzibah was there, reaching for me. I touched her fingers, and I saw you." He spread his fingers wide and closed his eyes as if reliving it. He shuddered. "You were covered in blood. I knew it was blood, even though it looked almost black. Everything around you was dark. And you collapsed on the ground. And screamed and screamed." His blue eyes opened and met her hazel ones in entreaty.

He continued, "I believe you when you say you're a target. I believe that you have a lead to Blue. But I think it might kill you."

Chapter Eighteen

Robin snorted and shook her head. Tom tilted his head in concern, as if expecting hysteria, but she was so wrung out that she was numb. Of course she would die: bloody, screaming, and probably soon. Why would she expect anything else? This whole jaunt away from her little head-in-the-sand life had been a mistake, but maybe it was for the best. The dull peace of recent years with Liam had tricked her into hoping for more, but it was just a dream, like her childhood had been before the onset of the curse.

Real life equaled the terror and confusion of being fifteen and thinking she was going crazy. It equaled falling in love and thinking that made everything better, only to find betrayal. It equaled giving up her baby to protect the girl, only to find she'd doomed her baby to a life of abuse. It equaled her uncle sacrificing first his finger, and then his life, at the hands of her boyfriend's homicidal father.

Of course she would die, and she didn't need Tom or his spirit guide to tell her that. It wasn't only her flashes that alienated her from the normal world, it was her rotten, bloody fate. So be it. Tom had told her all he could: no where, or when, or why. And he didn't know if it was simply a warning not to follow a certain path, or an inevitable result of whatever she did. Therefore, she just had to keep going. And first things first. She had a responsibility to find Blue.

"I'm so sorry," Tom said. "I wish I had something more useful to tell you."

"It's okay. But knowing that, do you want to come with me to look for Blue? Even though—well, things might go badly?"

He winced. "You're something else. Really. What can I say to that except, Danger is my middle name! Plus, I wasn't in the vision. So I'm probably okay."

She raised her eyebrows. "Corny. You tell me I'm about to die, and then subject me to terrible jokes?"

"I feel a little nervous for some reason. Maybe because I just got bashed in the head. Maybe because we're both in over our heads in something we don't understand. But I will help you. I wasn't there, in my vision. Maybe if I am, I can stop whatever goes wrong. Went wrong. Will go wrong?"

Robin wondered if he felt the same sense of doom in the pit of his stomach as she did. Prognostication was not a game for cowards. But maybe, if somehow what he'd seen came to pass, he could take it the rest of the way. Maybe if she'd succeeded in enlisting Liam in the struggle to save his parents, he and she would have succeeded together where she had failed alone.

She nodded. "Thanks. Let's get going, then. If everything's still locked up, we'll check with the others and see what kind of progress they've made."

Tom looked at his watch. "It's almost eleven. Some people might have decided to sleep through it. But we can check. We'll have to stick something in the door. Earlier, some people got locked out of their own rooms before we all realized the ID cards didn't work anymore."

"Shit. I didn't know that. I guess my room is off limits. But I wasn't planning to go back anyway."

"If it comes to it, you can sleep in here. I'll sleep on the couch." He patted the cushions.

"This is called a loveseat, and it's about two feet too short for anybody to sleep on. It won't come to that," she said. "We're finding a way out. There's no way I'm resting until Blue is found." Until all the lost children were found, she amended to herself.

****

Tom exchanged his leprechaun pants for jeans while Robin blew out the candles. Erin and Madeline both groaned at the news that they would be left tied up, and had to be walked to the bathroom one by one with their hands tied and then reattached to their chairs. Neither tried to make a break for it.

When they were ready to go, Robin peered through the peephole. The eerily lit hallway looked as deserted as she'd left it. They swung open the door. Tom shoved a sock between the door and the jamb, forcing it to stay ajar. They paused, looking both ways.

His room was next to the emergency stairs, which he'd said he tried earlier. She grasped the door handle anyway and twisted, then pulled, then wrenched. It was completely immobile. "Damn. Still locked."

"I have an idea. Let's look at the double doors at the end of the hall," Tom said.

Robin shrugged, and they walked the twenty yards to the end of the hallway. These doors had been locked since they arrived; they led into a section that the psychics had always been barred from, possibly employee housing or more offices.

She shook the doors. "Still locked too."

"I was wondering about the hinges. If the electrical and the supernatural are both failing us so far, maybe the mechanical…" He looked at the top right hinge and then crouched down to examine the one on the bottom.

Her heart leapt with hope. "Smart. Could we just unscrew those?"

He made a face. "I don't know. They're capped to make it difficult. You might need a special tool. They didn't stint on quality or security in this building."

"Shoot."

"I'm not saying I won't try. If we can find a tool kit, maybe there will be something we can pry the caps off with, and then I'll look and see what else we would need. Honestly, I'm not a handyman. Maybe someone else will know better."

"Who should we try? Do you know which rooms everyone is in?"

He shrugged. "I think some people got locked out of their own rooms, and others stuck together just because of the weirdness. I have no idea who would be where, by now. Let's just try all the doors."

The first few were fruitless, but then Robin noticed a pair of doors that were held ajar: one with a newspaper, the other with a corduroy slipper.

"Here," she said, and Tom joined her. "Do you know whose rooms these are?"

He shrugged. "Not sure. Doesn't matter, does it?" He rapped on the one with the slipper.

The door opened slowly to show Delia's worried face, which eased a little when she recognized them. She raised a finger and stepped out into the hallway, pulling the door partially shut behind her. Her bright orange hair looked like a bird's nest perched on top of her head, and her reading glasses were smeary. "Sorry, I don't want to disturb anyone. I was wondering where you two were, although there are others missing too. Those two funny women from New Jersey, and Sidney! Sidney's not here! Anyway, about ten of us decided to hang out together. So we don't hang separately!" She laughed nervously.

"We were indisposed," Robin said, not wanting to waste time on complicated explanations. "What's going on?"

Delia shrugged. "People are doing what they can. Master Leopold is dowsing for a way out in the living room. Leelyn and her nanny are locked into one of the bedrooms with Baby, who's fussy because Leelyn keeps trying to connect with the other side. Baby doesn't like the vibe. CeeCee and Loren have split the kitchen table down the middle and are doing tarot readings. There are a couple of others in the other bedroom doing who knows what, but it involves chanting. As hostess, I've been trying to feed everyone without the benefit of electricity. No coffee, no tea." She sighed. "This is such a travesty. Mr. Hartwin invited us here to help, and then he imprisons us while the poor girl is still missing?"

Tom asked, "No leads yet?"

Delia shrugged. "Nothing concrete, dear. Between you and me, a lot of these gifts are a bit impractical in an actual emergency. But come on in, you can see for yourself. Just be a little quiet."

Robin interjected, "Has anyone looked around for a toolbox? Tom was thinking we might try to remove the hinges from one of the doors, and get out that way."

Delia brightened. "Good idea. Let's see what we can find."

Robin still wasn't sure whose suite it was but in her

book it was even more luxurious than the others she'd seen. There was a large open living/dining area with a fireplace, plus a full-sized kitchen and two bedrooms. A whole family could comfortably live there. As in Tom's room, the surreal light from the emergency strips had been warmed and brightened by candles on every surface, and the honeyed smell of beeswax filled the air. Who traveled with candles, she wondered. These people were strange.

Tom followed Delia into the kitchen, and Robin paused to see what everyone was doing. She could hear the baby grizzling through a closed door, and the chanting that Delia had mentioned was rhythmic but very quiet, like a radio playing in a neighbor's house.

Robin nodded to the two tarot readers at the large oval table. They were seated next to each other, and seemed to be consulting in low, serious voices, gesturing at different points of the large spread of cards they'd created. Both nodded back and returned to the cards.

In the living room, two psychics knelt at Master Leopold's feet. He looked like a medieval Druid in his long pale robes, with his silver hair loose around his shoulders. He dangled a slender pointed crystal on a shining chain over the coffee table. As she approached, she saw that the kneeling ones were studying a hand-drawn map that appeared to be a sketch of the hallway and all the spaces adjoining it. Leo's eyes were closed, the planes of his face betraying deep concentration, but the crystal did no more than sway in slight aimless circles.

She hung back, watching with fascination. Dowsing was not an occult art she was familiar with. In fact, she'd believed it had something to do with finding wells. The two onlookers seemed to be eagerly tracking every microscopic twist of the chain, but Robin detected frustration in Leo's face.

Delia came up behind her and said softly, "We found a toolbox under the sink. Tom is taking it out into the hallway."

Robin turned. "I should help him."

Delia gestured toward Leopold with her head and lowered her voice to a whisper. "He insists there's a way out, but I'm beginning to have my doubts. I think we may just have to wait. But, people believe what they want to believe."

Robin nodded wryly. She too would like to believe there was a way out, but she wasn't sure she had the patience to wait for dowsing to work. "Well, let us know if you come up with anything in here. We'll be trying to tunnel through the wall with a file."

Delia snorted, which drew Master Leopold's attention. His eyes flashed open in annoyance. Simultaneously, the crystal made its first move, swinging abruptly forward. His eyes widened, and he stilled himself. The crystal jerked, more like a fishing line than a pendulum. Robin held her breath. The two at the table followed the direction of the crystal's pointing end with their gazes, and their eyes fell on her.

Had Leo's distraction caused him to swing the pendulum toward the sound of Delia's laugh? It had jerked so unnaturally.

Now it started following an equally unnatural arc, falling from near-perpendicular, then down to the table as gravity willed it, and then circling to point out at Robin again. It jerked at Master Leopold's hands like a leash.

Robin took an involuntary step back as he released it, and the crystal arced through the air and fell to the carpet at her feet.

"It's you," Master Leopold announced with satisfaction, his voice pitched to carry dramatically through the apartment. "You're the way out."

****

Blushing and protesting, Robin tried to explain that she was no such thing as the others gathered around her. Even Tom was summoned back from the hallway, and she was suddenly the target of more peer pressure than she'd experienced since junior high.

"My power doesn't work like that! Definitely not on command. And never directed." Even as she said it, she realized that was no longer true. Had it been only that afternoon when she'd flashed on Blue during the group meditation circle? It had inadvertently been a blood vision, terrifying her with the slow seduction of blood magic that had scarred her uncle.

Realizing the truth, Robin stopped protesting. She hadn't yet had time to process the flash she'd had after the lockdown alarm, but she felt like the way might still be in her. Could there really be power that was more like an attunement with the world rather than a bargain made with blood? She wasn't sure she believed in a free lunch.

But it might be worth a try. She needed to get out of here to find Blue. All her rules, all her boundaries seemed to be breaking. Maybe she could finally be useful.

In minutes, Robin found herself in the tiny bedroom from which the chanters had been expelled. She sat on the only thin strip of carpet not covered by furniture, trying to compose herself as she had in the Circle. She'd been skeptical then, and she had still gotten a flash. She held onto that, and breathed deeply, concentrating on finding a way out.

Her mind wandered despite herself, from a way out to searching for Blue, then to Kami and Angel, and then to Tom. Realizing that she was revisiting the way his hair curled along his collar, she reined herself in. She imagined an impatient crowd listening outside the door, even though she knew it wasn't true. They would know, probably better than she did, that it would take as long as it took.

She let everything fall away again, concentrating on her breath, but thoughts of her daughter invaded her mind. Kami as she'd seen her in the parking lot. Kami sucking down menthol smoke like the breath of life. Kami as a child, lying on the floor at the feet of Victor LeClair as he unlaced his belt.

Hush, she thought. Hush.

And with a slow and chilly expansion, as if the air that she breathed was stretching her skull instead of her lungs, the flash began.

Part of her flinched in recognition, then flailed in panic expecting chaos and pain. Expecting to drown in unbearable, uninterpretable sensation.

But another part of her, a cool observer, remembered a different way. She thought of the rock-face man, the mountain spirit.

Hush, she thought, hush. Breath, and wind.

Her lungs drew in a deep, easy breath that expanded her mind.

In the breath was a breeze, and in the breeze was a candle flame that licked and danced. And in the flame was more breath, not cool but coarse and quick.

Flickering shadows danced around her, thrown against golden skin. Sharp teeth nipped, and the scents of sweat, patchouli, and warm wax were so thick she could taste them.

The smell was overwhelming, and she lost it, lost the thread. Every color burned like desert sun against her eyes, every noise grated and made her stomach wrench.

She screeched Stop! And nothing stopped, all was chaos. And then she spoke to herself in a language newly learned. Hush. Hush, said the wind. She could find it; she could focus on it. It was in her breath, it was in her lungs, it was in her blood and the beat of her heart. It was a powerful presence in the earth below, that seeped in and helped guide her.

Her heart beat. The blood flowed. Ba-thump. Ba-thump. She let go of her panic. The sensations were intense, alien. But they weren't shaking the world. Ba-thump. They weren't happening to her. She was here. Breath and heartbeat. Blood flow and breath. Ba-thump.

And, at the same time, she was there. With clarity this time, the pieces came together:

Silken hair, a gleaming pale waterfall in candlelight, the curved alabaster neck, so fragile. The bones of his spine, right there under the thin skin, under her fingers, under her mouth.

The room was an eggshell around them, a force-field keeping out the world, remaking existence into this tiny bubble of delicious decadence. "I love you," she sighed, stroking his jawline with one long fingernail. It was true, if that dark red longing was love, if that sharp white lightning that leapt from her fingers was love. It leapt again, a spark cutting the gentle candlelit shadows, and he cringed while she laughed in delight.

Her body was curled around him where he'd retreated against the wall at the sight of the first spark. He was naked and trembling, and she teased him with bits of her own vast energy and wicked joy, even as she pulled from him. For her, it was like a drug. For her ignorant partners, it was a mysterious subtle high or a deep creeping exhaustion.

Usually, the movement of energy was invisible to all but her. And her father. But Angel was different. He could see what she was. He could see what she did. And he'd cringed away from every point of contact as soon as he figured it out. But she continued, her hands all over him, tugging, rubbing, zapping, drinking his energy like wine. She was powerful. She would do what she wanted.

"Stop!" he cried.

Robin shook again, almost losing her calm, almost losing her separation in her need to respond to the desperation in Angel's voice. But she breathed, and felt the presence below, and split herself again.

"I won't. I love you." Even as she said it, even as she felt it, the anger boiled up. Why did he resist? Why did everyone resist? She loved so deeply. She needed, so much. To have and possess, to hurt, to taste the sweat and the blood—wasn't that what everyone wanted? Wasn't that love?

He shoved himself backward against her suddenly, and taken by surprise, she fell clumsily away and collapsed onto her hip at the edge of the mattress. He kicked out, a quick two-footed push, and she was propelled off the bed, momentarily shocked by his sudden violence.

Gathering herself, she knelt on the floor, eyes narrowing. She still wore the satin confection that had temporarily distracted him from the truth of her aura, and her raven hair fell forward around her face as she caught her breath and wrapped herself tight around the familiar rush of pain and rejection. Dark shadows leapt across his face as she stared up at him, making him look ugly, making him look like everyone who had ever hurt her. He was standing on the bed, back against the wall, his gaze darting from her to the door.

Kami's hands hungered to draw all resistance from him. She could feel the ache in her heart, the impossible yearning to make him want her the way she wanted him. He stayed frozen, one brief decision away from leaping toward escape, his sky-blue eyes fixed on hers. She stayed frozen too, not certain herself if the wretched bleeding thing that used to be her heart would let him go—or if it would attack.

Angel leaped. And the door flew open.

Chapter Nineteen

A crash jerked Robin back to awareness, and she blinked.

Tom stood over her in the open doorway, his gaze bouncing from corner to corner before falling on her. "What's wrong? You screamed!"

Master Leopold peered over his shoulder, concern on his face. "Sorry," Robin managed. Her heart began to slow as she took in the candlelit room around her. Someone hadn't tucked everything into the suitcase next to her on the floor, and a fuzzy gray sock was caught in the zipper. A hairbrush with the kind of soft bristles her grandmother used to like lay on top of the small bureau. She shook her head, as if trying to shift her marbles back into place, then summoned a grim smile for Tom. "It's fine. I'm fine." The flash was over, painlessly if abruptly. Physically, she felt rested and well, as if she could leap up and jog to the gym for a workout.

She sprang to her feet. There was no space in the room, nowhere to go, but she had to move, had to think.

She barely noticed as Tom waved Leo away and came in, pulling the door shut. Superimposed on the world was Angel's terrified face, mouth pulled wide into a desperate yell. And she could feel the echo of Kami's twisted yearning, her neediness a yawning black hunger shot through with the crimson urge to hurt.

How could Robin live with what she had learned?

How could she act on it? Kami was so badly damaged. The way she had toyed with Angel—the way she had enjoyed it. Was there any hope of healing someone so messed up inside?

It was the saddest cliché in the whole fucked-up world, for the abused to become the abuser, and Robin refused to let it go at that, no matter what. She squeezed her fists. Kami was young. She could learn. She could turn her life around, like Robin had. After all her losses, Robin had been so hurt, so angry—and yet she'd grown into a relatively stable person. Not that her limited, pathetic existence was anything to aspire to, but she was at peace with herself, mostly. She didn't take pleasure in other people's pain. She'd only had the Foxes for a short while, and then only Liam, but it was enough. And Kami would have Robin, even if she didn't know it yet. One way or another, she would.

"Robin," she heard, and realized she'd been hearing it periodically, patiently, for the last few minutes. She looked up and noticed Tom still standing by the door.

She forced herself to stop and face him. Heat flushed her face. Talk about being self-absorbed. "Sorry. Yes. I mean, what?"

"Are you really okay? Did you find a way out?"

She took a deep breath. "I'm fine, I think. I'm just not good at this. At making flashes tell me what I want to know. Or at talking to people, apparently."

A quick smile visited his face. He sat on the edge of the bed, patting an invitation for her to sit beside him. She sat heavily, her excess energy draining suddenly into sobriety. The bed sagged under their weight, leaning them toward one another.

"Tell me," Tom said.

"Nothing about the way out. Master Leopold's dowsing was completely wrong about that. But something is happening here. My daughter, Kami—" she cut herself off. Her thoughts roiled with pieces of the present and the past, and her utter helplessness. All those arguments she'd had with Uncle Matt, him accusing her of being naïve, her accusing him of being paranoid— he'd been right on all counts.

She wasn't naïve anymore. Tom had described Victor LeClair as a nice old rich guy. Now that she'd felt even more evidence of Victor's effect on Kami, she shuddered to imagine the depths of his deception. She would tear his mask away for all to see. Out of revenge, yes, but also to free Kami from the monster who had made her into what she was. And to free herself from living in fear, regardless of the consequences.

She turned toward Tom, so close in the candlelit gloom. "Kami is here somewhere with one of the other psychics. Angel. Do you know him?"

Tom shrugged. "I know who he is. The kid with the hair, right?"

Robin nodded. "In my flash, they were together. I could feel her emotions. I could feel her power. She has this ability, I think her father had it, but I didn't recognize it at the time." She paused, fully realizing the implications. Daniel had always made her feel so good, so energized. He'd probably been feeding her energy, countering the effects of her depression, her fear. Had it been addictive? Had that been what she thought was love?

"She can transmit energy both ways—drain it away, or zap it like a taser, only it's like life-force energy, not like—you know, an electrical charge. She's torturing him with it." Robin swallowed, realizing the limits of her knowledge. "At least, in the flash she was, I don't know the timeline. It felt like now."

"He can't stop her?"

"He hadn't yet. He was trying to. I think she was toying with him, and he didn't realize what was going on at first. Or how far she would go." Robin raised her face to look at him.

"That's terrible. I mean, that's some power, but that's messed up."

"We have to stop her. We have to find them."

"Angel's not a little kid," he pointed out. "And probably less likely than most to freak out because someone has an unusual gift. Don't you think we still need to focus on Blue? I mean, your daughter—she won't actually…" he trailed off, reading her fear.

Robin closed her eyes. "I have such a bad feeling. God. Angel's face, you should have seen it. We have to find Blue, but I have to find Kami too. I don't know why she's doing what she's doing, but I have to stop her. And I'm her mother."

He took a deep breath, unable to argue against that. "Yeah. I see that. But it doesn't really matter now, does it? We're still stuck. Unless they happen to be here, in this hallway, we're just as helpless as ever."

She suddenly remembered what he'd been doing before all the excitement about the dowsing. "No luck on the hinges, then."

"I hadn't gotten very far. I'll go back. It's still worth trying."

"Especially if there's nothing else. But I hate to break the news that I have no quick and easy solution," she said, heart sinking.

"There's never a quick and easy solution. Almost never. And it was partly your idea to follow through with the toolbox, wasn't it? Wouldn't it be funny if that's what the dowsing meant?"

She got to her feet. "Hilarious."

He stood too, and they looked at each other for a moment in the dim room.

"Thanks," she said softly. "For, you know, talking stuff out. Listening. I feel somewhat more human now."

He smiled and reached for her hand. It seemed for one crazy moment that he might lean in and kiss her, and she leaned a little too, surprised by her lack of ambivalence. She had dated occasionally, but never more than two or three dates with the same guy. Her internal heckler, that little voice of constant criticism in her head, warned against relationships because someone might learn her secrets. But she'd known Tom for only twenty-four hours, and he already knew more than Liam. Her heart beat faster and she became aware of his breath, his warmth.

Then, like convicts on a failed escape attempt, they were bathed in the glare of bright overhead lights. Muffled yells came through the door, and loud slamming noises. Robin and Tom jerked apart. The baby cried, a thin wail that worked its way right through the wall.

"What the hell?" Tom said. "Power's back on, but—" He took a step toward the door. Robin stood still, feeling a dismal premonition.

There was a quick knock and the door opened before Tom could reach it. Master Leopold looked in, the electric lights making him look haggard.

"I'm sorry," he said to Robin. "I misunderstood. It wasn't you that opens doors, but doors are opened *for* you."

He was abruptly pushed aside by two figures wearing holstered guns and ballistics vests over black pants, T-shirts, and boots. No insignia. Robin recognized the one on the left, the woman in charge of security with the little girl who'd been sick.

"Sarah?" she asked. "What's going on?"

"You're coming to see the boss," Sarah Park said without a trace of humor.

They swarmed into the small bedroom, the two in front followed by two more. Sarah briskly spun Robin around and hitched a zip-tie around her wrists. Robin had a split second to decide whether to resist, but dismissed the idea even as it occurred. She was outnumbered and her self-defense classes hadn't covered what to do against a group of armed guards. The blank expressions on the faces of her captors scared her even more than their pseudo-military gear.

Two of them pushed Tom up against the wall. Robin caught a look at his bewildered face and knew it must reflect her own.

"I don't get it," she said. "What did I do? This has got to be a mistake."

"Boss says you know something about Blue," Sarah said. "Says you're in on it."

"That's crazy," Robin said. Could Hartwin really think she had something to do with Blue's disappearance? Or had someone else shared a psychic tip with him that had been misunderstood? "I'm not in on anything. But I do think I know where she is! Please, listen. I had a flash. A vision!" She stopped, realizing she just sounded desperate.

She was hustled through the narrow doorway and

stumbled into the main apartment, the zip-tie biting into her wrists. The black-clad figures outnumbered the psychics, who looked helpless and confused.

Behind her, Tom was trying to argue, but no one was paying attention. "This isn't right. You're acting like thugs! Even if you have grounds for suspicion, you don't just come in and grab people! Where are the cops?!"

One of the men in black seized Robin's shoulder and hustled her toward the front door. Behind her Sarah spoke loudly, addressing the entire group.

"I know this seems strange, but these are strange times. Don't worry. We're bringing your colleague to talk to Mr. Hartwin. He's sworn to do whatever it takes to find Blue as quickly as possible, and the nice way wasn't working. But you can trust us. Soon this will be over."

"Let me come with you, then," Tom demanded.

Master Leopold chimed in. "He's right. Let him go and be a witness."

"I'm sorry, I can't do that," Park said. "But we'll be back as soon as we can to release you."

Robin was pushed into the hallway, held between two men. Behind her, the outcry of multiple voices was pierced by Delia's high-pitched protest: "What do you mean, release us?"

The door to the suite slammed shut, and Robin saw the double doors at the end of the hall were now wide open. She was hustled through by her squadron of pseudo-soldiers. From behind came shouts, and she looked over her shoulder. Tom, Loren, and Leelyn were running towards them, but they were too late. The security team ignored them, slamming the doors shut despite outraged protests from the other side. The locking mechanism clicked as it re-engaged.

Robin met Tom's pained eyes through the window as she was pulled away. She thought he yelled, "Be careful!" and knew he was recalling his vision. He had no way to help her now, but that was okay, he'd probably be better off.

The security group moved forward swiftly and in silence along a hallway no different from any other hallway in this place. Robin's stomach was in knots, and with every step she felt like she was walking farther out over a chasm on a high wire. Stealing a glance to her left, she was startled to recognize the freckle-faced guard from the gate, Samantha Toofer.

"What the hell is going on?" she demanded, unable to hide the shake in her voice.

Toofer shot her a worried glance. "I'm not sure," she whispered. "But don't worry. Mr. Hartwin is a good guy. It will be okay."

Robin desperately wanted to believe that. "This doesn't feel okay," she told Toofer.

"Not one more word," Sarah Park warned from behind, voice cold. A moment later, Sarah traded places with Samantha. Robin looked over and was stunned at the loathing in Sarah's eyes.

Sarah said, "You're not actually 'Robin Fox,' are you? So we have a little trust issue. Why don't you just keep your lying mouth shut, and everyone will be happy."

Robin flinched. Had Madeline and Erin been spreading word of her past around? Why would they tell the Survival Unlimited people? And why would Wes Hartwin or his minions care?

She stiffened. Unless Hartwin, like Erin and

Madeline, was tied to the LeClairs. Which was a completely paranoid thought. Wasn't it? Or had the whole psychic invitation been a trap, especially baited for Heather Farrell?

She pushed the theory away for later consideration. "I'm still the same person you talked to the other day. I'm just a normal woman! Yes, I changed my name. You might too, if you'd been through what I went through. It's not some sinister conspiracy!"

Sarah walked in stony silence, then stopped in front of an elevator. One of the men ran an ID card through the reader.

Robin tried again. "Remember, we talked about my brother. And your little girl! She'd been sick. Is she better now?" However strange and awful this forced march was, she would give a lot to delay its culmination. Hartwin had been taken in for questioning, and when he'd returned, he'd immediately locked down the bunker. And locked in all his guests. It was hard to think of a good-guy reason for that.

So much adrenaline was shooting through her veins that her knees felt unglued.

"Don't talk about my daughter," Sarah said coldly.

Robin had a flashback to a self-defense course she'd taken with another trainer at Liam's gym. The woman had said, "Never, ever, get into a car with an assailant. Resist, resist, resist, before you're further in their power and harder to find."

The elevator wasn't a car, and she wasn't really capable of making a move, but it gave her a terrible sinking feeling to see the doors slide open. She twisted again, trying to look behind her, hoping against hope that Tom and the others had broken through the locked double doors and were coming to save her. But that was ludicrous. The security team was trained, armed and armored. What were a bunch of psychics going to do to them, throw curses? Say mean things about their auras? As far as she knew, Kami and Daniel were the only ones she'd met whose power had a direct physical impact.

Her resistance was as pointless as that of cattle balking at the killing chute. She stumbled forward with a single hard push, biting her tongue bloody as she slammed into the wall with her shoulder. Her mind raced wildly. There had to be something she could do or say that would change the situation. Scenario after scenario ran through her head. But it was too late, wasn't it? She was being taken against her will, and there was nothing she could do about it. The cold whoosh of the elevator sliding shut was like the cover of a tomb scraping home.

Had Blue felt this helpless when she was taken? Probably more so, considering she was a child, and that much more used to being protected, that much more vulnerable to the size and strength of the adults around her. Robin pictured that determined little face. Brave girl. She could not let Blue down.

One of Robin's guards programmed the elevator with a card-activated touchpad on the wall, but Robin couldn't tell if they were going up or down. She breathed deeply, reminding herself it was just Wes Hartwin who wanted to see her, a successful, charismatic businessman. But she felt as much dread as if she were about to set eyes on Victor LeClair, although yesterday she would have called that ridiculous paranoia.

The doors slid open, and she was led into another familiar-looking hallway. So many of the corridors were similar, despite shifts in artwork and color scheme, that she wasn't certain until she saw the lettering on the closest door: SECURITY. She and Grimley had stopped here to drop off her suitcase in their mad rush to Orientation that first night.

Park stepped forward to open the door with her ID card, and Robin looked back for Toofer, hoping for more reassurance. Instead, one of the other guards roughly grabbed her upper arm as if she was about to make a break for it, her zip-tied hands and all. As soon as the door opened, they moved her into the small office. One wall was covered with screens showing dozens of camera feeds, flickering as they cycled through view after view. There were two doors on the far wall, one of which was fitted with a large reinforced window, through which a closet-sized cubicle was visible. With a chair bolted to the floor.

Robin groaned as she was ushered into the cubicle. "You have got to be kidding me. This is ridiculous. You're putting me in a cell?!"

Sarah gave her a tight smile. "Yes. But if you promise to be good, I'll untie your hands."

"Blue's in a cave somewhere below us!" Robin blurted. "And Angel, did you talk to Angel's dad? I know where he is too, or at least who he's with. Please, don't do this."

"Last chance. Turn around and shut up, or keep the damn zip-tie on for all I care."

Robin shut up long enough for Park to slice through the plastic. She shook circulation back into her hands and turned just in time to see the other woman push the heavy door shut with a muffled thump. Robin stared after her. Her eyes prickled with heat. "Bullshit," she said. Then she slammed her hand against the window and yelled,

"Bullshit!"

The group outside rearranged itself. Five left the room, leaving Sarah behind. Robin watched for a few minutes, slapping the window to demand attention until her hand hurt, but she was studiously ignored. She gave up and sat in the bolted-down wooden chair, rubbing her temples. A minute later, she stood and went to the window again.

"This is ridiculous! You know that, right? Where is your boss, anyway?"

The door to the hallway opened and Peter Grimley appeared. His fuzzy blonde hair pointed in all directions above his haggard face. He still wore boots and jeans with a button-down shirt, but the shirt was badly wrinkled and the jacket and tie were gone. His gaze caught on Robin and his brows drew down. His muffled voice carried through the thick glass. "Are you bringing Fox to the boss?"

Sarah answered. Robin caught the word "Blue", and the words "knows something," but Sarah was facing away from her and talking more softly than Grimley.

When Grimley said, "We have no right to hold her. Just let her go back to the others," it came through just fine, and Robin held her breath.

Sarah turned to glare at her through the window and this time Robin could hear her perfectly. "She's staying right here until Hartwin's ready."

Grimley leaned toward Sarah, his face pained. "Don't you think this is a little extreme? I'm not sure about this lockdown, Sarah. This isn't a drill, we're not playing. Remember Waco? You and I have got to talk to the boss. He'll pay more attention if it's coming from both of us."

Sarah turned back to him, her face cold with fury. She hissed her reply, and Robin couldn't make it out. But Grimley stood, his face paling further, and squared his shoulders. "I'll talk to him myself, then."

He disappeared back into the hallway, and Robin felt cold. Her last, best hope was gone—somebody still sane enough to question Hartwin's actions. But at least she knew they hadn't all drunk the Kool-Aid.

Time passed slowly. Robin alternately paced, sat on the chair, and watched Sarah Park work on her computer. Another guard delivered coffee and a sandwich, then left. Robin wondered if the psychics were still locked in the hallway downstairs. Had the preppers at least left their power back on? Her fury at her own helplessness rose and ebbed in waves.

Finally, the door from the hallway opened again. Robin glimpsed the movement as she paced and shifted to look through the window. Grimley stumbled in, falling to his hands and knees. His ID card skittered across the floor. Park stood abruptly, her hand dropping to her holster, but it was already too late. The man behind Grimley levered himself swiftly over the desk, hip first, his legs sliding into Sarah's monitor and crashing everything to the floor. He had possession of Sarah's gun before Robin could blink, and Sarah was on the floor too, unmoving after a swift blow to the head. The man returned to Grimley, who now lay on his side, gasping and unable to fight back.

Robin backed away despite the locked door between them. He spotted her through the window and grinned, the expression reviving the boyishness that she remembered in the face of the fleshy, balding man.

Daniel.

Chapter Twenty

Blue giggled as they played a jungle game, creeping through dark musty passages as if through thick trees in hot humid sun. She could almost feel the brush of long feathery leaves against her bare arms and hear monkeys chittering above. The trees would be full of parrots, green and pink, and they would all say, "Polly? Polly want a cracker?"

She cracked up, and Georgina turned around with a grin and a finger to her lips. Georgina-Jennifer was her name now, Blue knew, but it was too long, so she called her G.J.. In the skywell, G.J. had finally found the perfect shoes and no longer went barefoot. She tripped along ahead of Blue leaving trails of sparkles like magical dragonflies for her to follow.

Blue's imaginary playmate had become a Helpful Spirit with the ghost of the bones. Daddy had been right, Helpful Spirits did exist! But when G.J. first took her hand in the skywell, Blue saw scary things she didn't really want to think about. Uncle Wes was a boy, probably close to her own age. He was chasing a little girl up the steep slope of Spirit Ridge, and they were both laughing and grabbing onto trees to keep their balance.

—I thought Wesley was my friend, G.J. told her sadly.—But when we found the hole in the mountain, he pushed me in to see what would happen. He thought he might get a wish. He said there were old stories about

236

magic in Spirit Ridge.

"What did happen?" Blue whispered.

—The mountain woke up. He was angry and shook to make Wesley fall, but Wesley ran away. And then the mountain spirit stayed with me and was my friend. He'll be your friend too.

"I don't understand," Blue said. She didn't like the idea of angry spirits that shook mountains.

—Don't be scared, G.J. said as Blue pulled away.

Blue turned and saw him, glowing in the gray light of the sky well. He was a kid, but as insubstantial as G.J. and had rocks where his eyes should be.

The boy had stillness rolling off him. If she took an ancient stone church and squished it into the shape of a boy, and it still had all that big quietness and oldness stuck to it—that's what he felt like. He made her heart feel awe. G.J. was a little strange because she was part ghost and part imaginary friend. Sometimes she was sad and sometimes she was angry but mostly she just wanted to play and Blue almost forgot she was a Spirit. That could never happen with the boy.

He stepped forward and took her hand. His fingers were soft as air, but undeniably there, and he felt as understanding as a grandmother. All her fear and her hunger and her weariness of this strange dark place bubbled over for a minute, and she cried a little. But when he released her hand, she felt better and dried her tears, and knew G.J. was right. He was a good friend to have. To him, they were fragile things out of place, needing protection, and he led them from the skywell onward.

The jungle game was his idea to distract Blue from her hunger and her thirst, and it worked. She saw the giant plants, and felt the sun and a moist humid breeze, and knew it was a daydream but she threw herself into it without question. The darkness could be a backdrop for anything, and her mind projected vivid pictures whether she wanted it to or not, so it was better to give it something happy to think about.

When they reached water, clean, deep water that tasted like pennies, they stopped. She washed her face after she drank, and then she sat with her hands in the water hoping to feel a cave fish. The water was icy, but she'd warmed up during the game, moving faster following the boy and G.J. further than she had dared on her own. She stayed perfectly still, hoping. If she felt a cave fish, she would grab it and eat it raw like sushi, which she liked even though most of her up-above friends thought it was gross. But she wasn't sure if she could just bite into a live fish belly—that did sound gross—and the other parts would be bony and prickly in her mouth. Or maybe the fish would be little, like a sardine, and she could just crunch right through? Her mouth flooded with saliva. She was so hungry.

No cave fish nibbled on her fingers, and finally she gave up and warmed her icy hands under her sweatshirt. G.J. and the boy waited patiently until she could bring herself to leave the water behind. She felt better, more awake, and proceeded again through cracks and tunnels.

In the pitch darkness, the mountain spirit showed her the way. His eyes weren't eyes, but he sensed the tunnels and cracks in the earth like she felt her own arms and legs. He helped her for a while, but more and more, he made her do it herself, focusing sideways so she could feel her foot reaching for the floor just as she could feel the shape of the floor beneath her and the jutting rock just in front of her forehead before she ducked. After a time, she started to feel like a balloon, floaty and soft. It was time to sleep, time to curl up in the blackness and let go.

—Just a little longer, G.J. said, and Blue pushed on.

In a while, they came to a place where more gray light seeped in, and Blue could see again. She came back to herself as if she'd been sleepwalking and looked around in wonder. The walls were covered with bumpy swirls of yellowish rock. She remembered the mean lady dragging a stick along the wall, making a line as she called "Halloo!" into the darkness ahead.

Blue found the line, a scar along the wall. She ran her finger along it, stepping softly with her heart going pitter-pat in her chest. G.J. and the boy hung back in the darkness but she kept going. She knew where she was, at the entrance to the secret tunnel Uncle Wes had showed her in the woods. The way in.

The way out.

If she'd ever hoped in her heart that it had all been a mistake, that Uncle Wes hadn't meant to leave her there, that he didn't know the mean lady was so mean—that hope shriveled up like a dead worm in the sun one second later.

The door, the pretty door with the greenish metal curlicues, the door that looked promising and magical like the entrance to a special Secret Garden, just like in the book Mom and Dad read to her—the door with the shiny metal old-fashioned key unlike all the cardlocks everywhere else in the bunker—had been padlocked shut again.

On hide-and-seek day, her last up-above day, Uncle Wes had pulled the key out of his pocket, grinning mischievously, and let her open the door herself. She loved it when he smiled like that, because usually he looked so serious and a little sad. Daddy said he was thinking of all the bad things that could happen and trying to prevent them. But once in a while, just for Blue, Uncle Wes would play, and his sad hangdog face would light up like he was a kid again.

On that day, the mean lady had moved from foot to foot as Blue fumbled the key into the shiny padlock, and the sun shone down on Blue's head, and the breeze played with her ponytail and smelled of trees and river. One of the other kids had laughed far behind them in the woods and that mixed in with all the forest sounds like the trill of a happy bird. Blue had finally got the padlock to slide off, and Uncle Wes took the key and the lock and stuck them in his jacket pocket.

Now, in the night, standing only inches away from where she had stood then, Blue pressed herself against the cold bars. She threaded her arm through and pulled at the thick metal lock hanging down smugly as if she had never opened it. It clanked against the gate, ungiving.

In the gloomy gray light that shone down from a few stars, she saw something even worse. Before, there had been brambles growing around the little dip in the ground that made the door almost invisible. The brambles had formed a green bower bright with early leaves on the tangled vines. Now there was a brush pile taller than the door, dense and thickly piled, full of dead branches, and she would bet anything it blocked the little gate.

The place where Blue and her uncle and his friend had stood was gone. For an instant, she felt like if she wished hard enough, she could switch places with her old self and make her say no. No special game with Uncle Wes. No leaving the other children behind. No descending deep into the earth, no matter how many treasures and secrets were down there.

Tears filled her eyes. There was no way out at this gate, wishful or otherwise.

She trudged back down the tunnel. G.J. and the boy waited in the blackness beyond the tiny bits of starlight.

—It's okay, G.J. said when she reached them.

The boy didn't say anything, but Blue took comfort from his stillness. She nodded and sniffled hard, then wiped her tears away with the sleeves of her hoodie.

—He says there's one more chance to go back up-above, G.J. told her.—But if it doesn't work, it's okay. You can stay here, with us.

Chapter Twenty-One

Daniel LeClair had been slender and floppy-haired back when they'd met as teenagers. Now, he was nearly double Robin's girth, thick-necked and crewcut. Despite that, she recognized him instantly and viscerally. Every cell in her body contracted as if trying to shrink out of his sight.

Back then, he'd never physically hurt her or raised his voice at her. In fact, she'd known him for six months, seventeen years ago, and they hadn't argued at all until the very end. Until she'd confronted him with the disturbing little pieces that had been piling up: finding her missing birth control case in his desk drawer when looking for stamps, an overheard phone call where he'd insulted her when talking to his mother, her uncle's suspicions of Daniel's father. Daniel had finally admitted, in a bored tone that contrasted with the strident denials of moments before, that his father ordered him to impregnate her. Everything from that first meeting on had been in service to that goal. She'd been in shock as she fled, and the horror of what followed overshadowed that revelation, but the betrayal cut so deep she still found herself unable to trust anyone.

She cringed away from the window, trembling with agitation. Was she going to vomit? If she did, her hysterical heart might land on the floor, still beating, among all the bile. A distant part of her observed her fight-or-flight response with impatience. There was no winnable fight, no possible flight, and the adrenaline was just making it hard to think.

Daniel approached, beaming, and she retreated until her back was against the wall. He examined her from head to foot. She could not look him in the face at first, but as the reality of his presence soaked in, she began to feel ridiculous, letting herself be so cowed. She forced herself to breathe deep.

So what, if he was the son of a killer?

So what, if he had perverted the course of her life?

So what, if he had played with her emotions for his own purposes? Not even his, but those of his father!

So what? She had grown up. She was not such an easy target anymore.

Robin squared herself and lifted her chin to stare back at him. She focused on the changes that nearly two decades had wrought. His mouth had a cruel twist and his eyes, which used to flash with mischief and good humor and in which she'd imagined patience and compassion, held only smug satisfaction. His attire, black suit pants and a black button-down shirt with the sleeves pushed up to reveal thick forearms, made him look like a movie gangster or a defrocked priest.

As she returned his scrutiny, his smile died. He disappeared from the window. When she moved to look, he was crouched on the floor retrieving Grimley's ID card. He ran it through the reader next to Robin's cell door, but she heard no click. Daniel shook the handle and narrowed his eyes. With one polished brogue, he kicked Grimley, who'd been feebly trying to rise to his knees.

Daniel switched his attention to Park's prone body and freed the card from her lanyard. Robin stepped to one side of the door, hoping to surprise him with a sudden kicking attack as soon as it opened, but Daniel moved with the quick grace of a boxer. His arm shot out and clenched her upper arm, thumb digging into a nerve bundle. Her knees went weak and she stumbled.

When he jerked her close, the same cologne he'd worn back then washed over her, summoning a ghost of her deluded teenage self. For a microsecond, her body remembered seeking comfort in his warmth.

Then she twisted away in revulsion. She dropped her weight to dislodge his grip from her arm and absorbed the move with bent knees to give herself leverage for an attack on his ankle. But he was more solid than she'd guessed, the fleshiness a deceptive layer of fat on thick, developed muscle. Before she knew it, she was immobilized with her back to his chest, his massive arms squeezing the breath from her lungs. Her head was well-placed to slam back into his nose, but he anticipated that and ducked easily out of the way, chuckling.

"Heather," he growled against her ear. "How nice to see you again." His voice had roughened, but was still slightly nasal with the trace of a Boston accent, and again her heart tugged with a strange mix of hatred and homesickness.

He'd always gone for the laugh, always played to an invisible audience. Maybe he hadn't changed much underneath. He'd also always underestimated her, counted on her gullibility. She forced herself to go limp as if in surrender.

From behind came a clang and a crash, and Daniel pushed her away so abruptly that she found herself on hands and knees in the middle of the cell, catching herself just in time to protect her nose from the floor. She leapt to her feet in a panic and found that Grimley was on his feet. The two men grappled, Grimley's thin frame over-matched by Daniel's bulk. Robin's eyes flew to Park's gun, which protruded temptingly from the back of Daniel's waistband.

Then she noticed the fire extinguisher lying on the floor, its bright red weight a promise of crushing force. The crash she'd heard—Grimley must have used it to attack.

She'd have to get close to Daniel to reach the gun, and the two men were wrestling now, clenched together and wrenching each other across the floor. She grabbed the extinguisher instead, swinging it as she rose to build some force behind her attack. But Grimley fell away as Daniel managed to break his hold and throw him off, and Robin's swing hit the wall. The reverberation from the blow twisted the extinguisher's trigger painfully against her fingers, and she released it despite herself. It clanged to the floor, and that easily she was disarmed.

Robin put her hands up. "You win," she said.

"No shit." Daniel was breathing heavily, red-faced, but he grinned in the way of a man who enjoyed a good fight. "These assholes aren't all that, are they?" He kicked Grimley again, and the man didn't react. "I'll have to tell Wes his training ain't worth shit."

Robin noted the sign of familiarity between Hartwin and the LeClairs. "Why are you here?"

"Heather, Heather, Heather," he mused. "Didn't you used to be smart? I have a date, my dear. A date—with our daughter. Have you met her yet? She's a piece of work, must take after you. Hey, you'd think there would be a nice stash of security-type items in this office..."

Robin stood in the cell doorway, keeping her face

blank and her hands halfway up, while Daniel lazily pointed the gun at her with his right hand. He made his way around Park's body to access the desk drawers, pulling them open to poke at the contents. "Handcuffs? Zip-ties? No? They must have an armory or something where they keep the good stuff." He slammed the drawers shut, then his eyes dropped to Park. Robin knew from recent experience that the Head of Security carried zip-ties in the utility belt at her waist and held her breath.

Instead of crouching to search Park, Daniel stared down thoughtfully for a moment then said, "We should get out of here. Don't know when the next security whatsit is going to stop by or check in or whatever they do. You'll be a good girl, won't you, my lovely?"

"Sure," Robin said, mouth dry.

Daniel scanned the screens on the wall. Robin followed his gaze. Several of them were completely black, some showed dim green emergency lighting, but others appeared normal. There were no visible teams of security personnel, but as the displays flicked to a different feed every twenty or thirty seconds, that might not mean anything. She searched for a view of the parking lot, hoping to see flashing lights. Were the cavalry here yet? Had they even been called?

Daniel shrugged and grinned at her. With a last look around the room, he noticed the door next to the cell door and reached for it. Her heart sank. It was probably the armory, because where else would you put that, if not the security office? But he seemed pleased rather than disappointed when it opened into a small bathroom.

"Stand by the door, turn around. Don't mess with me," he said. "I need to take a piss, but trust me, I can shoot at the same time. I've done it before."

Helplessly waiting, she fantasized about a fast back kick that would send him reeling straight into the toilet and tiled wall, but she knew it wouldn't work. He was quick, powerful, and on his guard. If he didn't shoot her, he'd grab her leg and she'd be face first on the floor, probably with a broken bone.

The sound of the stream ended, and she heard him zip, then flush, and the faucet started. She risked a glance over her shoulder, wondering if he'd been over-confident enough to put the gun down to soap his hands. No such luck. He grinned at her as he rinsed one hand, the other still roughly aiming the gun at her butt. Such a jovial guy.

She looked away angrily.

He poked the gun into her back. "All right, we're outta here. We're going down, down, down, my lovely. How do we get there?"

She froze. Down would be the cavern where Blue was. "What do you mean, down, down, down? You get in an elevator or go down the stairs."

"Further than that. There are caves down below, tunnels. Our dear daughter was supposed to take me, but she seems to have left poor Daddy behind. You know how to get there?"

Kami was down there. Robin's insides turned to water. Here it was, finally, everything she'd wanted yet feared to know. The fear was winning. "Tell me, how did you find her?" she asked, her voice small and choked.

He ignored the question, but massaged her shoulder and pulled her close. Moist lips brushed her ear and onion-scented breath blew against her cheek as he spoke. "We are going to have a little family reunion. I have been looking forward to this for years."

Robin stiffened. "I don't know anything about any

caves," she managed.

He pulled back and prodded her with the gun. "I don't have time for this. We gotta be there by midnight. Show me where to go."

"Fuck you," she said.

He swung her around by the shoulder and smacked her lightly across the jaw. Lightly for him, because he could have knocked her out, but way too hard for her. She reeled to one side, stars in her head, and caught herself against the wall. "I don't know!" she protested.

"Watch your mouth," he growled.

She straightened and rubbed her jaw. "Yeah. Right."

He caressed her reddened cheek. "Okay, okay, okay. You don't know, why would you? What are we gonna do, then? That girl, she's a snake. Give her an inch."

She would have to appease him, to buy time. "Did you, umm, did they give you the MapApp when you got here?" she offered. "To get around? I had it but my phone is dead."

A clotted voice rose from the floor. "It's not on the app." It was followed by a full minute of hacking and spitting, as Grimley rolled to one side and emptied his nose and mouth of blood.

Daniel smiled patiently down at the man. "Oh yeah? Tell me more. I keep telling Pops. It's smart not to just kill everybody. People can be very helpful, if they're motivated enough."

"Look at me. I'm motivated," Grimley said, and spat again. He climbed to his feet, clutching his left side. "I'll show you where to go. Just let me check on Park first."

Daniel shook his head, still smiling. "Forget it. Either she's fine or she's not, we don't have time for first aid, boy scout."

"Wes didn't tell many people about the cavern. As a matter of fact, he didn't tell anyone, I just happened to be paying attention. You need me. Give me one minute. Half a minute."

Daniel looked up into Grimley's bloody face. He stretched his lips as if considering. Then his fist shot out and landed in Grimley's gut. "Yeah? No. Now get us the fuck out of here or I'm going to fucking shoot you." He waved the gun loosely at Park. "Or I can shoot her, which will answer all your questions about her well-being."

Grimley's face blanched under the blood, and he turned to the door. "We have to go up to Wes's suite," he wheezed. "He's got a secret way down."

Robin shot a glance at his face, wondering if he was telling the truth or if he had a plan.

But if Hartwin's rooms really did lead straight to the cavern—the cavern where she was sure Blue was waiting, the cavern where Daniel believed Kami was—it settled the question of whether Hartwin was involved.

"There's no other way?" Daniel demanded. "Don't fuck with me. You serious? We have to go all the way up to go down?"

Grimley nodded and coughed. "It's an elevator ride, not a marathon. Five minutes." He swayed on his feet, and Daniel made up his mind.

"Let's go. What's your name, guy?"

"Peter Grimley."

"Pete. Fine. You're in front, leading the way. Go directly to Wes's place, do not pass go, do not collect two-hundred dollars. Any funny business, you won't know if you get the bullet or Heather here does. It will be a surprise. Heather, you're in front of me. It will be a real pain in the ass if I have to knock you out and throw you over my shoulder, but I will."

"I get it," Robin said. She wanted to scream with frustration. The best time to make a move would be while Daniel's attention was divided between herself and Grimley, but then how would she get down to the cavern? But if she was in the cavern with Daniel, she wouldn't be able to do anything to help anybody. She would have to save her strength and time her resistance.

Tom's scried warning was as vivid to her as if she had seen it herself, but she tried to find hope in it. She may have been screaming, but at least Daniel wasn't there.

Grimley limped into the hallway. He didn't hesitate, but turned left and walked toward the elevator Robin had been transported in. He reached for his lanyard and found nothing.

Daniel dug in his pocket and ran Grimley's card. The doors slid open. Daniel gestured, and Grimley and Robin stepped inside, Daniel a split second after.

Daniel faced them both when the doors shut.

"We're going all the way up," Grimley said. "You have to run the card again."

Daniel ran it, and Grimley tapped three digits on the keypad. "No funny business," Daniel reiterated, and Grimley said nothing.

Robin ventured a glance at Grimley's face, which was expressionless. Pale, one eye swollen shut, and smeared with blood, but expressionless.

Daniel positioned himself with his back against the side wall. The wall behind Robin slid open instead of the door in front of her—she hadn't expected that.

Grimley had. He slung his arm around her and pulled her down with him as he dropped to the floor, yelling "Intruder!"

She banged her knee and squeezed her eyes shut in anticipation of shooting and blood and flying bodies. Nothing happened. Robin opened her eyes. The elevator had opened into an atrium with floor to ceiling windows facing out and a basketball hoop on the inside wall. There were wicker tables and chairs here and there, and clusters of tropical plants and trees in massive cement pots. Across from the elevator, a narrow white door was nearly hidden by greenery. There were no people in sight, and nowhere for people to be hiding, unless they were crouched behind cement pots.

Robin had landed half on top of Grimley. His heartbeat pounded beneath her hand, his gasping breath blew against her face. Cautiously, she edged off of him. There was no one here. Terrified, she looked up at Daniel, knowing he would pull the trigger.

He stood unperturbed, looking around with interest. After a moment of nothing, he chuckled and kicked at Grimley's ankle with the toe of his boot. Grimley jerked away, swore and crawled to his feet. Still smiling and shaking his head, Daniel backhanded him across the face.

"Trying to get me killed, Pete? What, was there supposed to be a guard?"

Grimley spat blood on the ground. "Could have been. Sorry."

Daniel scanned the space, then put the gun to Grimley's head and a hand on his shoulder. "We'll go for a little walk, make sure no one's hiding in the corners. But you know, I think our friend Wes might have pulled all eyes off his place. I maybe heard something about that." He chuckled again.

Robin followed, at a loss, as Daniel steered Grimley close enough to the clusters of planters to confirm what they already sensed—there was no one else in the atrium.

They stopped in front of the narrow white door. Daniel put his face up to the taller man's and hissed, "No more tricks."

Grimley nodded. He'd sweated through the back of his button-down shirt. "The private elevator in the suite has an extra button at the bottom. Run my card," he said. Daniel swiped the card, and Grimley inserted a key that he pulled out of his pocket into a hidden hole in the side of the reader. When it beeped, he entered a numeric code into the keypad and turned the door handle when the light blinked green. He paused, looking at Daniel for direction.

Daniel said, "Anyone going to be in there?"

"Shouldn't be. Wes likes his privacy. I have the key and code in case of emergency. And security has a backup locked away. That's it. The only person who should be here is Wes."

"Well, Wes is busy tonight," Daniel said.

They entered and Daniel had them wait by the door while he scanned the room. Like the atrium area, Hartwin's apartment was roofed by the high curved dome of the bunker. The huge open area was furnished in stark contrast to the luxurious hunting-lodge feel of the lower floors. Instead of tribal art, natural fibers, and warm wood, there was black leather, glass, and steel, accented with abstract canvases in red and purple with matching throw pillows. A couple of oversized vases were filled with looming dried flower arrangements, completing a look more magazine-spread than home.

"Anybody here?" Daniel called.

Silence met them. "You first," Daniel told Grimley. "Heather stays with me. Any funny business, boom. Got it?"

Grimley headed across the room toward a whitewashed wall with a wide, arched opening, through which could be seen a further room and a hall area with multiple closed doors. Daniel looped his left arm around Robin's shoulders and followed, gawking like a tourist and gesturing broadly with the gun.

"Look at that. The man actually buys coffee table books and puts them on the coffee table. Who woulda thunk it?" The gun tapped Robin on the ribs. She stiffened. There was no doubt in her mind that Daniel would pull the trigger on a whim, and never feel remorse.

He swung the gun away again, apparently oblivious. "Hey, that's a nice bike! It's got the VR glasses, you can do the Tour de France, anything." They detoured to admire the exercise bike positioned by the window wall. Grimley lengthened his steps, spurred by Daniel's divided attention, and Robin tensed even more. Grimley had to know, as she did, that Daniel would have no need of him once the private elevator was found and opened. It would be far easier for Daniel to have only one prisoner to manage. If Grimley was going to make a move, which he had to for his own survival, she needed to take advantage however she could. All of her senses were on high alert, her pulse pounding, her mind calculating exits and obstacles and evaluating what could be used as a weapon.

Grimley was ten paces ahead when he passed through the archway. Instead of rushing forward like she expected, maybe to find a knife in the kitchen that had come into view, he moved instantly out of sight.

"Pete!" Daniel called. He released Robin and pointed the gun with both hands at the archway. "Show yourself." A crocodile grin split his face, and she realized with a shudder that he'd wanted Grimley to make a move, that he was toying with him—with them both— like a cat with a moth.

"Just a sec," Grimley called back.

"Now!" Daniel barked. He stepped forward.

"I'm getting the door…" Grimley trailed off. His voice sounded muffled, as if he were speaking into a closet.

Daniel took two giant steps toward the archway, gun held in both hands. Robin was left behind. She glanced back toward the elevator, tempted to run for it, but she might need a card to make it go down.

Instead, as Daniel stepped forward, Robin rushed to the thigh-high vase on the left side of the archway. She wrenched out the dried flowers and grabbed the rim of the glossy purple monstrosity. It was heavier than expected but she had no time to reconsider. A gunshot, impossibly loud, reverberated throughout the apartment, and she screamed and swung with all her might as if the unwieldy thing was a bat and Daniel was a baseball.

There was a terrible meaty thud and he crumpled, head smacking into the wall at full force. He fell awkwardly to the floor, fingers twitching, the gun leaving his hand on a separate trajectory with a frightening bounce and spin on the polished wood floor.

Robin didn't breathe until the gun stopped moving. Then she blinked. She was seeing double. Two guns lay on the floor within a few feet of each other. "You had a gun?" she whispered, and raised her eyes to Grimley.

He was leaning in the inside corner created by the

archway, pressing hard at a wound in his left shoulder. Blood seeped around his hand, dark in the fabric of his shirt.

He wheezed, "Hidden in the drawer. An emergency piece. Wes showed it to me during one of our drills. Who could ever penetrate this far into the bunker? But he's—paranoid." He tried to laugh, but it sounded like a gasp. His face twisted into a grimace as he let himself slide down the wall.

"Are you okay?" she asked. Obviously not, but he wouldn't be talking this much if he was about to die, right? The bloody red smear on the wall behind him was—she looked away quickly, feeling light-headed.

"Went through. Hurts—not bad." He spoke with little gasps. "Check on—him. Terminator."

Robin crouched and put her fingers to Daniel's wrist. His pulse felt normal to her, but his color reminded her of the awful grayish-green emergency lighting from earlier. "Did you shoot him?"

"No—all you," Grimley said. He sucked in a breath through his nose. "Okay. Okay." He seemed to be trying to gather his thoughts.

"I've got to get help for you," she said. "Where should I go? Will they listen to me?"

"You got to…get guns."

"Right, the guns, sorry." If Daniel came to right now, he'd end up with two guns and she'd have nothing, again. She picked them both up gingerly, looking for a place to put them, and then dropped them into the giant vase she hadn't used as a weapon.

As a further precaution, she unbuckled Daniel's belt and yanked hard to free it from his unconscious body, then triple-wrapped it around his ankles and buckled it tight. "Can I have yours, too?" she asked Grimley. He nodded, and she fumbled with his buckle and pulled it out gingerly so as not to jar his wound. Daniel had landed on his stomach and she was able to pull his arms together and buckle them behind his back. He groaned, but although his eyelids fluttered, he settled back into silence.

Grimley's eyes had closed too, his hand falling away from his shoulder. She forced herself to look more closely, but she couldn't really see anything but the torn shirt and blood. The blood wasn't spurting, which meant it hadn't hit an artery—but could he still bleed out if he wasn't treated?

She found a bathroom on the other side of the hallway, with a pile of towels on a stand next to the shower. She took them back to Grimley, who stirred as she unbuttoned the top of his shirt. He slurred, "I'm okay…"

"Yeah, you're fine. Let me just see—"

She unbuttoned the shirt further and gently pulled it away from the wound. She had some idea that the wound would be bigger on the back, but it looked about the same as the front. She held the towel so it was covering both sides, then told him to lean back and hold it. "Don't let go, okay? You've got to stop the bleeding. Grimley. Peter! You got it?"

He shook his head and then nodded. "Got it. Shock, I think. Cold. Any—blankets?"

She put a couple of towels over him, one on his legs, one across his chest, and bit her lip. She needed to stop whatever was happening down in the cavern, but could she leave a man to die in order to save someone else, even if it was a child?

"Help me—" he said.

"I'm trying to help you—"

"—lay down," he finished. "Be fine."

She helped him scoot down further and rolled another towel to put under his head as a pillow. He blinked. "Don't. Forget. Key."

"What?"

"Elevator override. Code eight, six, five…one, five."

"Grimley. Peter," she appealed. He opened his eyes again. "I don't know where the elevator is. I didn't see it anywhere."

"Bedroom."

The hallway doors led to two closets and a bathroom, and the open archway at the end of the short hallway led into a kitchen/dining area. She backtracked to the huge open living room, and found a door to the left of the archway, whose contours had been camouflaged by another ugly vase. She went in and saw a king-sized bed, a walk-in closet, an ensuite bathroom—and no elevator. Unwilling to go back and interrogate Grimley again, she kept looking, and discovered a keypad at the back of the closet.

Instead of amusing her with the foibles of the rich, this chilled her. Why would Hartwin hide an elevator? Considering it was already in his private apartment, which required a special access code known only to his closest associates.

Kicking herself for forgetting, she returned to the hallway for Grimley's ID card. Grimley was still pressing one of the towels to his wound. He opened his eyes to watch her.

"Forgot this," she said. She held up the card. "And I

need the other key too, that you used for the front door. Is it in your pants pocket?"

A grimace of agreement. "Hold the towel."

She kept pressure on the wound while he gingerly used the other hand to pull out the key.

"Not sure you should go," he said as he handed it to her.

"I have to," she said.

"It's dangerous. Something's wrong," Grimley's eyes fluttered.

"No shit. Your boss is in something up to his eyeballs."

"I'll get help," Grimley murmured.

She stared at him for a moment, frozen with indecision. Then the word dangerous clicked in her mind, and she tipped the vase so she could reach the guns at the bottom. One, she put far from Daniel and near Grimley's good hand. The other, she took for herself.

"I'll come back as soon as I can," she told him.

She sped back to the bedroom closet. The combination was still in her head. Eight, six, five, one, five. Easy. Eight, six, five, one, five.

The card swiped through and beeped twice. The key clicked and turned, making a green light flash. And she entered the numbers on the keypad. Eight, six, five, one, five. Nothing.

She tried again. Nothing. Could Hartwin have programmed this one with a different code? Of course he could have. Despairing, she tapped her head against the wall. She replayed Grimley's voice in her head, and realized the pause could have been for correction, not continuation. She tried eight, six, one, five and the door slid open.

Robin's heart rate doubled. She hadn't expected to succeed. What was she thinking? She was heading into a completely unknown situation. Daniel had implied some kind of ritual would take place at midnight. But Blue was down there, and Kami. She had no choice.

Chapter Twenty-Two

Stepping into the private elevator, lined with dark polished wood, felt surreal, as if Muzak was about to play her down to hell. She closed her eyes and drew deep breaths to center herself, but she felt hot and jittery with anxiety. The echo of Daniel's touch remained on her skin: his grip around her arm, his thumb caressing her cheekbone. His voice, while roughened by time was still that of the boy she'd thought she loved and then helplessly hated from afar. The father of her lost child.

Every painful emotion she'd tried to repress or process or cope with for the past sixteen years could no longer be ascribed to a distant memory, but to a flesh and blood man who lay unconscious only yards away. In his presence, she was raw again, scabs torn away to reveal the unhealed wounds underneath.

Not a helpful concept, she admonished herself. And it couldn't be true. She was older, stronger, smarter. And she was going to fight back. Somehow.

The brushed steel wall to the right of the door held a generic two column keypad, but this one had two buttons that hadn't been in the other two elevators. One said ROOF, the other B4. Her heart pounded. Was this really the best course of action? With cell reception blocked and the Survival Unlimited staff under orders to detain her, she had no one to turn to for help. She pressed the button.

The elevator descended. She turned the gun over in sweaty hands. Liam had tried to teach her, so it wasn't like she'd never held one before, but it had been so long ago. Maybe that was appropriate, since everything else was a shock from the past as well. She checked to make sure it was loaded by releasing the magazine: there were seven rounds. She slid the magazine back in and realized that she had nowhere to carry the damn thing. Sticking it in her waistband like Daniel had didn't seem smart, so she just held it, even though it felt awkward.

The floors eased by in smooth silence. She pictured Liam's earnest face, persuading her just days ago, that it was time to come out of hiding. Ha! If only he could see her now, falling apart in an elevator on the way to her doom.

She missed him terribly, and her whole life, all of it, from her crappy, mundane jobs to her runs on the beach. She'd give almost anything to go back. But Tom's vision haunted her. Black blood. Screaming. Alone. She didn't think she'd see Liam again, or any of her old life. Whatever waited down below, there was no coming back.

The elevator dinged, giving her a half-second to collect herself before the door slid open. She gripped the gun and stepped out, her eyes flicking everywhere but finding no one, just a boxy antechamber. The room was mostly concrete, but a wide set of stairs to her left extended upwards and ended in an unfinished wall, the two-by-fours and drywall unbroken by a door.

She sniffed, noticing a strange odor. Burnt plastic, like a spatula handle left too close to the burner. Not strong, but distinct.

To her right were a pair of sturdy gray double doors.

261

A fluorescent light above cast a dim, bluish light. No sign of anyone, no sound.

A card reader was embedded in the wall next to the doors, but the normally bright glow-strip at the top was dark and there was a burnt spot on one side. She sniffed again. Definitely the source of the smell.

The door handle twisted easily in her hand. Self-consciously, she held the gun straight out ahead of her in a copied-from-cop-shows move, flung the door open, and stepped forward. She was in an airlock-like area, six feet of dimly lit space capped by another set of double doors, this pair beige with narrow rectangular windows. On one side of the small room stood a metal coat-rack, empty except for a few hardhats and earplugs along the top shelf.

She let the gun drop to her side. There was no one in sight. The windows revealed a slim slice of gloomy, rocky tunnel, low ceilinged and scattered with piles of boulders and deep shadows. True, she had been expecting some kind of a cave, but the reality surprised her. It felt familiar, as if she had been here before. Maybe a field trip somewhere similar when she was a kid?

She shook herself. It didn't matter. What mattered was, why would Hartwin create a private elevator that led to a natural cave? No, what really mattered was, where was Blue? Where was Kami? She could detect no movement on the other side of the doors, except for a possible flickering of shadows at the far end where the darkness thickened.

Robin's hand was sweaty on the gun, and she wiped it on her pants. Did they know she was coming, were they waiting for Daniel to bring her down or had that been his own idea? She wished she had time to try to trigger another helpful flash, but she was just stalling. She tightened her grip on the gun again and cracked the door enough to slide through, gun first. Her heart hammered and her hand was sweaty again already.

Behind her, the door closed with a whoosh and a click. It was loud, too loud, and she turned and grabbed the handle as if to prevent it. Too late. Despite the damage on the other side, it had locked behind her. Her heartbeat re-doubled and she felt faint with fear. No backing out now.

The low ceiling brought on a wave of clammy claustrophobia, but when she took a deep breath an oddly soothing odor superseded the burnt plastic scent—cool, dusty, with a sweet hint of fungus. It brought to mind small things finding shelter in the cracks of the earth, rainwater seeping down, of peace and haven. She held that, breathed deeply again, and calmed, the rush of her own blood quieting in her ears.

Muffled voices echoed strangely, both unintelligible and impossible to pinpoint.

She edged her way around the cavern, seeing that it narrowed to a crooked black opening at the far end. The murmuring continued, maddeningly low, then rising to one brief peal of laughter. Robin froze. The laughter echoed, distorted against the rock walls and the low ceiling, but she had no doubt. It was Kami.

Up close, what had been a jagged slice of darkness became a narrow passage flickering with moving shadows. The murmur of conversation clarified into words.

"This is nothing, nothing like I wanted," a man insisted, and although she had expected it, Robin shivered to recognize Hartwin.

"This is everything you wanted," Kami said. "And more. Take off your shirt, I'll need to reach your heart."

"Where's your father? I want him here. This is not what we agreed!"

Another laugh from Kami. Then a moan, from someone else. Robin forced herself closer. Halfway through the narrow passage, with her back to the wall and gun pointed toward the opening, she made out a wider area ahead with an uneven ceiling descending sharply to a pile of rock on one side. A few candles flickered on the floor. As she hugged the end of the stone passageway to stay out of sight, the uneven edge blocked her view. She could see only a slice of trousered leg.

Another cautious step forward revealed the rest of Hartwin. He paced back and forth, checking his watch repeatedly, his face shining with sweat and his shirt half-unbuttoned. Beyond him, more candles formed a ragged circle around a figure on the floor.

Robin caught her breath. The figure was wrapped in white sheets, but she could see white-blond hair and a pale face. Angel, limply strewn with one arm out-flung, more still than any sleeper.

"You want to wait for my father, fine. But, FYI, that pretty much takes you out of the game because the clock is ticking. This is your chance, right here, right now, Mister 'Survival Unlimited', and there won't be another one."

"You don't know what you're doing," Hartwin said, but Robin could hear the surrender in his voice.

"I know midnight means midnight." Her voice changed to a croon. "Doesn't it, my love?"

Robin edged closer, and Kami entered her field of vision. The girl knelt at Angel's side, then straddled him, stretching the seams of her skin-tight jeans. No ritual robes, just a black hoodie and her crow-black hair loose around her shoulders. Robin couldn't see her face, but she could hear glee in her voice.

"All right, it's almost midnight now," Hartwin said. "Do it."

"Timing is everything," Kami said, and leaned forward to kiss Angel. For the first time, Robin noticed a dagger lying on the sheet beside him, gleaming in the candlelight.

Nearly frozen with horror, Robin opened her mouth. Her first "Stop," came out strangled. But panic and need pushed her forward and the next "Stop!" came out as a yell as she burst into the cavern with the gun waving wildly before her.

Hartwin jerked in shock. Kami merely looked up at her, mouth twisting in a sneer.

"Hey, it's my abandoning bitch of a mother. Hello, Mommy. Where's Daddy?"

Robin lifted the gun in front of her, arms trembling. "Get off him. Get off of Angel!"

Hartwin said, "It's not what it looks like, I swear to god, we're just helping him. We're helping him. She—"

He took a step toward Robin, his hands up like the victim in a mugging, and she swung the gun toward him. "Stop," she growled.

"Yes, do stop," Kami said. "You sound ridiculous. This is exactly what it looks like. I'm going to stab my lover here, so that Mister CEO can live forever, or at least for an extra decade or so. It's a special little method we've developed, isn't it, Daddy?"

Robin darted a frightened glance behind her, but there was no one there. Kami giggled. "Whoops, I thought I heard him. I guess Daddy's running late tonight. Or giving us time to catch up. Too bad I'm busy!"

Heart thumping so hard her body shook with it, Robin repeated, "Get off him." Hartwin edged forward, hands widespread, midway between her and Kami, and she swung the gun from one to the other. Would Kami stab Angel even if Robin shot Hartwin? But she couldn't bring herself to shoot an unarmed man, when Kami was the one with the knife. Would the bullet ricochet in the rocky cavern? And the sound—what if the sound caused a rockfall? Her gaze sped back to the far side of the cavern, where the ceiling was low above a line of loose rock, as if that side had fallen at least once before.

In the shadowy interstices between the boulders, her eyes fixed on a momentary glimmer of reflection. Glasses. And with them, a small, scared face. Robin was staring straight at Blue Gracen, who was crouched between two large rocks, hidden from Kami and Hartwin. Robin nearly flinched, but forced herself to look back at Hartwin and Kami instead.

Kami busied herself, pulling the loose sheet from Angel's chest. She was humming to herself, and Robin recognized "You Are My Sunshine," an old song Daniel used to sing.

Robin said more firmly, "Kami, put the knife down. You don't have to do this."

Hartwin looked again at his watch, then threw up his hands, abruptly shedding his pantomime of misunderstood Samaritan. "This is so fucked," he said to Kami. "We have two minutes. You better pull it off."

Robin pointed the gun at him.

Hartwin hurled himself at her, fast.

She squeezed the trigger.

The cavern boomed and shook, then shook some more, the floor tipping and dropping beneath her feet. A split-second impression of Hartwin falling, of Kami reeling, of boulders crashing and dust rising and screams echoing all around. As Robin lost her balance, shock tore through her at the disconnect—gunshot? Earthquake?!—even as her knees caught her full weight on the sharp uneven rock. The ruckus continued, loud and awful as a cement mixer, about to churn them into the bowels of the earth. Her hands mashed into the floor with another shock of pain, but she didn't care, she was desperately seeking the small face of Blue.

Something slammed into her back from above. She collapsed onto her stomach, her face scraping the floor. Hartwin was crumpled nearby, under an onslaught of falling rock behind a veil of dust. She glimpsed his ghastly face, eyes wide in a mask of blood, before a rock fell between them and another gout of dust blocked her vision.

The shaking slowed, then stopped. Robin heard humming that clarified into an ugly chanting and struggled to raise her head. The area where Angel and Kami were was mostly free of fallen rocks. Only a few candles still glimmered, and in their meager light Robin saw Kami on top of Angel. She had retrieved the dagger and sat upright with it held high above her head. Nonsense words flowed from her mouth like poison, and Robin tried to blink away a strange thickness that appeared in the air around Angel.

She turned her head. To her left, Hartwin was struggling to rise. Beyond him, Blue lay on the floor, a small figure in the midst of rubble. He was fixated on her and growling. His head looked wrong, uneven, and he moved slowly, but his intent was definitely not rescue.

The gun was nowhere to be seen. A hot lance of pain traveled through Robin's back when she tried to rise. She dropped her head to the floor, hot tears on her face. She had failed again, failed to save anyone, failed to help anything. For so many years, she'd held her pain close but told herself it was fate, not her fault. Wrapping herself in shame and resentment and despair at not being normal, at Uncle Matt wasting his life on her when she wasn't worth saving, at the way she had hurt her family and abandoned her baby.

She sensed a soft and blessed darkness waiting to welcome her, a place without blame, without pain, without memory. But something moved beyond Blue just as Robin's eyes were falling shut. With sudden awe, she made out two figures glowing in the dusty air; a girl with hair down to her knees and shoes that sparkled, and a boy with rocks where his eyes should be. But she met his blind gaze and knew him for a power of the earth. It was the spirit that waited on the other side of the flash. It had shown her how to use her curse without blood sacrifice, and it had not yet demanded a price.

The spirit had done what it could, bringing Blue here, bringing Robin here, shaking the ground of Spirit Ridge as if you could shake off evil. It had not been enough.

But it reminded Robin she had one more weapon.

Closing her eyes, she tried to breathe deep but was stopped by the fiery pain in her ribs. Hush, she told herself. Hush. Gritty dust filled her throat and she coughed, but stifled it. She must reach deeper, she must overcome the pain and fill her lungs from a place she couldn't sense but knew was there.

Hush, she thought. And she felt it, a bare trace at first, and then more solid. She drew in a breath of not-air from a place of not-time, past the pain and into the flash. But not a flash of elsewhere and elsewhen. Her attention fixed tight on the present. Everything around her froze in a tableau of falling rock and rising dust and dancing shadow. Kami straddled Angel with a knife in both hands. Blue cowered away from Hartwin, who reached toward her with murderous intent.

Usually a flash crashed over Robin like a tsunami, a chaotic wave of sensation that receded abruptly and left her reeling with only a few droplets in memory.

Here at Spirit Ridge, the spirit had offered her a way to slow the wave, to reduce the tsunami to a flow she could understand.

But she had to do more. She had to do what Uncle Matt had sworn their family could do with a big enough sacrifice: change the flow of events. She would sacrifice if she needed to, but she didn't know how. Sheer force of will? In all her life, wishing had never made anything work.

She studied each frozen figure again, wondering. Could she use some kind of telepathy to change the minds of Kami or Hartwin? Could she knock the weapons out of their hands? Give energy to Angel, so he could fight back?

Desperately, she looked again to the rock-faced boy, the mountain spirit. It watched her patiently with its eyeless face. It wanted her to do something, to agree to something, and she whispered, "I'll do it. I'll do anything."

All she got back was silence.

Hush, she thought. Hush.

And her mind dropped. It felt so physical she thought at first that the caverns were collapsing, but it was only her perception turning inside out. She couldn't see anymore—or maybe she could only *see* the way the spirit saw? Another level of reality.

The people were bright lights connected by threads. Or were they music? It resisted definition, and in the chords/glow/vibration for a moment she sensed a tsunami wave gathering above her ready to smash her human synapses to water.

Hush. Let it come. Ride the flash. Feel the slow ticking of the earth.

She was tied to each soul in the cavern. To Hartwin by fear and a respect frayed to disgust. To Blue and to Angel, with a braid of empathy and sympathy and protectiveness. To Kami most of all, with webs of the same, but wound around with horror and guilt and aching loss. And below that, stronger than that, a powerful love that had persevered in her heart through all the years of separation.

Robin sensed the path of the dagger in Kami's hand. When it plunged into Angel's chest, when it stopped his fiercely pounding heart, Angel would die and the remaining spark of humanity in Kami would sputter out. A kind of murder-suicide, which was about to happen/was happening/had already happened in her strange timeless vision.

She turned her gaze to Blue. Hartwin's hatred, his anger at having what he wanted stolen from him, was a dark force strangling Blue's remaining willpower and hope. A sickly despair pulsed around Blue, and the threads of love that pulled her toward her distant parents weakened as ties to the cavern and the otherworldly beings in it grew stronger.

Robin *looked* from Hartwin to Kami, from Blue to Angel, and her heart bled helplessly for each. She was about to slip back into real time, she could feel it. She had no more time to think, no more time to choose. All her will had to be poured into action. She had to change the music, she had to tug the threads.

She turned her back on Blue, and with whatever she had for hands, grasped the thread of love under all the wretched horror and pain and loss that connected her to Kami, and in some instinctive way, broadened it to a tunnel strong enough to pierce the English Channel. The love she pulsed through it would have reforested the Amazon, and it washed Kami clean.

The poisonous lines leading from Kami to Angel broke. The guilt and pain washed away. For one moment, Kami's presence became a full moon shining through the darkest night of the year.

Then intense pain seemed to turn Robin's inside-out mind right side in again, and she lost her grasp on it all, lost the thread and the lights and the music. Her hands screamed like burning meat and she fell back into her poor battered body lying under a pile of rocks on the floor.

Someone howled, with rage or loss. She was pretty sure it wasn't her, but she couldn't track it. There was such a wrenching feeling in her—was it in her mind or her body? Had her guts been torn loose? It was a terrible wrongness, and now the blackness was not a gentle invitation, but a—

Chapter Twenty-Three

Robin blinked grit out of her eyes and found a pale face hovering above her, dancing with shadow.

"Shhh," Angel whispered. His hand was smooth and cool, cradling one of hers. "You're okay. I can feel it."

She tried to believe him but both of her hands throbbed with heat as if the skin had been shredded away and the raw meat toasted over coals. That pain was slightly louder than the rest of her body, which felt beaten by a meat tenderizer.

Nevertheless, she smiled up at him. Right now, he looked more angel than teenage boy, but his voice broke, reminding her how young he was, how close he had come to death.

Tears gathered in her eyes. The after-image of all the glowing lines clung to her vision, and the universe felt fragile, held together by twining strands of love and hate, yearning and greed and anger and—

"Kami?" she asked hoarsely.

He shook his head. He must have moved the candle close, because light haloed his white-blond hair. He was still wrapped in the dusty white sheet, but he'd redraped it to be more toga than shroud. "Gone."

"Dead?" Her voice was strangled.

"A guy showed up and took her away. I didn't recognize him."

"God," she said, and squeezed her eyes shut. Then

they shot open again, and she twisted her head, trying to see around him. "Blue! Did Hartwin—?" She couldn't finish her question, and her eyes filled with tears.

"Blue wasn't here. I don't—She was?" Angel seemed to find the truth on her face, or maybe in her aura. "I never saw her. She's not here now, no sign of her. Mr. Hartwin, though…" He swallowed. "Dead. Definitely dead."

Robin became aware of noises, voices, something mechanical. She struggled to roll over and sit, but pain lanced through her side. Remembering the rock smashing into her back, she panicked and wiggled her toes. Not paralyzed, then. Just really hurt.

Angel squeezed her hand again. "There are rocks blocking the passage to the door. I've been hearing noises for at least an hour. Sounds like they're almost in."

She focused abruptly on a bloodstain at the edge of the shoulder wrap of his toga-sheet. "Angel—"

He followed the look and snorted. "That's nothing. Whatever you did—Kami dropped the knife on me. It just scratched me. I forgot all about it."

It looked like a big bloodstain, wet and still fresh. She hoped he wasn't being macho. "What did she do then? Did you grab the knife? Weren't you tied up?"

"My feet were tied. She scrambled off me like I was the one attacking her, and then she kind of stared around, all sweaty and sick. Then she grabbed the knife again and started crawling toward you and saying all this crazy shit. I was trying to yell, to stop her, but it was like a bad dream. I couldn't move, she'd sucked all my energy away. My heart was barely beating. And then—that guy showed up, and pulled her away."

She pictured Daniel as she'd left him, unconscious and tied up in Hartwin's suite. Grimley wouldn't have let him go. Plus, if the passageway was full of rocks, how could he have gotten in? Had Daniel escaped and been hiding down here even before the earth had started shaking? Or maybe someone else came for Kami. Victor. She shuddered. "Where did he come from?"

He shook his head. "I don't know. I was pretty out of it. I saw them leave though—they went that way." He gestured toward the other end of the cavern, just a shadowy blur to her now.

"Thank you," she whispered. She should let him rest. Hell, she should rest. She dropped her head back on the floor and her eyes drifted shut.

The rescuers crowded in, in hardhats and dust-masks, and when she opened her eyes, the cavern was filled with glaring artificial light from a powerful lantern too close to her face. She squeezed her eyes shut. They separated her and Angel and examined them both. Robin was strapped onto a stretcher. She heard radio chatter and voices talking about Hartwin's body, and then she was carried back to the elevator where her stretcher was snapped onto a waiting gurney.

Inside the elevator she kept her eyes closed even when the door slid open at the top. She felt herself wheeled out. Angel's dad, Jim, was there. She heard his tearful reunion with Angel, who told him to stop being such a baby. She cracked her eyelids open when Jim grabbed her hand and laid a scratchy mustache kiss on it.

"I owe you," he said. "Everything. Anything. Just ask." He waited for acknowledgement until she forced a tiny nod, then he stuffed something into her pocket and was gone.

Her eyes shut again. She was so tired, but she was trying to remember something. Her brain felt like the Little Engine That Could, pushing and pushing at…something. A storybook, about the engine almost too small to deliver toys to all the children on the other side of the mountain. But it chugged and it chugged and it chugged…

She startled awake, awash with panic, but she still felt the echo of Jim's scratchy kiss on her hand, and remembered. Angel was alive. Kami was safely away. Robin's mind tried to soothe itself, repeating it over and over. But it didn't work. Kami was alive, but she wasn't safe, had never been safe. But at least she was alive. At least she hadn't murdered Angel and finished off her own soul. Robin struggled to remember the certainty she'd felt in the grip of the flash, that by focusing on Kami and Angel she was saving two lives. She'd let Blue be lost, to keep her own daughter, already twisted and cruel, from becoming a killer.

She had made her choice. But something had stopped Hartwin anyway, because Angel told her he was dead. Angel had said—

"Wait!" she cried, trying to struggle upright. "Blue!"

"Shush," one of the stretcher carriers said. "Lie back. It's okay."

"Did you look for her? Why isn't she here? Is she dead?!"

The two figures, still masked, exchanged a glance. "The boy said you'd seen her, but there was no one else in the cavern. Blue wasn't there. Don't worry."

She struggled against the straps. "Please! Look again! She wants to come home, I know she does! She must be so scared."

They wheeled her gently out of the elevator and into a hallway, and one of them, with kind green eyes above the mask, said, "Okay, okay, we'll look again. We'll take care of it. Don't worry."

Robin felt the pinch of a needle, and then darkness again.

****

Sleep was warmth, and safety, and not having to deal with anyone, and she resisted waking even when Master Leopold's voice refused to go away. On top of that voice piled the smell of bleach and the feel of rough sheets and the sounds of rolling carts and beeping machines, and it became harder and harder to hold on to the wisps of a dream. Then she heard Tom, too, and forced her heavy eyelids open.

Leo was perched on a high stool to her left, Tom in a chair to her right. She was surrounded by the sliding curtain of a hospital bed, partially open, with a monitor of some kind beeping quietly behind her. Above, the tiled ceiling was pockmarked with water stains.

Tom's eyes crinkled, though he looked tired and disheveled. "Hey. You're awake!"

She would have rolled her eyes, but she had room for only one thought. "Blue?"

He shook his head. "Not yet. Angel told everyone you saw her, and the EMTs said the same thing, but are you sure? Her parents are here with the police. They've been wanting to wake you up but the doctor wouldn't let them."

"What hospital?" she managed.

"We're in Grants Pass. Angel's been checked and released but you were in worse shape. You have broken ribs on top of all the bruises, and your hands are all bandaged. You should rest."

She shook her head and started to struggle to her elbows. "I'm fine. I'll talk to Blue's parents."

"Whoa! You've been out for twelve hours. Sure you don't want to pull yourself together first, eat something? I think the docs might want to check in with you."

Master Leopold patted her shoulder. "Let her do what she needs to do." He smiled down at her. "Glad to see you're awake and alert. I'll fetch the nurse, he's around here somewhere."

"How did we get here?" Robin asked. Her voice was a rough whisper, and Tom poured water from the pitcher by the bed and held it so she could drink through the straw.

"Well, you and Angel and Jim came by ambulance. Some of us followed. The police want to talk to all of us, but they don't want anyone staying at the compound. So it's either twiddle our thumbs at the Days Inn or hang out here." He looked embarrassed. "I just wanted to make sure you were okay. You are okay, right?"

She managed a smile. "Of course. Just—it was pretty awful. And I don't know—" Hot tears came to her eyes again. "I lost Blue. And Kami's—" Her voice hitched.

"Hey," he whispered, and squeezed her shoulder through the sheet. "It's going to be okay. I want to hear all about it, when you feel up to it. Do you want me to reserve a room for you at the hotel for when they let you go? And maybe you and I can get dinner then. After you've rested?"

She looked down. "I really just—I want to go home. If they'll let me, after they talk to me. Can I have a raincheck? An email address?"

He looked embarrassed. "Of course you want to go home. God, I'm an idiot. Will you need a ride, can I drive you?"

She shook her head. "I'll call my brother. He'll kill me, otherwise."

"Okay. But I'm serious. Don't disappear."

"I won't." After a moment, she asked, "What happened with Madeline and Erin? Did the police arrest them?"

His face sobered. "I don't know how they escaped, but they did. I reported what happened as soon as I could, but they never turned up. It's incredible, because when the lockdown lifted, the cops escorted us all up to the cafeteria. We were all in there together, but no Madeline or Erin. The other crazy thing was, when the cops searched the whole compound, they found the two deputies that had been inside during the lockdown in an office, groggy and wrapped in duct-tape. They said Sarah Park brought them coffee, and that was the last thing they remembered."

"Sarah Park? Daniel attacked her, she couldn't have been part of it."

"She was part of something. When she came to arrest you, she wasn't acting like someone just following orders. She was scary-fanatical."

Robin nodded. "I'm not sure why she was so loyal, but she was a true believer. Hartwin wanted to sacrifice Blue for some kind of ritual involving extended life, which I would have thought was bullshit, but—after what I saw, I'm not so sure."

Even knowing that some psychic powers were real, Robin had never believed in such things. Surely there was a difference between unusual human abilities and magic. But the words Kami had spoken had been powerful. Robin had felt their wrongness and seen the awful darkness that had gathered around Kami in the cave. Robin would have to be more open-minded from now on.

Robin was still trying to understand the rest of what had happened. Kami lost Blue, the intended victim of Hartwin's sacrifice—or Blue had escaped her with the help of the rock-face boy. Kami decided to sacrifice Angel instead, to fulfill the deal between Hartwin and the LeClairs. And Daniel? Had he been there simply to oversee? Or possibly, his role was to capture Robin, who'd been lured there with the hope of helping a little girl. But how could the LeClairs have believed she'd take the bait? Half the time, she didn't even keep up with the news. If Liam hadn't pointed it out to her, she would have missed learning about Blue's disappearance until it was too late.

Unless they had someone who could foresee pieces of the future better than she could, and had known she would come.

Tom was apparently turning the pieces over in his head as well. "But why, when Hartwin was taken in for questioning—?" Tom began to ask, but was cut off by a distraction.

The doorway was suddenly filled with people intent on entering. Agent DiBlasi's voice, insistent, powered over the others for a moment but then fell in surrender. The only ones that made it in were dressed in scrubs. They shooed Tom away, and Robin found herself efficiently poked, prodded, and otherwise checked over, before she walked painfully to the bathroom on the arm of a plump male nurse.

When she returned to the bed, the nurse whispered, "Doctor says you're absolutely fine, but we don't have to tell them that yet. Do you want a few minutes?"

Robin shook her head, settling back into bed. "Thank you, but I need to tell them what happened."

When DiBlasi came in, this time accompanied by the Sheriff and two deputies who stood uncomfortably against the wall, Robin told them about everything from the onset of the lockdown through being attacked by Erin and Madeline, incarcerated by Sarah Park's security team and then captured by Daniel.

She interrupted her own story by saying, "I can't believe Erin and Madeline escaped. Did they disappear into the woods while you were blocking the road or something?"

DiBlasi exchanged glances with the Sheriff. "Yes and no," she said. "There was a lot of confusion when we were gathering statements. A deputy took their statement that they'd spent the lockdown sleeping in their suite, and then they walked away. Most likely they hiked through the woods and got picked up by the road, but we don't know yet. We'll track them down. There's still video feed to sort through."

Robin pictured them, with their outrageous makeup and big hair. Would Tom have recognized them in a crowded cafeteria full of stressed-out frightened people, if they had changed their trademark style? She wasn't sure she would have.

Shrugging, she continued. "Sarah Park seemed determined to hold me prisoner, supposedly on Hartwin's say-so. But Peter Grimley challenged her, saying Hartwin was acting weird. Park was determined to follow her instructions, though."

DiBlasi nodded. "Park's daughter has leukemia. We've talked to her. Hartwin promised her a cure if she kept a few little details about the security system private. When the lockdown started, he convinced her this was part of his plan, and you had the power to mess it up."

"That's terrible. She told me her daughter was sick, but then she said it was just a bug, that she was fine. And Park ended up getting attacked by Daniel for her pains. I'm glad she's alright. What about Peter Grimley?" Robin asked belatedly. "He was shot. Is he here?" No one had mentioned him, and she felt a moment of guilt and panic.

The Sheriff grunted. "He's going to be fine. He's a hero. If it weren't for him, we'd probably still be out in the parking lot waiting for a battering ram strong enough to get through those reinforced doors."

Robin didn't miss the disgusted look he shot toward Special Agent DiBlasi, who remained unmoved as she said, "Despite a gunshot wound, Peter Grimley managed to release the lockdown controls, allowing law enforcement access to the building shortly after the tremor. He told us that Daniel LeClair had forced the two of you up into Hartwin's suite in order to get to the cave. What can you tell us about Daniel LeClair? How did he know you? I'm still trying to get a lock on how you fit into all of this."

Robin rubbed her forehead. The last thing she wanted was to relate her life story. She floundered. "I'm not sure how I fit in. When I was a teenager, I dated Daniel. But I haven't seen or heard from him in sixteen years. For him to show up here, calling me by a name I used to go by—it's just bizarre. Angel said—I thought maybe Daniel escaped, with Kami? The girl who was working with Hartwin."

DiBlasi narrowed her eyes, plainly sensing there was more to it, but she shook her head slowly. "Daniel is under guard in the hospital. He's not going anywhere."

Robin had a momentary sensation of relief. "But— then who took Kami away?"

"We don't know. We haven't found her yet. And that may not be her name. There's no record of her, no birth certificate. The TV station had her listed as Kamilla Smith, but it appears to have been a fake name."

That wasn't surprising. Robin's daughter was truly the LeClairs secret weapon. And someone else had come for her, someone who knew another way into the caverns, someone who she went with willingly and who was able to evade law enforcement. Another employee of Victor LeClair, no doubt—or Victor himself. Robin shuddered.

Letting her history with Daniel slide for now, Special Agent DiBlasi questioned her further on what she saw and heard when she got to the cavern. Robin wanted to edit out some of the weird stuff—the thickness that had gathered in the air as Kami spoke, and the figures that had crouched by Blue's side—but DiBlasi already knew about her psychic ability. If they decided she was lying, so be it, but she gave them all the information she had.

DiBlasi and the Sheriff exchanged a glance when she got to the part about Blue.

The Sheriff said, "You'll be glad to know there was a credible sighting last night in Boise. We got a call, and there's some video. It's almost certainly Blue. We have a reliable witness who can tie Wes Hartwin to the truck driver."

Robin narrowed her eyes. "But we know Hartwin wanted to sacrifice her, not send her to Boise. Did this anonymous caller sound anything like the one who made you bring Hartwin in for questioning in the first place?"

DiBlasi exchanged glances with the Sheriff again, but neither answered.

"It couldn't have been Blue at the truck stop," Robin insisted forcefully. "She's in the cavern, I saw her. She needs help."

Agent DiBlasi rose. "We'll check it out," she said. "I promise. But please don't say that to the parents. They're scared enough as it is. That cavern is a mess. If anyone was down there, well—chances of survival aren't good."

Robin shook her head. "Blue's safe," she said, knowing she wouldn't be believed. "She's safe, but she needs help coming home."

****

Someone, probably Tom or Delia, had delivered Robin's suitcase and toiletries to the hospital, but her purse and cell phone were missing. She'd had them in the tiny bedroom where she'd brought on the flash of Angel and Kami just before Sarah Park had arrested her, and she supposed they were probably still there. Fortunately, she knew Liam's phone number by heart, and dialed him from the room.

He answered on the first ring, and from the background noise, she could tell he was driving. "Hello?" he said.

She couldn't speak, because she'd started crying in relief as soon as he answered, but he recognized the sound of her sobs.

"Robin! What's wrong? Are you okay? Where are

you?"

She sucked in a couple of deep breaths through her mouth, whispered, "Hang on a sec," and blew her nose copiously. "Okay. I'm okay. I'm just glad to hear your voice."

"I gotta pull over, I can barely hear you." In a moment, he switched the phone from speaker and she could suddenly hear him clearly in her ear. "Where are you?"

"The hospital in Grants Pass. I'm okay." There was so much more to say, but she just gripped the phone, overwhelmed.

"Robin? Are you there?"

"I found Blue."

"That's wonderful. That's great!"

"But no one will listen to me. Blue's still there. Under the bunker."

"They won't listen? Why not?"

"Well, it's a long story. Someone sort of tried to kidnap me. And there was an earthquake. A couple of my ribs are cracked, that's all."

"Oh. Okay. Wow. That's why they don't believe you?" He seemed confused.

"They think I was imagining things." She closed her eyes, too tired to explain any better right at that moment.

"Robin, if you're sure, you gotta keep telling them. Make them listen. Okay? I believe in you. You can do this."

She smiled, tears still slipping from beneath her lashes. "You are the best brother ever. Okay? I want you to get married and live happily ever after."

He snorted. "And why are we suddenly talking about marriage?"

"Because, Miri," she said. "And don't worry, I'll find my own place." Robin must be exhausted, because the challenge of apartment hunting on a temp worker's salary suddenly seemed every bit as daunting as finding Blue.

He laughed out loud. "Robin, stop. You're getting loopy. Do they have you on painkillers? Miri and I are not getting married."

"You're not? I was so sure you would say yes—"

"However much we joke, please remember—I do have some sense. You and I can talk about whether to let her move in, okay? But I will never, never, expect you to leave OUR house. It's yours as much as mine. Mom and Dad would have wanted that. Understand?"

She nodded but couldn't speak.

After a moment, he sighed and said, "Listen, I'm going to get off the phone and drive, okay? Just, sit tight. Wait there, I'll be there as soon as I can. It's going to be okay." He hung up.

She sniffled, wiped her nose, and looked at the phone. Had she really just come apart like that? It must have been the painkillers. She hadn't even realized how much she dreaded apartment hunting.

The nurse popped in. "Doc's signed off on you, but you can't drive, you have to be picked up. Do you have someone?"

She nodded.

"Okay, you need to sign some papers downstairs, then you can go. I've got to bring you down in the wheelchair."

He popped back out. Robin swung her legs over the side of the bed, wishing she could get a shower before they hustled her out of the room, but felt too out of sorts to request it. Maybe she would just sit in the cafeteria until Liam turned up, and then she could sleep in the car. Sleep, and sleep, and sleep.

Tom poked his head back in. She summoned a smile, or at least the ghost of one. He looked somber.

"Someone to see you, if that's okay," he said.

She nodded, and Marletta and Miller Gracen pushed past him, looking drawn and disheveled and somehow still larger than life. They stood together at the end of Robin's bed.

There were no niceties. "You're sure you saw my baby?" Marletta asked. She telegraphed anxiety with every line of her body. She glanced at the unused stool and the unused chair on either side of the bed, but did not sit. With her right hand, she twisted the wedding ring around on her finger, over and over.

Robin remembered DiBlasi's request, but she couldn't lie. "I saw Blue. I'm sure. She's there. She's okay. She was okay when I saw her."

Miller gently grasped his wife's hand. "Did you— Are you sure? I mean, I'm sorry. We're falling apart here." He took a deep breath. "Can you tell us what happened? All of it?"

"I will. And I'll take you there."

"They won't let us anywhere near the place," Tom warned from the doorway.

He was right but Robin knew she was right too. By the time the machinery of the investigation was ready to search for Blue under Spirit Ridge, it could be too late. "There's another way in," Robin said. "The cops probably have the back way guarded, the way they think Kami got out. But climbing up from the river park, there's a place I saw in a flash, a hole in the side of the mountain." She didn't add that it had been a flash about another little girl losing her life because of Hartwin's perverse curiosity. "We'll need a harness and rope. And Leo and his dowsing crystal, because the opening is overgrown and we want to find it fast."

Chapter Twenty-Four

Blue could understand the boy now without G.J. translating. It wasn't quite like words, but it was close enough.

—I'm sorry.

She didn't bother to answer. The tears kept coming, even though they were a waste of water. She was snuggled into a little crevice just her size, with her hood up and her sleeves pulled over her hands. Her glasses were lost, her flashlight was lost, her imaginary friend was lost, and she was just another tiny hurt creature, squeaking in the dark.

—You can stay with me, he said.

She nodded, still crying. She would have to stay with him. Just like G.J., who had finally been freed, Blue would waste away to bones.

When Uncle Wes had been squished, G.J. had disappeared from her floaty hair to her magic sparkly shoes. It didn't seem fair to lose her all the way, when only part of her had been a Spirit, but Blue couldn't summon the energy to make the imaginary friend part come back. Anyway, Blue could see in the dark now, even without the sparkly shoes to follow, and she still had the boy.

—You're part of this place now. We'll go over and under, in and out, and the people will be gone. Plants will grow in the bunker, and deer will jump the fences. It will be good.

Blue felt it in her heart; it would be good. It would be good for Spirit Ridge to be alone again. It would be good for the forest, for the animals and the crawling things and the river and the fish. It would be good for the blind boy who lived in the mountain and was the mountain and took care of the mountain.

But Blue still wanted her mom and dad. She wanted cheeseburgers and fries. She wanted sunshine and road trips in the convertible and being bored at grown-up parties. She wanted to change her clothes and take a bubble bath that smelled like strawberry ice cream.

And she knew something he didn't seem to understand. Now that the bunker was there, people wouldn't let it be empty, even with Uncle Wes gone for good.

"I'm thirsty," she whispered. "Can we go to the water?"

They wound through the tunnels. When G.J. balled up all her mad and sad and forced Uncle Wes to let Blue go, rocks fell down everywhere, and Blue thought she would be squished too. But the boy knew all the strong places and kept her safe. There were lots of skinny parts in the passages, though, places where it was hard to squeeze, even though Blue felt like a shadow of the girl she used to be in the up-above. And when they were close to the water, so close that she could smell it and almost taste it and her throat closed up for the need of it—they got to a fallen-down place where she couldn't quite fit.

—I'm sorry, the boy said.—I thought it would work. We'll try another way.

"I'm too tired." She sank down in the tunnel and

closed her eyes, leaning back against the rock, and he sat next to her, and she rested.

In her dream, she was out in the sunshine, playing hide-and-seek with the blind boy who wasn't blind at all, and they played among the trees and the breeze tickled under her ponytail and the world smelled of a woody piny life and she loved it. And then she heard voices, children playing nearby, and she was happy not to be alone. But the children sounded familiar, like they were not children at all, and a little tiny, scared piece of hope whispered maybe they were her parents. Calling her. The voices echoed through the tunnels, and she woke up.

The voices were far away, more like a vibration than a noise, but she knew.

"They're out there. They're calling me," she told him. Her heart was a dried out husk, but it managed to beat, just a little bit.

—I know. He looked sad.—Can you make it?

It was a very long way. She thought of all the tight places, all the parts she would have to force her poor tired legs to push through, but her heart ached to be with them. She nodded. "I want to," she said.

—Good. Let's go.

She rested for a moment longer, closing her eyes, and she almost forgot to move, but then she felt that vibration again, and she tried to get to her feet but she couldn't. She started crawling.

Rocks tumbled from the ceiling of the tunnel. "Stop it," she whispered.

—I'm trying, he said.

Her knee came down on a rock so sharp that it pierced her jeans, and she rolled away from it onto her back and all was dark for a few minutes. But something tugged at her and woke her up.

—They found the skywell, the blind boy said. His voice was so soft, she almost couldn't hear it, just a breeze brushing her ears.

Blue opened her eyes but bright light made her squinch them shut.

"Blue! Are you there, honey?" It was her mother's voice, echoing. Her mother's real voice.

"Blue!" her father called. "We're here, honey! Please, if you can hear us, say something!" She could hear his fear, and she tried to call out.

"Is that a shoe?" her mother shrieked. "Oh my god, those are bones!"

"That's not her shoe," her father said. "Marly, it's not her. Blue! Are you there?"

—Come back to me, the blind boy said.—Come back, someday?

"I will," she whispered. And then, as loud as she could, she called, "Help!" but it came out like a croak.

"I think I heard something. It's her, she's okay, I know it!" someone said, and Blue recognized the voice of the good lady, the one who yelled at Uncle Wes before G.J. smashed him.

"She must be in the side tunnel. Look at the crystal!" someone else said, and she thought she must be dreaming, because it sounded like Master Leopold, who should be far away at the reincarnation camp.

"I'm going down," Daddy said in his no-arguing voice.

And one minute later there were arms around her, and Daddy held her close saying "Blue, Blue," and she barely noticed when they both swung up into the air through the skywell on a rope because she burrowed into his warm shoulder and she could feel his stubble prickling her face and his sobs shaking his whole chest. Another minute and they were back on the ground again, with real fresh air and a little breeze, and Mommy was squeezing them both together, smelling like flowers and oranges and home, and they were crying and laughing at the same time. Blue opened her eyes, but even through the tears it was too bright. She shut them again, but not before she saw the sunshine.

Thank you for purchasing
this publication of The Wild Rose Press, Inc.

For questions or more information
contact us at
info@thewildrosepress.com.

The Wild Rose Press, Inc.
www.thewildrosepress.com